RUN RIOT

RUN RIOT

STATE OF GRACE 1

COLETTE RHODES

CONTENT WARNING

Violence, Drug References,
Sexual Content

"I HAVE LOVED THE STARS TOO FONDLY TO BE FEARFUL OF THE NIGHT"

-SARAH WILLIAMS

GRACE

PROLOGUE

The ruins at Ephesus were oppressively silent at midnight. Gone were the human tourists who visited this place during the day to admire the achievements of civilization and architecture this site represented, though there weren't so many this time of year anyway — it was cold. I shivered in my wool coat, hands scrunched into fists inside the pockets, wishing I'd worn gloves.

There were no other agathos or daimons here now. Sometimes they would secretly visit these ruins, disguised as human tourists, to make a pilgrimage to their respective goddesses, the mothers of creation. It was never a pilgrimage I intended to make, even though many agathos did. I'd always felt too twisted inside, too tainted to contemplate visiting such a sacred place.

Only the very desperate would be at this place at this time of night.

And yet here I was, by invitation of the divine, to visit one goddess that I served, whose image I'd been made in, and one I was supposed to hate, but couldn't. One who'd given me life, but the other who'd given me *purpose*.

I was standing on a precipice from which I couldn't return, and I wasn't alone. I would never be alone again.

Maybe I'd walk out of this as the first agathos to fall from the light, or maybe I'd already fallen. Perhaps I might be the first daimon to be *made,* not *born*. As I looked between the four men standing stoically at my side, ready to face off against the divine without an ounce of fear, I wondered if that would really be so bad.

I was born to serve the light, but the dark had brought them to me. My friends. My lovers. My soulmates. The dark had given me life and hope and *meaning* when I'd had none.

Once upon a time, their kind had been my enemy. Now, it was my own people I had to fear.

GRACE

CHAPTER 1

"I could have sworn my wallet was in here!" the woman in line in front of me wailed, frantically digging through her oversized purse.

Oh no. Already, my palms were itching with the urge to help her. My instincts insisted that she was a human in need, and that was what I was here for. What *every* agathos was here for. To ease the suffering of humans in need and silently guide them towards the path of light. To the goddess Anesidora's path.

All I'd wanted to do was grab some cupcakes from the store for Verity Mae's baby shower.

"Sorry, just give me a couple of minutes. I swear it's in here. I need this stuff, it's for my son's birthday party," the woman said in a rush. She didn't look much older than me, late twenties perhaps, but there were huge shadows under her dark eyes, and her black hair was pulled up in a very mom-like messy bun.

I'd really hoped to get through today without anything bad happening, but that wasn't the reality of my life. I was a dispenser of luck, and I couldn't walk away from a human in need of some. Even if good luck for them meant bad luck for me.

"Let me help you look," I offered quietly. I'd pushed some of my agathos gift into my voice to soothe her and make her more amenable to my help, so she didn't object as I stepped closer and rested my palm on her exposed forearm. While I pretended to help her look in her purse—probably raising the eyebrows of everyone else in the store—I opened the well of my magic, letting some luck flow through me to her.

My palm tingled where it rested on the woman's arm, but she wouldn't feel anything except a pleasant, unexplainable heat that she'd promptly forget.

"I don't see it here," I said with a frown as I pulled my hand away. Apparently her good luck wasn't going to be finding her wallet at the bottom of her overfilled purse.

"Here, let me," a baritone voice said from behind me. A fancy looking middle-aged businessman stepped around me, holding out his credit card to pay for the woman's groceries.

"Oh, thank you, sir," the woman said, eyes welling up alarmingly fast. He gave her a tight smile before stepping back, looking immensely uncomfortable as the lady gathered up her bags, thanking him the whole way out of the store.

I paid for the cupcakes before making my way back to my car slowly, hoping something terrible happened between the store and my vehicle because otherwise I was about to have a very unfortunate afternoon at Verity Mae's baby shower.

3

The car door unlocked easily.

I didn't trip on anything on the way out.

No one had scratched the paint while I was inside.

So far, so good, which was also kind of bad.

The last few miles to Verity Mae's parents' house where the shower was being held were likewise uneventful. It was an enormous brick colonial mansion in central Auburn, surrounded by manicured lawns that didn't have a single leaf on the ground, despite the fact it was fall.

Huh, I even managed to find a parking space not far from the house. These were probably all bad signs. I checked my makeup in the rearview, finding nothing amiss in my heavily made-up-to-not-look-made-up face. My brown skin was appropriately highlighted and dewy looking, opal-colored agathos eyes framed by natural-looking false lashes and winged eyeliner, long black hair perfectly curled at the ends, nothing between my teeth.

Suspicious.

I quietly let myself into the mansion, following the sounds of laughter coming from the formal sitting area. If my bad luck was that I was running late, I'd happily take it. Perhaps Anesidora would be feeling generous today.

"You *guys*!" Verity Mae squealed, clapping her hands once over her enormous bump. She was a tiny woman who was *all* belly at the moment, and I smiled to myself at seeing her in this stage of life she'd been so looking forward to.

Verity Mae's blonde hair was looking particularly thick and lustrous, and she was dressed impeccably elegantly in a beige bump skimming dress that matched the party's color scheme. She was standing at the front of the room, in front of an entire wall that had been turned into some sort of white, beige and gold balloon display with globes of all different sizes. It kind of reminded me of bubbling caramel. The balloons continued up the wall and covered half of the ceiling, growing increasingly large in size, with plush teddy bears dangling from gold ribbons like they were being hanged from the rafters.

Or carried off into the clouds, which was probably what they had been going for.

Sugar, the amount of money they spent on balloons for this party could have probably furnished a whole nursery. *Which was their prerogative and not my place to judge*, I chastised internally. Today was a happy occasion. Verity Mae had finally found all four of her soul bonds and was expecting her first child. No need to be negative just because I was single and lonely and bad luck was about to come crashing down on me at any moment.

Negativity was very un-agathos, and I was *really* trying to work on that.

The balloons matched the tasteful cream-on-cream decor that every agathos seemed to share. The whole party was the epitome of neutral elegance, since Verity Mae had made a huge to-do about not finding out the sex of the baby.

"You have all *spoiled* me today," she gushed, gesturing at the pile of gifts in the corner of the lavish living room.

I hovered awkwardly near the food table by the door at the back of the room, not wanting to pick through everyone's outstretched legs to find a seat on one of the sofas. That was definitely inviting bad luck.

Verity Mae continued her thank you speech, expounding on all the many ways the goddess, Anesidora, had blessed her while I set the cupcakes on the table, wishing I'd improved my piping skills enough to actually bake for these events, and unnecessarily smoothed over the pleats in my pale pink skirt. A few of the guests had already noticed me enter and were giving me the discreet pitying looks I should have been used to receiving, but never failed to make me uncomfortable.

I was surprised Verity Mae had even invited me. Plenty of the other women in this room stopped bothering years ago, to avoid the awkwardness of my presence.

"I *need* to get into that cake, like *right now*," Verity Mae continued to a chorus of giggles, gesturing at the cream-colored five-tier cake, complete with fondant teddy bear topper on the table next to me. "So, I'll keep this brief. My guys and I are *so* excited to meet this little one," she said, smiling genuinely as she rubbed her belly.

The hard edges of the bitterness I was trying to suppress at feeling like the odd one out, and surrounded by reminders that I'd probably be alone forever softened a little at seeing her happiness. "We are so honored that he or she will have such a wonderful community around them, and we are so grateful to you all for this amazing day," Verity Mae added, beaming at everyone in the room. She had a carefully honed talent for making someone feel like she was speaking just to them, even in a crowded room.

I clapped along delicately with the rest of the women present—my agathos peers, the women I'd grown up with, played with, volunteered with and visited the temple with—smiling along like I fit in with them.

Truthfully, I didn't and we all knew it. That was why I didn't blame them for not wanting to invite me to celebrate their milestones when I was so far behind on reaching them. That I'd moved half an hour to Milton was just an additional convenient excuse for all of us to avoid these situations.

"One more thing. It felt like my journey took so long," Verity Mae sighed, unnecessarily fluffing her hair as her eyes went glassy. Her pupils were the same inhuman swirl of lavender, teal and gold as mine, as everyone's in the room. Agathos eyes, a mark of the goddess Anesidora.

Idly, I wondered what color humans saw Verity Mae's eyes as. Blue, probably. I'd been complimented on my dark brown by humans before, though I'd never see them that way. *Láthe biōsas* was one of the goddess' primary commandments for the agathos.

Live hidden.

Humans were never to know about us.

"...and that is why I wanted us all to make a special prayer to Anesidora for Grace Bellamy."

My wandering attention returned to the room instantly as every set of eyes swiveled to me in what was possibly my worst nightmare.

"Oh, that hardly seems necessary," I protested weakly, shrinking in on myself as though I could disappear into the decor. Maybe I could hide in the balloon wall?

Was it hot in here? It felt hot.

"Grace B!" Verity Mae laughed. "Don't be embarrassed. I've been in your position—well, not *quite* your position—but it took so long for me to meet Marcus, it felt like it would never happen, and I appreciated all the prayers people gave me to help me on my journey."

I didn't miss the chastisement in her tone, and I doubted anyone else did either.

"You're, what, 25 now?" Grace M. asked sympathetically, sitting the closest to me. She was also pregnant, with her third—or was it fourth?—child. *Sugar,* I should definitely know that. When we used to play tennis together as kids, I couldn't have imagined the different directions our lives would take.

"Yes," I replied, clearing my throat. "25. And no bonded," I added with a strained laugh like it didn't bother me at all. *No sirree, I am fine. Nothing to see here. Please, everyone stop staring at me.*

"Maybe you're looking in the wrong place?" Serenity asked from Grace M.'s other side. "Have you ever felt the call? Perhaps you should consider visiting your ancestral home. Where's your mother from again?"

"Canada," I volunteered with a tight-lipped smile, very familiar with where this conversation was going.

"Before that. Her *ancestral* home," she pushed impatiently, like she was on the verge of a major breakthrough. Auburn wasn't the most diverse of places, and my mother—a woman of Indian descent who'd been born and raised in Saskatoon—had been quite the topic of conversation when she'd felt called here to meet her final soul bond and had chosen to stay.

"One of my fathers is from Wisconsin, and I couldn't *believe* it when the call led me there to meet Noble. You need to be open minded about these things, Grace. Maybe your bonded are in your mother's *ancestral* home." Serenity gave me a pointed look, like the three-day trip she'd taken to Milwaukee with her three existing bonded was exactly the same as me going to India—a country I'd never been to and knew almost nothing about. Not that I'd ever felt any soul bond *call* to go there anyway.

Her heart is in the right place, I reminded myself unenthusiastically. I should have made an excuse and stayed home today. All the pity made me feel the kind of rage my kind weren't supposed to be able to feel, and I didn't need yet another reminder of all the ways I was different. Defective.

"Let's pray," Verity Mae called, bringing the conversation to a halt. The room fell silent, everyone's head dropping diligently downwards, eyes closed. "Anesidora, thank you for the blessings you have provided us all. For our soul bonds, our children, our families, our health, and our happiness. Please guide Grace B., a good and devoted daughter of yours, on her journey to discover her own soul bonds, so that she may experience the overwhelming happiness of your gift. *Láthe biōsas.*"

"*Láthe biōsas*," I murmured along in response with everyone else, twisting my fingers roughly in my beige cashmere sweater. A constant, daily reminder that our purpose was to serve the humans who knew nothing about us.

They just want what's best for you, I reminded myself as I smiled thankfully at Verity Mae for the prayer. My internal voice was beginning to sound suspiciously like my mother, chastising me for my ingratitude and general array of personality flaws.

These kinds of events had challenged my self-control for the past three or four years now, I should have gotten used to it. Used to showing up alone, used to pitying smiles and well-meaning prayers. Why wasn't it getting any easier?

"Okay, everyone," Verity Mae said with a clap, shooting me another painfully sympathetic look. "Let's cut that cake!"

And because being the focus of their prayer and pity wasn't embarrassing enough, my bad luck kicked in the moment I leaned over the table, knocking over the whole thing. Including the five-tier cake that was on top of it. Right before I fell butt-first into the mess.

Fortunately, after apologizing *profusely* and explaining that I'd gifted a woman at the store good luck before I'd arrived, I was able to make a fast escape. It was no secret among the agathos in Auburn that I had the gift of good luck, *Eutychia*, and therefore bad luck followed me around like a bad smell.

And while I wasn't ungrateful—I *wasn't*—my life would certainly be easier if I had the gift of moral virtue, *Arete*, like Verity Mae did. Little slips in my own moral virtue in return for guiding a human were a lot less unpleasant as far as consequences went than bad luck.

Basically, I drove home in a borrowed dress and a cloud of shame, sniffling the entire way.

It wasn't like I would have stayed late anyway. Most of them lived within walking distance of the party, and acted like I lived across the country since I'd finally convinced my parents to let me move to Milton to be closer to my job at the shelter and get away from the judgmental stares of the agathos community.

It was a decision that exactly one person in my life was happy about, and that person was me. Never more so than in that moment, smelling like vanilla sponge cake and tears.

The smooth roads out of Auburn were lined with well spaced colonial mansions and hundred-year-old trees, but as Auburn gave way to Milton, the scenery changed rapidly. Mansions became abandoned factories, row houses and crumbling condos. Smooth roads were suddenly filled with bumps and potholes.

Driving into Milton always felt like entering a different world. It consistently ranked as one of the worst cities in the country to live in, with a high crime rate, high unemployment and a weak job market. It was a city that had peaked in the late 19th century and had been struggling along ever since, but it called to me for some reason. Not *the call*, like my friends had felt towards their soul bonds, but some other kind of calling. The short commute was definitely a plus, but I worked with plenty of other agathos, and none of them had felt called to hang around here after the work day was done. They all happily rushed back to their brand new SUVs and kept their foot pressed to the gas until they got back to the safety of Auburn's city limits.

Fortunately—thanks to my mother's diligent PR work—the wider community believed I had moved to Milton because I had a servant's heart for helping others. That it wasn't enough for me to just *work* at the agathos-run shelter during the day, I had chosen to *live* in the community I served because I was just that selfless. I wasn't sure my motivations were that altruistic. She couldn't lie, but she was selective about the truths she told.

Marvin Gaye on the radio cut off as my phone started ringing through the car speakers and with a heavy sigh I hit 'accept call' on the dash.

Speak of the... shmevil.

That was an unkind thought.

"Hello, Mother."

"Terrible news," Mother began with no preamble as per usual. "Joy Lyon died."

"That's awful," I breathed, genuinely surprised. I barely knew the woman, but she was only 40 with three young kids and four bonded mates. Her death would rip a lot of people's worlds apart. Sugar, those poor children.

"It is," Mother said, and I could hear the grimace in her voice. "Just happened today. Car accident. I'll let you know when the public memorial is. Next week, I assume."

"Yes, keep me updated," I murmured, although I'd probably hear it from my boss first, since she'd roster all human staff on that day. It was unusual for a bonded agathos woman to die young, or at least to die alone. We didn't suffer from human illnesses—a trade-off for dedicating our lives to humans I supposed—and usually, women were cosseted and protected by their bonded at all times.

"How was the baby shower?" Mother asked. "What did you wear? You were meant to send me a picture of your outfit before you left your *apartment*."

Mother had a way of saying 'apartment' like she was saying 'prison', it was genuinely impressive, even as I fought the very *not sweet* urge to roll my eyes. I supposed, compared to the five-bedroom, five-bathroom sprawling home in Auburn where the rest of my family lived, my one-bedroom apartment seemed quaint.

"The pale pink pleated skirt Mercy found for me and the beige cashmere sweater I got in the city."

I was sure she'd hear about the food incident at some point, but I wasn't going to volunteer that information. I would *definitely* cry again if we talked about it now, and nothing frustrated my mother more than my tendency to weep whenever my emotions got the better of me.

Mother hummed disapprovingly. "You know I don't like you in beige. Pale colors brighten your complexion."

"I like my complexion."

There was an indignant scoff on the other end of the phone that made me cringe. I wasn't about to fight that particular battle again, though. At this point, I felt I was better focusing off my energy on preserving my own self-worth and my cousin Mercy who lived with her than trying to convince my mother she was beautiful the way she was— that we all were. At least she wasn't as hard on my brothers about their appearance. Yet, anyway. Maybe once they hit middle school.

Be sweet. You know it was difficult for her when she first immigrated to Auburn.

"You could have stopped by the house," Mother added. "You were just around the corner. Mercy will be disappointed that you didn't want to see her."

My jaw was starting to ache with how hard I was clenching it, so I forced myself to relax. I saw my family *every* Friday night for dinner. My cousin, Mercy was only 17, but incredibly understanding about why I didn't visit more frequently than that. Each dinner I would sit silently at the table and have my self-esteem ripped apart, one shred at a time, and spend the entire week building it back up again.

"Oh well," Mother continued. "We all knew this would happen when you moved so far away. You'll have to come here to get ready before the memorial so your dress doesn't wrinkle on the way."

That was a more creative version of 'I need to approve your outfit' than I usually got.

"Of course," I murmured. "I should concentrate on driving now, Mother."

"Indeed. We've lost enough of our women to car accidents today," Mother replied absently, and I flinched at the bleak assessment. It wasn't *wrong*—agathos couldn't lie even if they wanted to—but it was still callous. Poor Joy Lyon.

As always, Mother hung up without saying goodbye, and the soothing sounds of *I Heard It Through The Grapevine* came through the speakers again. I exhaled a long breath, forcing myself to concentrate on happier things, like what early 2000s rom coms I was going to watch tonight to pick myself up after my emotionally exhausting day, or the mint chocolate ice cream in the freezer I was going to indulge in for dessert.

Every conversation with my mother required breathing exercises and relaxing music afterward to aid the recovery process.

That probably wasn't a sweet thought either, but I was feeling particularly irritable after my disastrous afternoon. Maybe I'd gotten too comfortable over the past six months. Living in Milton meant I didn't have to wear my serene mask all the time, and it got increasingly difficult to put it back on.

I parked across the street from my building as the sun was setting and trudged up the stairs to my second story walkup, carrying my ruined clothes in a grocery bag. It was just a little one-bedroom apartment, but it was the first place that had ever been *mine*, and I adored it.

I'd been working for years and Milton's property prices were so cheap that I'd been able to buy it. Slowly, I was working on creating the perfect little oasis where I could be myself and pretend I wasn't some combination of cursed and broken. It was ideal. Plus, there were only three other apartments in the building, all occupied by regular humans. Being *near* their territory, but not actually on it, seemed to be fine with the surrounding daimons.

So long as they had access to corruptible humans, they didn't care much about what we did or all the ways in which we tried to redeem those same humans.

I unlocked the door and leaned against it with my shoulder to heave it open, the comforting scent of all the wax melts I liked to use hitting me instantly.

My feet practically exhaled with relief as I slid off my too-tight heeled ankle boots, arranging them neatly on the shoe shelf by the door before making a beeline for the laundry to deal with my stained clothes.

After a quick shower to wash off the cake smell, I dressed in a matching loungewear set—my number one indulgence—braided my hair, and gave myself permission to relax for a moment.

Usually, Sundays were reserved for cleaning, organizing and grocery shopping. I'd run out of time for the latter because of the baby shower, and just knowing my pantry was half empty and my pretty storage jars weren't topped right up made me panic a little. Six months later and I hadn't lost the fear that Mother would barge in unexpectedly and point out all the ways I'd failed my homemaker training. Those comments were often accompanied by a pointed remark about not having any soul bonds, like there was no question the two facts were related.

The sun was setting, and I flipped on a lamp as I walked into the small living area and pulled the curtains in front of the balcony shut. The quiet of my apartment was both a relief and a reminder of my almost constant loneliness. It was nice not to have to fake happiness or perform for anyone, but agathos weren't meant to be alone. All the women I'd spent the afternoon with would be going home to their bonded, some of them to their children, while I had returned here all on my lonesome to a grilled chicken breast with steamed vegetables, and to rewatch *10 Things I Hate About You*.

I lit the vanilla soy candle at the center of the coffee table and flopped back onto the cushion-laden navy velvet couch with a groan. My houseplants craved attention, but I needed a minute to sulk first. Verity Mae was the last of my age group to have her first baby. Even then, she'd met her first soul bond when they were teenagers. It was only because it had taken so long to find her fourth that Anesidora hadn't gifted her a pregnancy before now.

I was mostly content with my life, but events like today's threw my fragile happiness off-balance. I had been waiting and waiting, demonstrating my patience and piety or so I'd thought, but maybe Verity Mae had the right idea. Maybe I should pray more. Maybe Anesidora wasn't convinced that I *wanted* it enough.

My thoughts drifted to Joy Lyon, who'd done everything right and found the four loves predestined for her, only to be ripped away while her children were young, leaving a hole in all of their lives that could never be filled. The dark selfish part of me that I tried to ignore was *envious* that at least she'd experienced that kind of all consuming, life changing love, even if it was only for a short time.

I wanted that. I wanted to be the center of someone's universe. Anesidora had designed it so that could *only* happen with my soul bonds.

A prayer couldn't hurt. Perhaps if I prayed more, I wouldn't have such selfish thoughts all the time. I straightened on the couch and clasped my hands in my lap, bowing my head respectfully.

"Anesidora, Sender of Gifts, Great Mother, I need your guidance. Perhaps the path you have set for me does not lead to me finding my soul bonds, and I understand that." I swallowed thickly, a sharp stab of heartache running through my chest at the words. They were true, but they were agony. "I ask you humbly if you could maybe give me some direction? Show me where you need me, where I can best be of service to you. I am your vessel. *Láthe biōsas.*"

I glanced around the room like Anesidora might give me a sign then and there. I'd settle for a howling wind, a flickering light, *anything* to make me feel less like I was screaming into a void.

Nothing.

If it weren't for the feel of Anesidora's magic traveling through me when I helped humans in need, I'd wonder if I was agathos at all.

She was always right there when it came time for me to pay the price for using my gift. I didn't hear a peep when I prayed, but the bad luck was infinitely reliable.

The flame of the candle in front of me felt like it was calling my name, the warm glow offering me some comfort as the scent of vanilla saturated the room. I'd often wondered if the relief I derived from fire was normal. It wasn't like I could ask—everyone thought I was broken already, and I didn't want to add to the speculation.

If they knew the kind of dark thoughts I had sometimes—the very much *not* sweet, *not* virtuous, *not* selfless thoughts—I'd probably be restrained in the basement of the temple for corrective behavior training for the rest of my life.

While I was usually good at suppressing it, I could feel the darkness—my inner monster, as I thought of it—rising in me now like a sinful tidal wave. Where was Anesidora when I needed her? When I'd followed the rules my entire life and fought against all the instincts I wasn't meant to have in order to please her?

Why was she always, consistently *silent*?

The dark had never scared me the way it scared my friends and family. There was something...*welcoming* about it.

Don't do it, I told myself internally, resolve weakening by the second. But I wanted to do it. I wanted to be a little bit reckless. I wanted to indulge the selfish part of me that demanded answers. That demanded *action.* That was tired of drifting through life waiting endlessly for something that I'd already accepted would never come.

"Goddess of Night," I whispered, a shiver of dangerous excitement running through me at doing something so forbidden. "If you can see something in my future, please..."

Please, what? I served the light. I will only ever serve the light, an alarmed voice in the back of my mind screamed. My voice of reason, perhaps.

"...please share your wisdom with me. I serve Anesidora, but I hope to find my place in the world, my calling."

That yearning hunger inside me that always demanded *more* seemed to unfurl and spread the longer I spoke, and I hastily wrapped up my ill-advised prayer before it grew so monstrous I wouldn't be able to contain it.

"Thank you, Goddess of Night."

There was a moment of perfect, complete silence, not even the sound of traffic or the noise of my neighbor's blaring television cut through the strange bubble of quiet I was suddenly engulfed in. The candle in front of me extinguished suddenly, making me jump at the unexpected darkness, and the background noise rushed back in like someone had suddenly turned up the volume dial.

I clutched my chest as my heart pounded double time in my chest, a tremor of fear running down my spine.

It was probably a coincidence, right? Right. Maybe I was just...tired.

No way would the Goddess of Night, La Nuit herself, respond to the desperate pleas of one tragic little agathos.

That would be...impossible. Wouldn't it? Improbable at least. I'd prayed to Anesidora thousands of times, and had never received such a response.

My empty apartment suddenly felt oppressively quiet, and I quickly turned on the TV and flicked through the menu until I found *10 Things I Hate About You*. I exhaled with relief as Kat's stereo blared *Bad Reputation* and settled into the corner of the sofa, tugging a cream throw over my legs. It was fine. I'd probably imagined whatever I thought had happened. I shouldn't have been talking to the Goddess of Night anyway.

I'd watch the movie, reheat the grilled chicken from last night, undo my healthy dinner with a pint of ice cream and binge romantic comedies until I couldn't keep my eyes open any longer. Everything would be fine, and I'd pretend I hadn't temporarily lost my mind and asked for help from the main source of human misery.

I didn't relight the candle though.

RIOT

CHAPTER 2

I was having a good dream.

I was racing someone I couldn't quite see on loud as fuck motorbikes we'd acquired somewhere, heading west on the quiet winding roads that led to Devil's Den. The adrenaline rush was better than any high, making my limbs shake with pent-up energy.

The black cloud that followed me around every day of my life was gone. The numbness had cleared. I felt each swoop of my stomach as I went over a particularly steep drop, the burn against my palms as I gripped the handlebars harder, pushing for more speed.

Whoever I was racing was gaining on me, but I couldn't turn my head to see them. They laughed, and it was a familiar sound. I knew this person.

Just a little further, and we would get to our destination. To our prize. It was something good, I could feel it.

"Get up, you lazy sack of shit."

I groaned as the remote Dad threw hit me in the head, rolling towards the back of the couch and giving him my back. Damn it, why had he woken me up? It had been such a good dream. I had been *so close* to winning.

I didn't need to see him to know exactly what he looked like right now—arms crossed, brows drawn down, jaw clenched. He was an older, rounder version of me, with hair that was more salt than pepper, and a beer gut that I had sworn to the goddess I would never develop. Every night he left the house in dark jeans, a t-shirt that was stretched a little too tight, and a leather jacket he'd acquired in the 90s and would wear until his dying day. Mostly because it had plenty of internal pockets to store his *merchandise*.

"You need to move some product tonight, Riot. I'm not joking," Dad warned, sounding as irritable as usual. "Or don't bother coming home. You're a curse on my reputation."

I grunted in acknowledgment, but didn't bother arguing. What was the point? My time was up. I'd been living here for ten years—which was about nine years longer than I'd intended—and my general uselessness to him was always going to be a deal breaker. We were a line of salesmen, and I wasn't fucking selling, nor did I intend to.

I didn't give a shit either way how my old man felt about that. I wasn't intending to die of guilt before my 30th birthday because I'd left a line of dead and dying humans in my wake.

"Get it together. I'm not running a fucking charity here, Riot," Dad groused as he let himself out the front door of the apartment, slamming it shut behind him hard enough to rattle the liquor bottles on the shelf.

I massaged the spot on my skull where he'd got me with the remote before rolling onto my back, staring up at the cracked plaster ceiling, yellowed from years of smoking indoors. The street outside was coming alive as the sun set, growing noisier as the neighboring daimons and a few of the particularly deadbeat humans who lived around here woke up. I knew if I looked on the kitchen counter, I'd find a selection he expected me to push tonight. Weed, pills and coke were the usual suspects, though sometimes he threw in little bonuses to surprise me.

Fuck, this would all be so much easier if I could just mindlessly follow orders, sell the shit I was supposed to sell, and ruin lives like a good little daimon.

For years, I'd faked it pretty well. Everyone who lived around here— human and daimon alike—knew who my old man was, what the family business was. If someone had approached me and asked for something, I'd give it to them and justified it to myself by saying that they'd asked. They had come to me.

When I watched humans get fucked up over the shit *I'd* given them, I told myself that they'd asked for it. Even when the Goddess' gift whispered in my ear what their weakness would be, their particular brand of poison, I ignored it. I only ever gave them what they asked for, and told myself they knew what they were getting into.

Until six months ago when I'd stopped selling anything at all. The excuses hadn't been flying even in my own head for a long time, and I'd finally made the call to do something about it. Apparently, the timer on Dad's patience had run out.

It was probably a good thing. I needed a push to get me out of my comfort zone. Homelessness was a push.

I reached blindly on the floor next to the couch until my fingers brushed over my cracked phone and grabbed it, squinting at the bright screen. Five pm, probably time to get up. There was a missed call from what probably passed as my only friend, Dare, and I hit 'call' not really expecting him to answer.

"Hey, man," he said distractedly. The phone crackled as he set it up somewhere, the sound of his equipment clinking against the bench in the background. "You're on speaker, but there's no one here."

"No one there? Are you losing your touch?" I joked. Dare was booked solid with clients almost every hour he was awake. He was the best tattoo artist for miles.

"Fuck off," Dare scoffed. "Just cleaning up in between bookings. Where are you planning on sulking tonight?"

"Onslaught," I replied, lips twitching as I felt the comforting rush of my self-destructive tendencies making an appearance. "Thought I'd mix things up."

There was a pause where it sounded like Dare stopped what he was doing before he let out a long, low whistle. "You're getting brave, my man. Or you have a death wish, which wouldn't entirely surprise me. I thought Wild banned you from all Underworld clubs?"

"That was ages ago," I replied dismissively. Two years maybe? Wild, club owner, big bastard, and king of a string of nightclubs known as the Underworld hadn't liked me since I'd sold coke at one of his clubs *one time*. He frowned upon that sort of thing. It wasn't like I'd *wanted* to sell it. "Besides, Onslaught is a shit hole. It's the chip in his crown, I doubt he's been there in years."

Dare snorted. "Wild's got eyes everywhere and he still owns the place, but whatever. It's your funeral."

"It might be my funeral soon anyway," I replied flippantly, feeling around in my jeans pocket for the bumpy carved exterior of my copper lighter. I fished it out and popped the lid reflexively, the familiar sound of igniting calming me down.

"You still not selling?" Dare asked. The concern in his voice was impossible to miss.

"Do you think I'm crazy?" I asked, smirking at the ceiling as I extinguished the flame then immediately lit it again. I felt fucking crazy. "It goes against everything I'm supposed to do. What we're supposed to be. What *I'm* supposed to be."

The darkness. The sinners. The Pied Pipers for sad and desperate humans. Those were the daimons. The Moros line in particular.

"I don't think you're crazy," Dare replied quietly. If anyone understood what it was to find a loophole in our programming, it was him. "But I think you need to get the fuck out of your dad's place before he kills you. Don't pull that bullshit about having no money, you can crash at mine until you figure something out. You sleep on a couch anyway. Sleep on mine."

"I might have to take you up on that," I replied, my chest tight. Not many daimon offered something without requesting a deal in return. "He said move some shit tonight or don't come home."

"Then I'll see you later," Dare replied firmly. "This could be good for you, if you don't destroy your life first. Gotta run, my client is here. Stay out of Wild's way. Don't get arrested. Or killed."

"Aye aye, sir," I chuckled, hanging up. *Ye of little faith*. No one was arresting anyone in Milton, this place was a fucking wasteland.

Besides, I sort of had a plan. My old man wasn't welcome in any Underworld-owned clubs either. So long as I kept my head down and didn't cause any trouble, I was better off in the viper's den than anywhere else in Milton, and I could burn off a little steam. *Win win*.

With a groan, I rolled off the sagging couch and headed for the bathroom to make myself look at least somewhat presentable and pack my toiletries, since apparently I wasn't coming back tonight. Or ever.

Fuck it, there was something quite freeing about that knowledge. No more waiting for my dad to reach the end of his tether and wondering what would happen when he did. I'd skim some of the good stuff Dad had left on the bench and spend the next few days living hard and hoping I didn't die young.

I splashed my face in cold water and roughly dried it before glancing up at my reflection in the mirror, gripping either side of the small porcelain sink. The devil stared back at me. Dark red irises that bled to purple around the edges. The mark of a daimon. No human ever saw these eyes or even knew we existed, but the goddess didn't let us hide our true nature from each other or ourselves. Even if we wanted to.

I ran my fingers through my messy black hair and left my stubble as it was, not particularly caring about what I looked like at that moment. On the one hand, there was a sense of freedom I hadn't experienced in years, so close I could touch it. On the other, if I wasn't doing what I'd been born to do, *designed* to do, then what was the point of *me*?

It's not like I could just pretend to be a human. Well, I *could*, they wouldn't know, but I didn't know how to be a regular human with a 9-to-5 job and a minivan. I had no idea how I was going to make money, and no legitimate work experience. Maybe I could spin a decade of slinging drugs for my dad as ten years sales experience for the family business? Or figure out how to hawk protein powder and sunglasses on social media.

I was pretty good looking, I could probably pull it off.

I grabbed a duffel bag and shoved in the few clothes I owned—stored in the entertainment unit since I didn't have my own room—my phone charger, and a selection of wares from the kitchen counter. Just because I wasn't going to sell them didn't mean I couldn't enjoy them. I'd just have to stay out of my dad's way for... ever.

It'd be worth it. Fuck knows I didn't have anything else in my life to enjoy.

Onslaught was on one of Milton's worst streets, tucked between a Daimon-owned liquor store and a human-owned barbershop. The sign above the pulled up roller door was falling off, and the whole place had a general air of desperation about it. It was exactly the kind of establishment where people went to forget about their lives for a while.

"Riot, you shifty little fucker, you know you're not allowed in here," Crow groaned, crossing his tattooed arms over his chest as he guarded the entry to the shittiest club in Milton like it was a fucking Ritz-Carlton.

Except instead of a fancy suit, Onslaught's bouncer wore a tight buckled up leather vest over a too-small black t-shirt, both of which he'd probably owned since the late '80s. Crow's head was completely shaved, but the gray in his beard gave away his age. I still wouldn't want to take him on in a fight, though. Daimons from the Keres line were not to be fucked with, even if they were old enough to remember the days before TV was in color.

"Looks like you could use the business," I replied mildly, looking past him at the half empty bar. Goddess, it really was a dump. The walls were covered in peeling posters and graffiti, barely visible under the dim overhanging lights, and none of the furniture matched. Basically the only things it had going for it were some decent tunes and a pool table.

"Fuck off," Crow groused without much heat. "You're more interested in pushing your own *business*."

I raised an eyebrow at him, because Crow had definitely bought from me before. Daimons only got the highs from drug use, not the lows. It was the goddess' way of making it look more appealing to the regular humans she despised, who had no such tolerance. They didn't know we weren't human, they just saw cool-as-fuck people like me getting high and making it look easy.

"Come on, man. You know I don't make the rules," he muttered, looking a little sheepish. "I bet if I looked in that duffel bag—not shady at all by the way, bringing that on a night out—that I'd find shit. Wild cares about keeping his establishments above board."

"No one is coming to investigate this place," I scoffed. "And anything I have is for personal use. I'm a good boy these days."

"You've never been a good boy a day in your life," Crow chuckled, not sounding concerned in the least about that.

He looked like he wanted to let me in, but Wild had a way of inspiring loyalty among his staff, so I wasn't surprised when he didn't move for me to pass. I leaned back against the graffitied brick wall next to him, all my worldly possessions slung over my shoulder and crossed my arms, making myself comfortable.

It wasn't like I had anywhere else to be, and I enjoyed a challenge.

"You're a pain in the ass, Riot," Crow groaned, though he was grinning at me.

"You enjoy the company," I replied with a smirk. Crow was from the Keres line, like Wild and most of his staff. They liked violence and destruction. For centuries, their kind had been on the front lines of battlefields, stirring up bloodlust. It must have been boring as fuck being a bouncer most of the time.

"I heard your old man is pissed at you," he remarked, pulling out a cigarette and patting down his pockets.

"Here," I offered, pulling out my copper lighter and flicking it to life. "Yeah, he's not my biggest fan. How'd you hear that?"

"You hear a lot standing here all fucking night," Crow replied with a shrug before taking a long drag of his cigarette. "Your old man has a big mouth and a bad temper."

And wasn't that the truth? Dad was just as inclined to sample the merchandise as I was, and he got chatty when he was high.

"Heyyyyyyy."

I glanced disinterestedly at the trashed redheaded woman who stumbled up next to me, accompanied by Buck, a younger daimon I didn't have much to do with. The human woman was totally wasted and reeked of booze, but I knew that wasn't her poison of choice.

That was the curse of the Moros. We felt *doom*. We knew just what it would take to send a human down a spiral they couldn't return from. It was like a dark whisper in my mind that I couldn't ignore.

"What's your name? My name is Rae," she continued, oblivious to my silence and Buck's grunt of irritation that she was talking to us. "This is my friend, Buck."

The kid gave us a smug grin while Crow glared at him. I doubted he was having the same moral crisis as I was, but she did look about five minutes away from vomiting over whoever was in her general vicinity. I was pretty sure Wild, and therefore Crow, didn't like those sorts in his glowing establishments either.

"Oh my god, I love your tattoos. You're so pretty," she continued, running her hand down my arm in what was possibly meant to be a seductive way. "You should party with us. Buck has some treats to really get things going."

Fuck my life.

It was fucking twisted that the goddess gave me this ability to sense weakness, encouraged me to exploit it, but also gave me a guilt complex about it.

I could walk away. She wasn't my responsibility, I didn't know her.

I fucking *couldn't* though. If I left her with Buck, he'd give her the pills she was so desperately craving and she'd be dead before midnight.

My dad never felt guilty about the lives he destroyed. No other daimon seemed to either. It was a curse unique to me.

"My name is Riot. Wanna come chill with me for a bit?" I asked in a low voice, leaning in to speak right in her ear. "We can catch up with Buck later, yeah?"

"Really?" Rae asked excitedly, stumbling against me. One wandering hand moved up to my chest, fondling my pecs through my shirt.

"For sure." *Just saving your life here, handsy lady. You're fucking welcome.*

"Fuck you, Riot," Buck muttered as I wrapped an arm around the sickly woman's shoulders and pulled her away from Onslaught.

I rolled my eyes as Crow chuckled at Buck's misery. I was sure the kid would find someone else from the meager pickings inside Onslaught. Humans came to us, whether we wanted them or not. Impatiently, I led Rae across the street to a grassy lot in the shadows, picking through the empty bottles and trash that covered the ground. Anyone who'd seen me lead her in here would think we were hooking up, which was a pretty solid cover.

"What do you want to do?" Rae asked in a husky voice, groping my biceps while running her hazel eyes down my body and stopping at my belt.

Not that.

"I want you to call a friend to pick you up," I replied flatly, extricating myself from her grip. "I'm going to wait here with you until you do."

"What? Why?" she asked, blinking in confusion. "Do you not have a condom? It's cool, I'm clean."

Hard pass. Even if that was true, I wasn't interested in either her, or potentially creating little Riots. No fucking thank you.

"You're wasted, you need to sleep it off."

"Fuck you, dude. I'm going back to see Buck," she muttered petulantly, turning to leave.

"He was going to sell you fake pills," I lied, smoothly stepping in front of her. "You're done for the night. Call a friend."

"You're no fun." She pouted at me for a moment, looking up at me with puppy dog eyes like she thought I might change my mind before sighing dramatically and pulling an old phone out of her jeans pocket.

Were those...*buttons*? Did they still make phones with buttons?

Rae stared at me sulkily as she aggressively stabbed the buttons and cocked her hip while the phone rang, looking put out the entire time. Honestly, I had no idea why I bothered helping people when they were such assholes about it. Probably because it made me hate myself one percent less.

Now I just needed to wait for her poor friend to come get her so she could spew in their car and I could go back to annoying Crow. Once I was comfortably inside the walls of Milton's worst club and out of my dad's reach, I could lose myself to oblivion and forget about everything else for a few hours before crashing on Dare's couch like the leech I was.

At least I'd ruined Buck's night. That was a nice bonus.

GRACE

CHAPTER 3

The problem with watching excellent romance movies is that they reminded me of all the things I didn't have in my own life. For every moment I'd grimly resolved to myself that I was completely fine being alone forever, there were ten more moments where I just craved that early aughts, teen romance kind of love.

The messy, giggly paintball kiss in *10 Things I Hate About You*. The overly dramatic kiss-the-star-football-player in the rain moment of *A Cinderella Story*. The foot pop at the end of *The Princess Diaries*.

I doubted it was possible to grow up expecting to have four soul mates and *not* have grand ideas about romance, but I'd had more time than most to ruminate on exactly what it was that I wanted.

The occasional grand gesture? Good.

Small, intimate moments that only meant something to us? Better.

I didn't want a fairytale kind of love. I wanted a two-person-pedal-boat-on-the-lake kind of love.

It didn't look like I'd be getting either.

Still feeling weirdly off-balance after my dabble with the darkness, I'd finished my movie and was eating my grilled chicken and steamed vegetables while standing in the kitchen. My phone was on the bench, and I idly scrolled through my news feed, which was almost exclusively pictures of Verity Mae's baby shower. The bubbling caramel balloon feature had obviously been popular.

Moments like these felt like a small act of rebellion. Mother would probably need to be hospitalized if she found out I regularly ate my dinner standing at the counter to minimize cleanup, scrolling through my phone. She'd expect me to set the dining table for one and sit myself down nicely with a napkin over my lap and my phone in another room. She'd instructed me as much when I'd finally successfully pleaded my case to move out.

I did a very unladylike snort over my bland plate of chicken. All those years making dinner for my parents to practice my future housewife skills for naught. I had no one but myself to be a housewife *for*. Not that I particularly minded *not* being housebound all the time—I liked my job, and I knew I would be expected to give that up for the foreseeable future if I found my soul bonds and had children.

Stop it, I chastised silently. It would be a privilege to have those things.

My contentment was an ongoing work in progress.

My phone vibrated noisily on the counter with an incoming call and I forced back an unkind groan when Rae's name appeared on the screen. So much for a peaceful night in.

Rae was a human who had been in and out of the shelter for years, even though she was a little younger than me. Most of the shelter staff were much older, and she'd formed an attachment to me in particular.

She was snared in the web the daimons had woven for her. A life of sex, drugs and rock 'n roll. The daimons made it look glamorous—they were built that way by their shadowy goddess. Regular humans couldn't help but feel enticed, it was what the daimons were called to do.

Devour. Destroy. Desecrate.

The agathos existed to pick up the pieces.

"Good evening, Rae," I said quietly, already knowing what she'd need. I'd received this call many times before, though usually not at this time of night.

"Graaaaaaaaaace!" Rae wailed dramatically, and I pulled the phone away from my ear with a wince.

"Are you okay?" I asked cautiously. Usually when Rae called, it was because she was coming down from something, or brutally hungover and needed help undoing the life choices she'd made. Her tone was generally more what-have-I-done than I'm-still-doing-it.

"Tonight is so trash, I can't even. Can you pick me up?"

"Of course," I replied instantly, even as dread unfurled in my stomach. I could hear the sound of car horns and laughter in the back, and the distant thump of bass. "Where are you?"

All the clubs in this city were daimon-owned and therefore considered daimon territory. I'd never interacted with one, but I'd been told my entire life that daimons were just looking for an excuse to destroy agathos at any given opportunity, and walking right into their lair definitely felt like I was giving them the opportunity.

"I'm at Onslaught, just chilling outside. I was going to party with this guy and have a *really* good time, but then this other guy was like nooooooooo," she continued, her voice a little slurred. "Then I thought we were going to have a different kind of fun, if you know what I mean."

I could practically hear her exaggerated wink through the phone, and I scrunched my eyes shut to regain my rapidly slipping composure.

"Anyway, he was like 'call your friend,'" she rambled on, dropping her voice an octave. "And now he's just waiting here with me until you get here."

Oh, sugar.

"Right. Okay. I'll be right there," I said weakly, dropping my fork in the sink and racing to the door, shoving my feet into my bright white sneakers. Why was everything I owned so blinding? Why didn't I own some rebellious looking black clothes? I may as well have a neon flashing sign above my head that said 'agathos'.

"Can you stay outside? Is it safe for you?" I asked, holding the phone between my shoulder and my cheek.

Surely, so long as I didn't try to enter the bar, I'd be okay? I'd driven down the street Onslaught was on before, there were human businesses on it, and no one had ever tried to stop me or anything...

It wasn't like I really had a choice anyway. To be an agathos was to make sacrifices for humans, Anesidora's favored children. My instincts demanded that I go to Rae's aid.

"What?" Rae laughed like the question was ludicrous. "Of course it's safe. See you soon, byeeeeeeee!"

In a way, it was a blessing I didn't have time to overthink things. I glanced down at my outfit—a matching knit white sweater and lounge pants—and realized I couldn't look any more out of place outside a daimonic club if I tried, but I didn't want to waste time changing. It wasn't like I had any other options in my closet that were more suitable. There was exactly one black dress in there and as per my mother's instructions, it was only for funerals.

I grabbed an olive-colored wool coat from next to the door as well as my tan purse. At least the coat was a semi inconspicuous color. I *really* hoped Rae would still be outside when I got there. It wouldn't matter what I was wearing if I had to go inside, the opal-colored eyes would give me away immediately. Humans might not be able to see them, but daimons certainly could.

Anesidora, watch over me, I asked silently as I closed my apartment door behind me with a click as the lock engaged and rushed down the silent stairs. The air was chilly as I let myself out in front of my building, keys in one hand, pepper spray in the other.

No one approached me as I jogged across the street and jumped into my car, blasting the heat as I reversed out onto the road. Fortunately, Milton wasn't a huge place. I had expected Rae to be downtown where most of the clubs were, and even that was only fifteen minutes away without traffic. Onslaught was a small, disreputable bar located between a liquor store and the world's saddest barber shop on East Main Street, and less than ten minutes away.

It was also the closest club to the shelter, which was convenient. Possibly she'd fallen prey to the daimonic lure as she passed by, already on her way to Hope House. The best of intentions could be thwarted by that call of the forbidden, and Rae rarely had the best of intentions.

I slowed down as I approached the club, chewing nervously on my lower lip. There was an enormous sex store on the corner of the street painted a garish pink, and my cheeks heated at the small glimpse of what I could see displayed in the window.

There was that dark part of my brain that wasn't meant to exist, flaring to life. I shouldn't even *notice* that kind of thing. It was even worse than usual—my face was increasingly flushed, heartbeat picking up in my chest, mouth suddenly dry.

Be sweet. Think...sweet thoughts.

The pale opal on my ring finger flashed in the streetlight shining through the windscreen, reminding me of my obligations and the promises I'd made, making guilt churn uneasily in my gut. Perhaps I'd never find my soul bonds, but I had sworn to Anesidora that I'd keep my thoughts pure for them.

It shouldn't have even been a struggle, it wasn't for anyone else I knew. My brain was twisted.

I pulled over quickly, glimpsing a hint of Rae's bright orange hair. She was waiting blessedly on the opposite side of the street to the club in an empty grassy lot, leaning on a metal fence with barbed wire coiled around the top of it.

Sugar, this really was my least favorite part of town.

My heartbeat continued to pick up even as my stress levels went down, the blood rushing in my ears almost enough to drown out the bass pumping from the club. The sensation was bizarre, bordering on painful. Rae was here. She was fine. So why was my heart thundering against my ribs like it was trying to break free?

Was I still that affected by the *adult* store? My mouth was drier than ever, an achy feeling forming low in my body, and my breasts felt... strange.

Oh no. This was definitely my punishment for asking the Goddess of Night for help. This must be some sort of...*curse*. I had to get Rae and get out of here, drop her at the shelter, then get back to the safety of my apartment to endure whatever the effects of this curse were in peace.

Maybe I was dying? Most people who tangled with daimons in any capacity ended up dead. I had asked the Goddess of Night for her insight into my future, and perhaps this was it. A meaningless life, leading to a meaningless death.

Get it together, Grace. Just because you're having a heart attack, that is no excuse for this morbidity. Rae needs you.

I quickly cut the engine and flicked the lights off, not wanting to draw attention to myself. The incessant throbbing got worse, and I looked around instinctively, feeling like there was a source that I was missing. A reason for the chaotic, overwhelming things my body was doing without my permission.

And then I found it.

My gaze snagged on the man standing in the shadows next to Rae. He was leaning casually back against the fence, further in the shadows than she was. Rae was about my height and he was at least a foot taller, wearing all black. His hair looked black too, and messy. I couldn't make out his features, though he kept playing with a lighter that illuminated pale hands covered in colorful ink.

If I got close enough, I knew what I'd find on his face though. Eyes rimmed in dark purple that bled to red around the iris. The Mark of the Daimon. *The enemy,* I reminded myself, though it sounded more like Mother's voice in my head than my own.

He didn't feel like my enemy. Why didn't he feel like my enemy?

I was opening the car door before I had time to question my actions, needing to get closer, like I wouldn't be able to breathe unless I was near him.

He was already looking at me as I exited the vehicle, posture tense like he was deciding whether to fight or flee.

"Here's my ride," Rae announced, bounding energetically towards the car and throwing her arms around me. The man stepped forward, brow furrowed like he was going to rip her off me before forcing himself to stay still.

Absently, I returned Rae's hug, my hand finding an exposed patch of skin on her back where her too-small top had ridden up. I flattened my palm and was vaguely aware of my magic—Anesidora's magic—working through me, but it was hard to concentrate on anything other than the beautiful man in front of me.

And *oh my word*, he was beautiful. I could see his features more clearly in the dim streetlight. Messy black hair, olive skin, dark stubble that covered his jaw, and a spectacularly kissable mouth. Not that I'd ever *done* that before, but I imagined his mouth would be *great* at it. I attempted to remind myself not to think that way, but I couldn't help it. I didn't want to rein in my inappropriate thoughts at that moment.

I wanted to *act* on them.

While his posture was protective, it wasn't overly confident. He didn't strut around like the world couldn't touch him the way most daimons did. And he was definitely a daimon.

His daimonic eyes, the fascinating blend of purple and red that Rae wouldn't be able to see, didn't detract from his features. It made him *more* appealing, if anything. I was definitely wired wrong. Other agathos didn't think like me.

Or *this* was the Goddess of Night's curse.

Or perhaps Anesidora's punishment for praying to a goddess other than her. I was experiencing attraction for the first time—something that was only meant to happen with my soul bonds—with a *daimon*.

"Hellooooo, Earth to Grace," Rae sang, gripping my shoulders and shaking me slightly. "Oh, are you checking him out? He's hot, right? His name is Riot. He doesn't want to have sex with me."

Riot. Goddess, even his name suggested trouble on an epic scale.

41

"Riot, this is my friend Grace. You should be *so* flattered she's checking you out. I've known Grace for years, she's practically a *nun*—"

"You shouldn't be here," he interjected, looking at me like I was the only thing he saw. His voice was low, with an almost melancholy lilt to it. "It's not safe."

My heart beat harder, like the organ was trying to escape my body, to close the distance between us.

"Come with me."

Was that strange, breathy sound my voice? Had I just suggested he leave with me? No, I hadn't even suggested it. I'd *demanded* it.

"Ooh, that was *sex* voice," Rae teased, half falling into the passenger seat. She was trying to kill me, I was convinced of it.

Riot was silent for a long moment, staring at me like he wasn't quite sure if I was real or not, his lips turned down.

Rejection clawed at my insides like a living, breathing beast, ready to consume me at the first opportunity. I couldn't understand this *need* for him to stay with me, this burning urge to keep him close. It couldn't be the pull of a soul bond. Agathos only bonded to other agathos. Whatever this was...it wasn't that.

I didn't think I could just walk away though.

"Alright," Riot agreed cautiously, moving towards the back seat. I blinked twice, startled at his easy acceptance. He was carrying a bag that seemed a little too big for a night out. Maybe he was going somewhere? Would it be inappropriate to ask?

Probably. I'd met him all of five minutes ago and I wanted to get inside his head and understand everything about him.

I exhaled the breath I didn't know I'd been holding as I rushed around the car to the driver's seat. He was right to say I wasn't safe here, and I'd already spent too long hanging around.

"Are you taking him home?" Rae all but screamed as both Riot and I got in the car. I winced at the sound in the confined space, focusing on turning the car on and getting the hell away from this street I had no business being on. "Are you going to lose your virginity tonight, Grace?!"

I actually hated her a little when she wasn't sober.

I shouldn't. We were meant to be guiding lights and safe harbors for regular human beings, to keep them away from the darkness. Hatred was meant to be reserved for those like the man sitting in the backseat of my car.

But Rae wasn't a nice person to be around when she was wasted, and I wasn't good enough to overlook it.

"That's an inappropriate question," I forced out, hands gripping the steering wheel as I looked both ways before turning out on the main road that led to the shelter.

"You've got *big* virgin energy," Rae persisted, twisting in her seat to look at Riot. "Girl, I think you're being a little ambitious. He's going to want someone with more experience. I bet he's got a big dick too."

"I'm glad that you're at least equal opportunity with your offensive comments," Riot said wryly, though there was no mistaking the censure in his voice. Apparently, his chastisement was more effective than mine, because Rae was silent the rest of the five minute drive to Hope House, and practically threw herself out the door the moment we pulled up in front of the enormous brick building.

43

"I'll see you tomorrow," I called after Rae, who pointedly ignored me.

Hope House slept 32 adults, taking singles only, and was open 24 hours for people to come in. There was a good chance they were full for the night, but I had no doubt whoever was on the front desk would be able to accommodate Rae now she was armed with a little of the good luck I'd slipped her during our hug.

Now I just needed to get home before I had to pay the cost of her good fortune, because I really couldn't afford bad luck with a daimon in the back of my car.

Even though it was usually the human staff rostered on at the shelter at night, it was no safer for Riot to hang around here than it was for me to hang around Onslaught.

"My place isn't far from here," I murmured, pulling away from the curb after I was confident Rae had been let inside. I glanced back at a quiet Riot in the back seat who was nodding his head absently, the purple in his irises catching in the street light.

He was breathtaking, and visibly confused.

"Do you often get in cars with strangers?" I joked weakly as I navigated the quiet streets, attempting to ease the awkward tension in the car.

"No," he replied thoughtfully. "Do you often make strangers feel like they're about to have a heart attack?"

"Never before," I said faintly. Though my heart rate seemed to be dropping now that I was in his presence. Silver linings, I supposed.

I didn't know what to make of his tone. He didn't sound—or look—upset. He just seemed curious about what was going on, head tilted thoughtfully to the side as he examined me in the rearview mirror.

His calm made me feel calmer, which was an unexpected bonus. Usually, I needed a cup of hot tea and several hours to overthink everything before I accomplished this level of zen.

This certainly *seemed* like the magic the elders told us we would find someday. The perfect symmetry we were promised in our soul bonds, the reason we dreamed about finding them someday. Except it couldn't be that. It was impossible for it to be that.

I pulled into my regular parking spot opposite my building and cut the engine, my hands shaking slightly as I undid my seat belt and pulled the key out of the ignition.

Riot was out of the car before I was, swinging his duffel bag over his shoulder and looking around with his brow furrowed. "Is it safe for you to live here?"

He didn't seem *surprised* that I lived here, which confirmed a lingering suspicion I'd always had that the daimons in the area were perfectly aware of my presence here and just didn't care.

I wished my community had that level of apathy sometimes.

"So far, it's been fine," I replied, locking the car and leading him across the street into my building, walking a little faster than usual. We were more likely to be seen by his people than mine in this area, but neither option felt good.

Whatever this was...we should probably keep it to ourselves.

45

"That is not very reassuring," he muttered, sticking close to my back as I led him up the stairs and into my one bedroom apartment. Would he like it? I didn't have people here often—none of my community liked to visit Milton socially—and I was suddenly questioning every decor choice I'd ever made.

"Would you like some tea?" I asked with a strained smile, pulling off my jacket and sneakers. Why did I have to be wearing the all-white knit loungewear? Could I look any more agathos if I tried?

The corner of Riot's mouth twitched as he dropped his duffel bag and pulled off his black leather jacket and combat boots, leaving him in just black jeans and a fitted black t-shirt. Without the jacket, the amount of ink on him was more obvious. Every inch of his arms, even his hands, was covered in beautiful, intricate designs, all done in vibrant colors that stood out against his monotone outfit.

"You don't have anything stronger?" he asked, eyes scanning the wall of photographs above my low bookshelf. Most were of me and my family, a few of my friends from back in Auburn like Verity Mae, but they tended to be from our teenage years.

"Um...Prosecco?"

Sugar, why was that little lip twitch thing he did so adorable? My mooning was reaching teenage girl levels.

"Sure," he replied, those unique purple-red eyes sparkling with amusement. "Prosecco sounds great."

Make that two. Drinking was allowed in moderation and only around others, both as a social activity and so they could hold you accountable. The Prosecco was in the fridge in case I ever had to entertain at the last minute, and while this wasn't quite the kind of emergency I'd planned on breaking it out for, I couldn't think of a more appropriate time.

"Take a seat," I said hastily, remembering my manners. "I'll just grab our drinks," I added unnecessarily, backing up and knocking my elbow on the wall that divided the kitchen and living room in the process. I forced a smile when Riot frowned like he was going to inspect my injury, before spinning on my heel and rushing into the small kitchen, silently mouthing *'ouch'* as my eyes watered.

Maybe that was the bad luck I was owed for helping Rae? A small physical injury was the most common form of payment.

I wiped my palms on my thighs, trying to compose myself while I had a moment alone in the kitchen. I'd never felt so *nervous* before. Not in a fearful way—I was absolutely convinced that he was no danger to me—just in an unsure, embarrassed kind of way.

I had a grand total of zero experiences with romance, as was expected of me, but I *had* watched a lot of romantic comedies, and I was the nerdy teenage good girl crushing on the high school bad boy right now, which at age 25 was all kinds of mortifying.

Plus, embarrassment aside, it shouldn't have been possible.

I glanced around the room as I pulled the chilled bottle out of the fridge, like I was expecting to find the eyes of one or both of the goddesses on me. *Absurd.* With a deep breath to steady my shaking hands, I set the bottle down and pulled two champagne flutes out of the cupboard.

Guilt was twisting painfully in my chest, tying my lungs into knots. Had I done this? I did ask the Goddess of Night for help in a moment of weakness.

No, it hadn't even been a weakness—I'd known exactly what I was doing. I had let that dark, reckless voice in the back of my mind win.

Had I brought this on myself? On *Riot*? He didn't look angry, but he didn't know what I'd done. He was just minding his business, going about his evening, and now he was here. Ripped from his real life because of the desperate pleas of a stranger to a goddess. Surely, neither goddess was cruel enough to punish *him* for my actions?

I regularly gave thanks to Anesidora and asked for guidance, and I'd never had any kind of reaction. No sign that she was listening, no vague open-to-interpretation clues...*nothing*.

Surely a half-baked request shot off to the Goddess of Night wouldn't result in a soul bond *with a daimon* appearing out of thin air an hour later. Did she even have that kind of power?

Anesidora and the Goddess of Night hated one another, that was common knowledge for both agathos and daimons. Surely, there was no way our souls could be tied together without cooperation from both of them? It couldn't be done.

Whatever this connection was...it wasn't a soul bond.

What scared me most was how little that bothered me.

CHAPTER 4

Grace.

It suited her. She'd been gracious to drunk-as-hell Rae, who'd been fucking rude to her. She moved with gracefulness. She was *grace* personified.

I didn't know why I was there. Why I was even in her *presence*. It felt like the universe was laughing at me. Or maybe the goddesses. I'd just known as soon as I'd seen her that I couldn't walk away. There were a million reasons why I should have—for both of our safety—but the moment she'd asked me to come with her, my decision had been made.

I couldn't even blame drugs for my reckless decision this time. I was completely sober and aware of the risk I'd be taking by leaving with her.

Grace was moving around in the kitchen tucked behind a wall off the living room, making our drinks, and I took advantage of the time to look around her apartment. It was *nothing* like the shithole Dad and I lived in above the tobacco shop.

The sofa was a dark blue velvet, layered with artfully placed black and white cushions and a fluffy white throw. Fairy lights were strung up above the couch, underneath an enormous mirror with a dark wood frame. Most of the furniture was polished dark wood, from the trendy coffee table to the low bookshelf. And there were plants *everywhere*— hanging from the ceiling, in cream or terracotta pots all over the surfaces and the floor.

I thought people only lived like this on Instagram.

My heart, which had slowed from the alarming level it had been at, picked up the pace again when Grace reemerged, two glasses of fizzing Prosecco in her hands.

She was so fucking pretty in her weird white knitted pants and matching crewneck sweater. Her brown skin looked impossibly smooth, and her black hair hung almost to her waist, curling slightly at the ends. Everything about her features was *elegant*—pale, jewel-colored eyes, thick curled lashes, a dainty nose, pouty mouth, and a pointed chin.

I felt like a filthy heathen in her presence, but judging by the fluttering pulse at her neck and the blush on her cheeks, she didn't mind that so much. Maybe Grace was the one agathos uptown girl who wanted to know what a daimon downtown man was like, and if that was all she was willing to give me, I'd probably take it.

"Um, shall we sit?" Grace suggested nervously, setting my glass down on the coffee table near where I was standing and motioning at the L-shaped couch. She perched herself daintily at one end and I sat at the other, pushing some decorative cushions out of the way to make room. I kept my distance, not wanting to crowd her even though it felt like every cell in my body disagreed with that sentiment.

Goddess, her apartment was so nice I felt like I was dirtying it up by just existing here.

"So, er, the heart attack sensation," she began, before taking a generous swig of her wine and placing the flute down on a coaster on the coffee table. She folded her hands into her lap, her knuckles turning pale as she twisted her fingers nervously.

I'd never wanted to hold someone's hand so much.

She must have cast some agathos magic on me.

"It's still happening," I noted, my heart still beating faster than usual in my chest, though it wasn't as urgent as it had been. It wasn't just that either. Every inch of my skin, every nerve in my body felt hyper aware of her presence. I definitely wanted to have sex with her—she was stunning, regardless of whatever else was happening to me—but whatever this feeling was, it went deeper than that.

"For me also," Grace replied with a tight smile, smoothing her hands over her white pants. "I can see you're hoping I have answers, and honestly...I don't. Not really."

Comforting.

"You didn't do some kind of agathos voodoo on me?" I asked skeptically.

"We don't do voodoo," she replied, stricken. "Our gifts are only for good—"

"I was joking," I assured her wryly. "I don't really know what you do, but I assume it's not black magic."

"You don't know what we do?" she asked, tipping her head to the side.

51

"No more than what you know about us, I assume." I leaned forward to grab the glass and did my best to ignore the fizzing bubbles as I took a long pull of the Prosecco. "You think we do bad things to hapless humans," I guessed, raising an eyebrow at her.

"Don't you?" Grace asked with a nervous laugh, glancing at an enormous white candle in the center of her coffee table like it held all the answers to the universe.

"We don't influence humans to do anything they don't already want to do." I shrugged, tipping back the glass to finish the sweet wine. Our curse was that we were driven to help them along that treacherous journey whether we wanted to do it or not, but we only encouraged their worst existing instincts.

"Oh."

"Oh?" I asked, feeling the corner of my mouth twitch.

"Sorry, I'm...having a breakdown, I think," she laughed weakly. "I sort of want to pretend that you aren't a daimon, which I know is stupid, but it would be less overwhelming. I feel this...this *connection* to you, and the only kind of instant connection I ever expected to feel like this is a soul bond."

I laughed humorlessly because there was no way that was a fucking option. I knew agathos women had multiple lovers that their goddess chose for them, but we didn't have an equivalent.

I wasn't even entirely sure I had a soul.

"Daimons don't have soul bonds," I replied eventually, shaking my head. We weren't meant for a life of monogamy. I'd never had any kind of long-term relationship. No one I knew ever had. We fucked around, made little daimons with humans who had no idea they'd spawned devil children, and that was that.

"I know," Grace said quietly, staring at the white candle like it was the most interesting thing she'd ever seen. "Agathos only have soul bonds with each other. It can't be that."

I flopped back on the couch, pushing my hair out of my face and tipping my head back to stare at the ceiling. I didn't want her to see my face at that moment. I felt weirdly exposed. There was part of me that was *disappointed* by her answer, which made no sense. I should be *grateful* if anything, like every other daimon would be.

If I'd ever wondered if I was a faulty daimon, there was no fucking doubt in my mind now.

"So, where are *your* soul bonds? You have a few right?" I asked the ceiling. It had always weirded me out that agathos were all about purity and morality and yet their women had multiple lovers. They were discreet about it because it didn't fit in with their country-club-and-picket-fence vibe, but it was knowledge that was passed down from generation to generation when we learned about the agathos.

"I don't have any," Grace replied, and the sadness in her voice was enough to snap me out of my own funk. I straightened up to look at her, noting that she was twisting the ring on her left hand so aggressively I was surprised she hadn't ripped her finger out of the socket. "I'm meant to. I'm 25, so I should have met them all by now, and I haven't even met one."

That seemed a little too odd to be coincidental.

"You, uh, you sure we can rule out the soul bond thing then?" I asked, brow furrowed. "How do you find out for sure if someone is your soul bond or not?"

If we had to fuck for answers, that was a sacrifice I was willing to make that also wasn't a sacrifice at all.

"I really wish I knew more," Grace said quietly, looking a little wistful. "It's deliberately not spoken of so we can experience the *magic* of it for ourselves. All we're really told is that we'll know when it happens, but the process is considered sacred. I've probably said too much already, considering..."

Considering I was a daimon.

"Anyway, I don't know much. Just that there's a call that's meant to be undeniable. I'm supposed to feel it and follow it to where he is. And then the process repeats until I've found all four of them."

The reaction I was having to hearing her describe a process happening with hypothetical dudes was fucking irrational. Whatever this thing was that was tying us together, Grace was never going to have agathos soul bonds. I'd make sure of it.

I'd kill them before they got to her.

In the back of my mind, I realized that my response wasn't healthy, but I could at least partly attribute it to my daimonic nature. We were selfish. Greedy. Covetous.

I wanted to possess Grace. To keep her to myself.

"And what are you supposed to do when you find them?" I asked, my voice hoarse with barely suppressed jealous rage.

The noise she made could best be described as a squeak. Her long black hair fell in front of her face and she didn't bother to push it back again.

Was she...embarrassed? That did help a little with the rage. I never wanted her to feel uncomfortable, and that in itself was a startling realization.

"I've heard from friends that the bond pushes them together. They said I'd feel, er, a sense of urgency until we, you know." She gave me a pointed look and I stifled the urge to laugh.

I didn't know. Got married? Lit a unity candle? Sacrificed a baby lamb to her megalomaniac goddess? I didn't understand anything about her people and how they did things.

"Consummate," she whispered, eyes wide.

There was that jealousy again. I didn't want her consummating anything with anyone other than me, and obviously that wasn't happening. Just saying the word had made Grace look like she was about to pass out.

"So there's supposed to be this overwhelming push to do that," I surmised, attempting to focus and speaking slowly, not wanting to spook her more than she'd already been spooked.

I wanted to feel Grace's body under mine more than I'd ever wanted to with anyone else, I wanted to taste her, hear my name on her lips, but I feel like I'd push her to do that when she was obviously comfortable with the idea.

The only logical conclusion was that this wasn't a soul bond, no matter what weird hopes I'd harbored that perhaps it could have been.

"From what I've heard, what's been hinted at, the feeling is supposed to be quite all consuming," Grace agreed uncomfortably, twisting the ring on her left hand again. The stone appeared to be an opal, it was the same unique color as her eyes.

"Right, so it's probably not that," I sighed.

"Probably not," she murmured, glancing up at me before returning her gaze to the candle. "But..."

"But?" I pressed.

"I want to, *you know*," she whispered conspiratorially, eyes wide. The pale turquoise in them sparkled almost silver when they caught the light.

"You want to what?" I asked, leaning forward and resting my elbows on my knees. There was still enough space on the couch between us to fit another person, but it didn't feel that way.

It felt like there was barely enough oxygen in the room for the two of us.

"I want to *kiss* you," Grace hissed, like the idea was mortifying. This girl was a brutal hit to my ego. I kind of liked it.

"I want to kiss you too, but we're probably thinking of different lips," I replied drily, suppressing a smile.

"Riot!" Grace squeaked, clapping both hands over her face. Why was she so fucking cute? Since when was *cute* so attractive to me? If I didn't get to keep her—soul bond or otherwise—then the goddess was playing a cruel trick on me. "Do you mean...actually, never mind."

"You sure? I don't mind elaborating," I teased, sitting back on the couch and crossing my ankle over my knee.

"I'm sure you don't," Grace said, shaking with silent laughter as she peered at me through spread fingers. "I can't believe you said that," she added, voice muffled by her palms.

"We can start with the mouth, if that helps," I replied with a shrug.

"Um, that won't be necessary," Grace mumbled. "I mean, I want to. But there are rules around that kind of thing."

Rules? What kind of rules were there for kissing?

There was a long moment of pause where Grace stayed in the same position, and I raised a questioning eyebrow at her as she groaned dramatically. *Cute. So fucking cute.* "I've committed to the face hiding thing now, and I don't know how to stop without being awkward. Why am I always so awkward?"

Shit, I couldn't even remember the last time I'd laughed, but the sound escaped me for a moment before I could rein it back in. For a second I hated myself a little less, because she felt so good and pure that I almost believed it could rub off on me.

"Don't overthink it," I advised her seriously.

Grace pulled her hands away and tucked them under her thighs, shooting me a disbelieving look. "You may as well tell me not to breathe or blink. Overthinking social interactions is a core function of my being."

"You're kind of delightful," I murmured, marveling at her. "Did you know that?"

Grace blinked at me, her face flushing again. "I'm fighting the urge to hide again."

Did she not receive compliments often? That seemed insane. Maybe there were rules around that too.

"Back to the, um, me-wanting-to-kiss-you thing," Grace said shyly, shifting her gaze back to the coffee table. "That's not a normal thing for agathos."

"You guys don't kiss…?" I asked slowly. "I assumed that with all the lovers, there'd be a lot of kissing."

"Maybe. I mean, I assume so. Between bonded." Grace cleared her throat. "Sugar, I am not explaining this well. Okay, so agathos are only meant to experience, er, *desire* with their soul bonds."

What in the sex-controlling-cult fuck was that about? Their goddess was the worst.

"So you've never experienced sexual attraction before?" I asked, struggling to keep the incredulity out of my tone.

"Not…not like this," Grace settled on. She looked uncomfortable, so I didn't push even though I sensed there was more to it than that.

"That seems like a pretty big point in favor of us being soul bonds," I pointed out, running a hand through my hair as Grace's eyes followed the movement.

"It does. But you being a daimon is a pretty big point against it," Grace replied softly. Maybe it was my imagination, but Grace almost looked as disappointed as I felt.

What did that mean? What was I supposed to do now? Get up and leave?

That was probably the smart thing to do. I didn't want to though. Everything in me rebelled at the idea of just walking away. Of leaving Grace here alone, living on the outskirts of what she should probably consider enemy territory.

What was for certain was that we were no closer to an answer than we had been when we'd started this conversation. Sex might give us answers, but that was *definitely* not on the table.

"Do you want to watch a movie or something?" Grace mumbled into her lap. I got the impression she needed a minute to clear her head, but maybe she also wasn't feeling ready to say goodbye just yet. "I had planned on watching a movie before bed, before Rae called. Maybe *Freaky Friday.* You probably don't want to watch that though, I'm sure I could find something more..."

I should have probably jumped in to reassure her that I didn't care what movie she picked, but I really wanted to hear what she thought I'd like.

"More serious? Like a documentary or something?" Grace settled on, looking at me like she wasn't sure if I was going to be offended or not.

"A documentary, huh?" I asked, lips twitching.

Grace bit her lower lip as she tried to suppress a smile, eyes sparkling with amusement, and fuck, if I thought she was beautiful before it was nothing compared to when she smiled.

"You seem like you'd like documentaries. Maybe about rock stars. Or true crime," she added, sounding like she was trying not to laugh as she turned on the television.

"Well, now I'm a little embarrassed to admit I like both of those things," I said drily. I was rewarded with a breathy laugh that sank into my bones, burrowing into whatever passed for a daimon's soul. Goddess, Grace was exquisite. "For tonight, *Freaky Friday* sounds good."

Grace glanced at me, giving me a beaming smile as she navigated to the movie. "It must be so nice to be able to lie."

I hadn't thought much about it, but fuck it must be terrible *not* being able to lie. The soul bonds sounded kind of cool, but maybe being an agathos wasn't all sunshine and roses after all.

"It comes in handy," I replied, settling in on the couch as the movie started. "You really can't lie at all?"

Grace shook her head. "Honesty is one of Anesidora's virtues. We're designed to model it by example," she added sheepishly.

Huh. That idea didn't sit particularly well with me.

"Since we have this mysterious connection and all, maybe we should get to know one another a little," I suggested, keeping my voice deliberately casual even as I sweated a little internally waiting for her answer.

If she said no, if she wasn't interested in exploring whatever this was, it would sting, which was an alarming thought. I honestly couldn't remember the last time another person had the capacity to hurt me. I didn't give a fuck what my dad thought. My human mom had succumbed to her addiction years ago, but she'd been in the throes of it my whole life, and I'd barely known her even when she'd been "raising" me.

It was foreign and sort of unpleasant to crave someone's approval, even though there was nothing unpleasant about Grace.

60

"That's a good idea," she replied, tucking her foot under her knee and angling herself more towards me on the couch. "I've never met a daimon before."

Her eyes widened so fast, it was comical. I was guessing she hadn't meant to say that part aloud.

"I've never met an agathos either," I said, suddenly feeling that strange urge to reassure her again. "Though your revelation is a little more surprising, considering where you live."

"Well, I've only been here six months, and this part of town is predominantly human."

"You weren't worried at all when you moved here? Wasn't your family concerned?" *I* was concerned, and I'd just met her.

"Not as much as you'd think," Grace replied carefully. "I'd always been told that daimons wouldn't care in the least about me unless I provoked them." That was true. We mostly didn't give a fuck about anything. "Besides, I think my family were a little relieved, though they'd never admit it. Maybe not that I came to Milton specifically, but that I left Auburn."

I let out a low whistle. "Auburn, huh?"

It wasn't particularly shocking—Auburn was the nearest big agathos settlement—but shit, Grace was really slumming it living here. There wasn't a single home in Auburn for under six figures, and the whole place gave off a distinctly *Stepford Wives* vibe that only a lot of money and cult-like leadership could achieve.

"I dread to think what kind of ideas you've come up with about me already," Grace said with a tentative smile, slumping back against the couch.

"None, actually," I replied, surprising both of us. I had a lot of ideas about what Auburn in general was like, but I hadn't applied any of them to Grace. None of them fit her. "Why don't you tell me the things you want people to know about you?"

The look she gave me was so startled, I briefly wondered if she'd misunderstood the question.

"Um, well I guess I'd like people to know that I have two little brothers, but I'm closest with my cousin, Mercy. I have a Bachelor's of Social Work that I did remotely, and I've worked at Hope House since I was 18, but I started there full-time after I graduated. I love rom-coms. Hate peanut butter. Love matching loungewear sets. Hate heels..."

She tilted her head to the side thoughtfully like she was coming up with more things, totally oblivious to the way she'd just put me under her spell. There was something *happening* to me. There was an unfamiliar, fluttery feeling in my stomach, while at the same time my chest tightened and my brain turned to mush. It was bizarre and addictive at the same time.

She was just so...*kind*. And entirely unaware of how sweet she was.

I mean, the peanut butter thing wasn't ideal, but no one was perfect.

"Are you close with your parents?" I asked, wanting to know every single thing I could learn about this mysterious woman.

Grace wrinkled her nose thoughtfully, tilting her head to the side. "I have one dad out of the four that I'm definitely closer to. My mother and I don't get along."

"That's a lot of parents," I said with a low whistle, slightly mind blown at the concept. "I only have one parent, and he's hard work most of the time."

"Your mother?" Grace asked sympathetically.

"Dead," I replied with a shrug, subconsciously pulling out my lighter. It was the one thing I had from my mom, and while I wasn't a particularly sentimental guy, I'd grown attached to this thing.

"I'm sorry," Grace said softly, some of the nervous tension in her posture relaxing the longer we spoke. "Um, same question for you. Riot, what do you want people to know about you?"

"The less the better, probably," I replied drily. Where to begin? With the homelessness or the drug dealing past? The options were endless.

Grace gave me an assessing look—a glimpse of the woman she probably was when she wasn't filled with nerves—before her face softened into a small smile. "You think about it while I make some popcorn then."

Fuck the consequences. I was going to keep her.

RIOT
CHAPTER 5

I woke up groggy—which wasn't usual for me—but I had to blink a few times before I remembered where I was. The light filtering into the room was painfully bright, and everything smelled a lot better than my dad's place.

Grace's apartment.

I was slumped uncomfortably into the corner of the sectional, propped up by the roughly fifty decorative cushions that covered the sofa. Grace had curled up on her end of the couch, but our hands had sought each other out in sleep, our fingers loosely intertwined between us. *That was an unexpected development,* I mused, staring at our hands. Had I ever held hands with anyone? It wasn't in my nature to seek out that kind of non-sexual intimacy, but I didn't hate it.

Grace's hand looked so dainty next to mine—smooth golden brown skin, slim fingers, nail polish that reminded me of ballerinas or candy floss or some shit. The moon phase tattoos stood out strikingly on my fingers in comparison, all done in dark shades of blue and purple that Dare despised but did anyway, because he was good like that and he needed the practice working with color.

How could Grace and I be total opposites—from our appearance to our very natures—yet fit together so well? What was that if not some divine, soul tying magic?

I didn't want to risk waking her, but I was about to piss myself if I didn't get up soon. The moment I shifted my hand away, Grace woke with a start, pastel-colored eyes blinking sleepily up at me. Fucking hell, she was even prettier in the light of day.

"Oh, did I fall asleep?" she asked, seemingly talking to herself as she pushed up into a sitting position, and looked around her like she was surprised to find her couch there. "Shoot, what time is it? I have work today."

She patted the couch, looking for her phone while I pulled mine out of my back pocket, squinting at the clock through the cracked screen. "It's eight am."

"Sugar!" she squealed, finally finding her phone in the cushions and snatching it up. *Fucking adorable.* "I have to be there in half an hour. Why didn't my alarm go off? Oh, the battery died. Fudge, I don't even have time for a run."

She ran? Around here? That didn't seem safe.

I was mostly confident that daimons would leave her alone—we didn't really give a shit about agathos unless they made themselves a problem for us—but humans were plenty capable of doing bad shit without daimonic influence, and Milton was full of those kinds of humans.

Maybe she had some sort of protective gift from her goddess?

I was not used to caring about other people's safety. It made my chest hurt.

Grace leaped off the couch, oblivious to my internal struggle, and made for what I assumed was her bedroom, while I quickly let myself into the small bathroom to take a piss. Like the living area, the bathroom was mostly neutral colors with green houseplants on every available surface. The more I thought about it, the more unusual that struck me.

Agathos notoriously did not give a fuck about anything other than *human* life. The more humans the better according to their ideology, the planet be damned. It was the basis of the falling out between the founding goddesses that had led to the creation of their own armies—daimons and agathos. Maybe the agathos made an exception for houseplants.

By the time I'd finished and washed my hands, Grace was waiting outside the door, looking obviously anxious. I added '*doesn't like being late*' to the mental file I was compiling on this mysterious woman who'd bowled into my life like a wrecking ball. Not that there was much to wreck, I didn't have any concrete plans anyway, but she'd smashed all my vague ideas apart by just existing.

I lounged on the sofa, pulling out my morning pick-me-up from my pocket and carefully arranging it into a neat line on the silver card holder I kept handy for these kinds of situations. My movements faltered as Grace reemerged from the bathroom, dressed in agathos, Sunday-best chic. Swishy berry-colored knee-length skirt, white long-sleeved blouse tucked into it, hair pulled back into a low ponytail with a gingham scrunchie, makeup so subtle only the slightly thicker eyelashes and light sheen on her lips gave it away.

Goddess above, she looked like she was doing a modern *Little House on the Prairie* cosplay, and I was weirdly into it. Maybe I had a secret good girl kink that I didn't know about?

It struck me then as I was staring at her like a lunatic that this was probably goodbye. I hadn't even meant to stay as long as I had, we'd just happened to fall asleep next to each other. There was a mysterious connection to one another that made me want to stay, but there wasn't any reason for me to, really.

"Do you think you could come back tonight?" Grace asked hurriedly, grabbing items haphazardly and shoving them in her purse. "To talk more?"

The fist that had been quickly crushing my heart seemed to ease its grip. That probably would have been a good moment to tell her I was currently homeless.

"Sure. I'll come back," I said instead. No need to drop the in-between-houses bomb so early.

"My phone is dead so I can't get your number, but my, uh, parents still pay my bill so that's probably not a good idea anyway," Grace muttered, sounding embarrassed about that fact. "I don't know if they can see who I message. It's never been a concern before."

"What are you doing?!" she shrieked suddenly, turning to face me and startling me out of my reverie.

"Staring at you?" I hedged, confused by her panicked tone.

"Is that," she began, before lowering her voice dramatically. "*Cocaine?*"

"This?" I asked, glancing down at the neat line of powder. Possibly I hadn't thought this through. "It is. I'm guessing you're not asking because you want some?"

"No," she gasped, looking appalled. "Why do *you* want it?"

"It's morning?" I suggested, and far earlier than I was used to getting up at that. "It wakes me up."

Grace's brow furrowed with irritation and I wanted to smile at the unexpected reaction. She'd been unfailingly polite since the moment I'd encountered her opposite Onslaught last night. Sweet as pie, even when Rae had been obviously getting on her last nerves.

There was a secret passionate side under that perfectly demure façade, and I wanted to see it.

"Drink coffee like a normal person," Grace snapped, before seeming to catch herself, muttering something like *'be sweet'* under her breath. "That was rude of me."

"No, no," I replied easily, trying not to smile at her sudden display of temper as I collected it back into the bag. "Your house, your rules. I'll refrain."

"Would you?" Grace asked, wincing apologetically.

"I'll give coffee a try." I shrugged. I wasn't convinced coffee would be as effective at waking me up as coke, but I could respect her boundaries.

"Great," Grace breathed. "Okay, shoot. I really have to go." She rushed over to the door, grabbing a pair of tan ankle boots and shoving her feet hastily in, snatching her purse off the side table. "Stay here as long as you like. Do you have to get to work too?"

"I'm a freelancer," I replied evasively. Surely, there was a daimon around here hiring. Maybe that asshole, Viper, needed a hand running the gym.

"Okay, well just lock up when you're ready to go. There's a spare key here," Grace said hastily, gesturing at a hook on the wall. "You should probably be careful coming and going, though this area is pretty quiet in the morning. There's a balcony out back if you want fresh air. It's quite private."

Grace hesitated for a moment, her hand resting on the door handle, and a foreign sensation brushed at my skin, making me startle. It was like whispers of emotion that weren't mine, seeking me out. Communicating with me. Grace's emotions.

It should have felt weird, or wrong—unsettling, at the very least— but it felt kind of *nice*.

I could feel what she needed—the sense of longing that was there that she wasn't ready to articulate. Like her body was silently issuing mine instructions. Letting that instinct guide me, I pushed off the couch and crossed the small room to her, resting one hand on her lower back and pressing a kiss against her hair. It was the chastest kiss I'd ever given anyone, and it felt amazing.

If Dare could see me now, getting all worked up about kissing a girl's *hair*, he'd laugh his ass off.

Grace exhaled softly, her entire body relaxing at my touch. I lingered longer than I needed to, memorizing the floral scent that might have been perfume or was maybe just her, the feel of her next to me, the way the top of her hair brushed against my nose when she turned her head.

It wasn't an overwhelming urge like Grace had described soul bonds as experiencing, but that need to touch her, be near her...it wasn't nothing either.

"Have a good day," I murmured in her ear, a little shiver running down her body as she breathily returned the sentiment, then fled the apartment like there was a monster on her tail, which was close enough to the truth.

It was fascinating. I'd always known that agathos were weird about lust, but Grace seemed borderline *afraid* of it. *Which made sense, if she'd never experienced it before,* I reminded myself.

The moment she left, the warmth she radiated vanished with her. This whole area of Milton was a little more upmarket—which in reality meant a little less decrepit—and it lacked the screaming neighbors and street brawls I was accustomed to waking up to, sometime closer to mid afternoon. Wanting to be true to my word, I tucked the drugs back in my jacket and poked around her tiny but fancy kitchen until I found a coffee press.

The kitchen was U-shaped, with a glossy wooden countertop, stainless steel appliances, fancy looking blue-gray cabinets, and an elaborate tile backsplash that made me think of Morocco. It was about as opposite as possible from my dad's apartment with the formica countertops and peeling beige paint on the cabinets.

It was all very fancy, and she obviously had good taste and cared about this kind of stuff, which was cool and a little intimidating. While something about Grace felt familiar—like I'd known her my whole life, or maybe in a previous one—her life, her *home*, her world made me feel incredibly out of place.

Coffee in hand in a fancy glazed cup that looked like it had been handspun by angels on a pottery wheel, I opened the curtains that covered the french doors out to the covered balcony.

Roses, I realized with surprise. There was a line of terracotta pots, each housing a rose bush. Grace's interest in plant life was *fascinating*. It directly contradicted everything I knew about agathos.

More puzzled than ever, I returned to the couch. We needed answers for this bizarre connection—or at least a starting point—and while I was basically useless in every way that mattered, there was one guy I knew who might be able to help. If he was feeling cooperative, which heavily depended on his mood.

71

Blowing out a long breath, I pulled up the contact on my phone and hit the video call icon. *Bullet*. I thought he was a fucking space cadet most of the time, but he had a strong connection with the Goddess of Night and maybe he could find some answers. Maybe he already *knew* the answers. Bullet was a descendent of the Oneiroi line, but I wasn't entirely sure how his gifts worked even though we'd known each other for years.

He picked up the call quickly, but there was a black screen where his picture should have been while my puzzled face stared back at me from the small box in the corner.

"Are you alone?" Bullet asked instantly.

"Er, yeah?" I replied. I supposed it was a fair question, he knew I lived with my dad. *Had lived* with my dad. Besides, I didn't really question Bullet's odd moments anymore. He lived out in the countryside, entirely isolated, bombarded with vague dreams of the future, with only his tarot cards for company.

What little social skills he'd gained while we were growing up, he'd lost as soon as he retired to the Farm of Tortured Psychics, or whatever they called it.

I'd be a little weird too.

"I thought it would take longer for you to contact me," Bullet greeted, grinning broadly at me as he switched the camera on, shoving his floppy pale blonde hair out of his face. He'd always taken an interest in fashion, so I wasn't entirely surprised to see him wearing a black t-shirt and charcoal blazer in his own home at 8:30 in the fucking morning. The gold 9mm bullet he always wore around his neck glinted in the light.

"So you were expecting me?" I asked flatly. He'd probably dreamed about this exact moment last night.

"Of course. I know what you're going to ask me, and no I'm not going to do a reading for you over the phone. That's not how it works," he sang. Goddess, I forgot how high energy he could be.

"Can you try?" I groused. "How different is video calling versus in person anyway? I don't know what you've *seen*, but I'm not in a position where I can just drop in right now."

Visiting Bullet was a nightmare at the best of times, since it involved a long drive through agathos territory, and they were a bigger threat to us than we were to them. Their non-violent rules didn't seem to apply when it came to daimons.

How nice of their goddess to include that convenient exception.

Bullet nodded solemnly, all traces of humor gone from his face for a brief, unsettling moment. "A reading on your own won't do you any good either."

I stilled, eyes narrowed on the screen, wondering what he knew. Either he'd *seen* something, or someone had watched me leave with Grace last night, though I thought we'd been pretty discreet. The former was a more terrifying idea. As far as I knew, the Oneiroi's visions were limited to their fellow daimons. His visions were a gift from the Goddess of Night, and she had no control over humans or agathos.

Daimons couldn't have visions about agathos, just like agathos couldn't have daimonic bonded.

Right?

A frisson of fear ran through me that whatever was going on here was bigger than just Grace and I. What if this was some kind of divine task? Back in the old days, the goddesses were always meddling with mortal lives, but they'd grown bored of that centuries ago.

Besides, it didn't seem likely that any deity would select me for anything. The Goddess of Night would be more likely to punish me for being a particularly terrible daimon. Grace, though...maybe she'd caught the attention of the goddesses. She was interesting, and beautiful and compassionate, and nothing like what I'd expected an agathos to be.

Fuck, I wondered how Grace felt about weed? Surely I could smoke a little of that to dull all these feelings. That was way less potent than coke.

Bullet tilted his head to the side, examining me with eyes similar to my own. "I wonder who you are."

"You know who I am," I replied flatly, his vague words pulling me out of the panic spiral I'd been heading towards. "We've known each other since we were kids."

Bullet scoffed. "I know you're Ryan Garner."

I cringed at the use of my birth name. Our nicknames were earned in our teen years by other daimons and we went by them for the rest of our lives. I should hate mine. Riot was an ironic nickname, given to me sarcastically. *Oh, Ryan's in the corner smoking by himself again. He's a riot.*

"What I mean is *which* one you are—The Devil, The Chariot, or The World?" Bullet continued, looking genuinely perplexed at his nonsense question. "Temptation, addiction, that sense of being trapped have always followed you around, at the same time you've always exercised more control and willpower than some of our *peers*, even when it makes you miserable, which is always. A sense of completion and accomplishment I probably *wouldn't* associate with you..."

"This isn't making me feel any better," I deadpanned, irritation coursing through me. "I called you for advice, not to listen to you list all my flaws."

Bullet hummed, grinning cheerfully again. "One man's flaw is a certain woman's kryptonite. Anyway, I'm sure my dreams will reveal who you are soon enough. Steps need to be taken, Riot. Don't wait too long."

The call ended and I cursed under my breath. *Fucking psychics.* Now I had more questions than answers, and I felt shittier than usual about myself. He couldn't have *seen* Grace. It wouldn't make sense for her to feature in his visions. Then again, nothing that had happened so far made any fucking sense so what did I know?

I almost trusted Bullet—more than I trusted most daimons with the exception of Dare—but the idea of visiting him with Grace for a reading was terrifying. Could I trust him with Grace? Could I trust anyone with her? With the knowledge of this *thing* between us, whatever it was?

Her people were meant to be the *good* ones. The kind and benevolent guardians of humanity. Yet if they found that one of their own had some kind of connection to a daimon, I doubted their kindness and benevolence would extend to Grace.

Fuck, how did people live with all this stress? How did they just go around making decisions all the time? No wonder humans were always hitting me up for temporary escapes.

I unlocked my phone to check my messages, realizing there was one from Dare that must have arrived when I was sleeping. I'd totally forgotten he was expecting me.

Me:

Hey, I found someone to crash with. Thanks for the offer though.

Dare:

Who? I'm your only friend.

He must have an early booking to be replying at this time of the morning. Dare slept less than anyone else I knew.

Me:

Bullet could be my friend.

The three of us had hung out a lot when we were young. Daimons didn't have friends, but those two were the closest I'd ever had to it I guessed.

Dare:

Fuck off, we've barely seen Bullet since he went full country hermit. Who is it? A girl?

As much as I trusted Dare, this wasn't just my life, or my secret to divulge.

How would I even explain it? *Oh yeah, I met this beautiful woman outside Onslaught and I felt like I was about to have a heart attack while being electrocuted, but I wanted to make out with her at the same time. And she's an agathos, so there's that.*

He'd probably wonder if I'd gone a little too wild with the stash I'd skimmed from my dad.

Dare:

Actually, tell me in person. If you're not working for your dad, you can come help me out. I need an errand boy.

Me:

Fuck off.

Dare:

See you in an hour then.

I scoffed even as I pushed off the couch to find clean clothes in my duffel bag. I knew Dare was being a dick to cover up his act of charity, and I appreciated him for it.

Besides, I had *some* pride. I couldn't just mooch off Grace and lie on her couch all day, even though that's all I'd been doing at my dad's place for months.

Maybe some of her good girl charm was rubbing off on me already.

"Hey," Dare said, straightening up from the bench of equipment he'd been cleaning and giving me an appraising look over the half wall that separated his work area from the front of the studio. "You look...a lot less shitty than I expected, honestly."

"Such little faith in me," I scoffed, even though it was entirely reasonable of him to expect I'd gotten shitfaced last night to avoid my problems. "You look terrible," I added with a smirk as I shut the door behind me. "You should consider sleeping this week."

"I'll sleep when I'm dead," Dare replied, rolling his eyes. He was wearing a black t-shirt that showcased the symmetrical ink down both arms and roses which climbed up the sides of his neck from his chest to finish behind his ears.

The neck tattoo wasn't new, but the roses hit differently today having seen Grace's collection. I was pretty sure I'd be seeing reminders of her all day. Already, my skin was itching with the need to get back to her which was...unexpected.

My entire life had been so thoroughly upended that it felt weird to see Dare looking the same as usual. Dare was at least half Japanese, raised by his Japanese daimon mother who never talked about Dare's father, and always looked too fucking cool for shitty Milton. Straight black hair that was shaved on the sides and longer on top, styled in an artful mess because he was vain like that. He had sharp features and shadows under his red and purple eyes from lack of sleep.

"What do you want me to do?" I asked, moving towards the glass desk in the corner where he kept his laptop and a pile of receipts that he probably considered an accounting system.

Most of his studio was stark white and glass, which showed off the black artwork in white frames covering almost every inch of wallspace.

I didn't like to tell him too often in case he got a big head about it, but he was crazy fucking talented.

"Deal with that shit," Dare replied, tipping his chin at the chaos on the desk. I wasn't surprised he didn't have the patience or attention to detail to sort out his admin work, he was descended from the Philotes line after all, and fighting against his nature as it was. "Greet the clients. Aftercare instructions. Take the payment. Get my lunch. But first I want to hear about where you're staying and what happened last night."

"No can do," I said, picking through the papers. Shit, the receipts here must go back a year at least.

Dare made a disgruntled noise under his breath. "Riot, don't be a dick. I'm guessing you swiped whatever you were supposed to sell last night, and your dad was raging before you even left the house. Plus, Goddess knows who you pissed off at Onslaught last night."

"Who says I pissed anyone off? I was on my best behavior. I didn't even go inside," I replied with mock offense.

"I really think you should crash with me," he pressed. "You have no self-preservation instincts, Riot. You're already in trouble before you consider the consequences."

I didn't argue because he wasn't wrong, but I was feeling more motivated to keep myself out of trouble than I usually did.

"Just be careful, okay?" Dare sighed, relenting.

The hint of concern in his voice made me turn around. Dare wasn't a Moros descendent like me, naturally prone to being as objectively miserable as possible. Philotes descendents fucked a lot, they were usually pretty cheerful.

"I'm good, man," I reassured him, feeling deeply unsettled while doing so. "Things are a little weird right now, but I'll tell you more when I can."

"Don't get killed, Riot," Dare muttered, turning his attention back to his equipment. "I'd miss you, like, one percent if you died."

"Cute. I'd miss you one percent too. Maybe two. It'd be more if you put out sometimes," I joked.

Dare scoffed. "With the amount of time you spend lying around moping, I bet you're a total starfish. I like my partners less...dead fish-like in bed."

"I'm not kink shaming, but that's two ocean-related metaphors in a row. Is there something you want to tell me?"

"Fuck off," Dare laughed, moving behind the half wall where the chair was. "Sit down at my desk, in my studio, and sort out my life. I'll have your sexy secretary uniform ready for next time."

GRACE

CHAPTER 6

I moved around the empty rooms at Hope House almost mindlessly, changing bedding and cleaning up for the next occupants, counting down the minutes until I could leave.

I loved my job, really.

I found it incredibly rewarding, even when my boss tested my resolve to be sweet and patient. Usually, getting home to my empty apartment was the last thing on my mind, but today it was like the hours couldn't pass fast enough.

Was Riot okay? Had he gone to his mysterious freelance job? Should I have asked more questions about that? How was he feeling? Was there enough food in the house for him? Did daimons even eat normal food? He ate popcorn last night, but what if he had dietary requirements? *Fudge*, I should have checked before I left.

What if he was hungry?

I hadn't even done my Sunday grocery run, I wailed internally. The *one* time I hadn't gone to the store, I had an overnight guest.

I wished I could message him, but it was probably a good thing I hadn't gotten his number even if my phone had been charged. My parents insisted on still paying for my phone plan, and I wasn't sure how much they could see. Probably a lot, since I was sure that was the only reason they did it.

That was one area of independence I hadn't achieved yet, and I was determined to rectify it.

At least the distance between Riot and I gave me a moment to process the possibilities of what this...*connection* between us meant without being distracted by his presence and his beautiful face, or all the things I wanted him to do to me that I didn't quite understand and wasn't allowed to feel.

Sugar, when he'd kissed my head this morning...

Logically, I remembered it was how my grandmother had used to kiss me, but it hadn't felt grandmotherly when he'd done it. It had felt... like the promise of something more.

I *desired* him, and agathos were programmed to only feel desire for their soul bonds. That Riot *was* my soul bond was the most obvious answer, yet the least plausible. It should be impossible. I'd never heard of it happening before in all the years of Saturday morning lessons at the temple when we'd been taught about our history and as much about bonds as the Elders were willing to share.

Then again, most agathos probably didn't dabble in prayers to a certain dark goddess.

I should have told him. Riot deserved to know what I'd done. He looked at me like he felt bad that I was stuck with him or something, which was madness when I was probably the one who'd got us into this situation in the first place.

My boss, Constance, was downstairs and moved around the place like she was trying to make as much noise as possible, so I took a moment to sit down at the end of the bed, exhausted from my poor night's sleep half upright on the couch.

I really needed to be on my A-game today. I couldn't afford to draw attention to myself while I was *entangled* with a daimon. And Constance disliked me already.

Get up, Grace.

Could Riot really be my soul bond, or did I just *want* him to be? Maybe I was just entertaining the idea to cover up my own depraved desires? My entire life, I'd known I was not as *good* as I should have been. As much as my mother had diligently worked to train the darkness and disobedience out of me, it obviously hadn't worked.

Maybe I'd sown the seeds of darkness that were already there by reaching out to the Goddess of Night, and she'd somehow connected Riot and I.

If he *was* my soul bond, that presented its own set of questions for me to overthink. What did that mean for the future? Would I have four soul bonds like other agathos? Would they all be daimons? If that was the case, it would make sense that I'd never met them. Or maybe one daimonic bond was the equivalent of four agathos, and it would just be Riot and me.

That might be better. Less people to organize when my community found out about this and banished me from their territories.

I couldn't expect the daimons to accept me into their ranks—if that was something I'd even want. I wondered how Riot would feel about living in unclaimed neutral territory, far away from the disapproving agathos...

Siberia, perhaps.

"You are useless today!" Constance snapped, standing in the doorway with her hands on her hips. I shot to my feet instantly, my stomach dropping out of my body. *Impossible.* Constance never snuck up on me. She was a slim woman who moved with the grace of an aging hippopotamus.

That was an unkind thought. I couldn't muster the energy in that moment to balance it out with a positive one.

"It's like you don't even want to help the poor unfortunate souls who rely on us," Constance sighed dramatically.

Sugar. This must be my bad luck for helping Rae yesterday.

"I'm sorry, I'll work faster," I murmured, bowing my head against her criticism. Constance managed Hope House—owned by her and her bonded—and was one of the most unpleasant people I'd ever encountered in my life.

She didn't even try to hide the blatant superiority she felt over the people we were bound to serve. Agathos like her were the reason I'd left Auburn and its riches and elitism behind.

"Look at me when I'm speaking to you," Constance ordered coolly.

I lifted my head and folded my hands demurely in front of me as my mother had always taught me. *Don't give them more reasons to look down on you. Our family is new and not well respected in Auburn. Earn your place.*

"Work faster," Constance instructed, her harsh glare on me. Her thin eyebrows were permanently raised, gray hair swept back into a slick bun, mouth *always* downturned. She terrified me just as much today as she had when I'd seen her at community events as a child. "Need I remind you that no other employee has taken so long to advance from the monitor role, Grace? You should be in a higher position by now."

With a final pointed look, she swept out of the room, her pale silver skirt swishing after her. I huffed a silent laugh under my breath at the *audacity* of that statement. I would never get a promotion, because Constance was in charge of doling them out, and Constance didn't like me.

Yesterday, that would have seemed like the most dramatic thing that could ever happen to me, but today I knew better.

There were far more dramatic things happening in my life than not getting a promotion at work.

By the time I'd finished making the beds and taking the laundry down to the basement, I was due to do another round of health and safety checks.

"Grace!" Rae called as I passed the common room. She was lounging on a bright red couch at the back of the room, watching the family movie we had playing on the screen in the corner. *Hercules.*

Someone on the front desk today had a sense of humor. Our experience of the Greek gods was *not quite* how the myths memorialized them. The Olympians may have the best stories, but it was the Primordials that held all the power.

"Get over here, Grace!"

I plastered a smile on my face and wound my way through the couches and armchairs to where Rae was relaxing, and sat in the small space at the end of the couch next to Rae's crossed ankles.

While I had mixed feelings about her last night, my agathos instincts didn't care about my personal feelings. Rae's pain was calling to me, and I couldn't *not* take some of it as my own, even if I was a little annoyed with her.

"How are you feeling today?" I asked, leaning over to rest my hand on her exposed arm and skimming her emotional anguish, gritting my teeth as her pain burrowed into my psyche like hot needles.

Unlike using my good luck gift, paying the cost for easing physical or mental suffering was at least short and instantaneous. It was an ability all agathos were blessed with. Or cursed with.

"Me? Fine," Rae replied, waving her hand dismissively as I sat back and folded my hands in my lap. It didn't surprise me that she hadn't thanked me for picking her up in the middle of the night—she'd never thanked me in the past—but perhaps my inner monster was feeling particularly petty today, because it *irritated* me.

"I wanted to see if you were walking okay this morning," she added with a sly smile.

I blinked slowly at her. "Why wouldn't I be?"

"Seriously?" Rae laughed, yanking her orange-red hair up into a messy bun. "That guy was giving off crazy Big Dick Energy, don't tell me it was all a front."

My face was definitely hot, but it wasn't *just* embarrassment like I usually experienced when it came to anything remotely sexual. I was offended? Or at least I thought I was. She had no right to talk about Riot's...*energy* like that.

"We were just talking," I replied diplomatically. Far more diplomatically than I felt.

"Suuuuuure," Rae laughed, before shooting me a sidelong look. "Oh shit, you're serious? Girl, *why*?"

"That's a very personal question," I deflected, smoothing out my skirt.

"Boo, you're no fun." Rae pouted, turning her attention back to the screen. I sat there awkwardly, not entirely sure if I'd been dismissed or not. Eventually, she turned her sullen attention back on me. "Can I have his number then? If you're not going to fuck him?"

Oh, sugar. The darkness rose up so swiftly I clutched my chest like I could physically restrain what I knew existed only inside my head. I wanted to yell at her. To be...*mean* to her. Riot was a *person*, he didn't exist for her sexual gratification.

"I don't have it," I replied through gritted teeth, suddenly grateful I hadn't asked for it since I wouldn't be able to lie if I had. "Excuse me, I need to finish my rounds," I added, standing up and giving her a tight smile.

Rae shook her head sadly, giving me a pitying look. "Probably for the best, girl. You're so sweet, you know I think the world of you, but a guy like Riot would eat you alive."

I held my head high as I walked away, forcing down the lump that was rapidly forming in my throat, warning me that Rae might be right.

By the time I arrived back at my apartment—Rae's warning still ringing in my ears—I felt like I'd run a marathon. Not that I'd been particularly physically active—I'd driven the short distance between the shelter and my apartment—but my heart was racing, lungs burning, breath coming in short pants.

I climbed the staircase feeling like there were lead weights in my shoes, dragging my feet down. Usually I didn't touch the bannister because *germs*, but today I was prepared to risk it and douse myself with sanitizer because I couldn't physically climb the stairs without pulling myself up.

What was *happening* to me?

The moment I stumbled inside, within reach of Riot, surrounded by his scent, some of the panic eased. I could hear him moving around the kitchen and a huge breath whooshed out of my lungs.

He was here. He was real. The past 24 hours hadn't been some kind of fever dream.

"Hi," I breathed, after ditching my coat and shoes and hovering in the doorway of the kitchen.

"Hey." Riot glanced at me, his thick black hair falling into his eyes, the corner of his mouth kicking up in an almost smile.

I almost melted into the floor. I'd always assumed women in romance movies were overdoing it with the swooning and sighing, but I was swooning and sighing with the best of them.

He was just so...*swoony.* All dark hair and cut cheekbones, like the movie villain with the tragic backstory who you hated as a kid, but were *curious* about as an adult.

"I'm making dinner, I hope that's okay," he said, gesturing at the cutting board in front of him. He didn't look much more energetic than I felt on closer inspection. There were dark shadows under his eyes, and his hair was sticking up everywhere like he'd been shoving his hands through it.

"Was there anything to cook?" I asked, cringing at the state of my fridge. I usually bought exactly what I needed every Sunday, since it was hard to keep fresh food from going off cooking for one.

"Well if canned soup and grilled cheese are okay, then yeah we're good," Riot replied with another soft smirk. How did he make that expression so effortlessly attractive? He really had the bad boy heartthrob look down pat.

"Sounds amazing. I was going to order in, but I wasn't sure what kind of things you ate as, you know..."

"As a daimon?" Riot asked, cocking a brow at me. "We prefer raw heart in the evenings to replenish us before our shadowy nighttime activities. Washed down with the blood of virgins, naturally."

My eyes were as wide as saucers, I could feel it. I was pretty sure my eyeballs were about to fall out of my skull.

"I'm kidding," Riot replied with a raspy laugh, giving me a sidelong look. "Though you totally believed me, which is...alarming."

"Sorry," I said sheepishly, feeling my face heat. Obviously they didn't eat raw hearts or drink blood. *Get it together, Grace.*

"No need to apologize," Riot said easily, far more forgiving than I would have been if someone had entertained for even a second that I drank the blood of virgins for sustenance. "It's not like I know much about the agathos. But daimons are vegetarians, just so you know."

"Really?" I asked, eyes widening.

"The Goddess of Night has very few expectations of the daimons, but that is one of them. She feels that we shouldn't hold ourselves above other creatures by consuming them," he explained casually, removing the saucepan of soup from the heat. "Unlike humans. Your goddess' creation, as far as I know."

"That's right," I volunteered, grabbing cutlery from the drawer and taking it out to the small white circular dining table I rarely used, sitting just outside the kitchen area. The two rattan dining chairs had mostly been for aesthetic purposes since no one visited me here.

"Let me finish up here and we'll talk," Riot said, looking thoughtful. I turned to walk away, wanting to change into comfortable clothes when I *felt* concern. *His* concern. It slid uneasily against my skin, somehow feeling both faint and entirely clear. I could identify the emotion instantly, even if it was only the echo of it.

"Everything okay?" Riot asked, brow furrowed as he looked at me, frozen in place.

"I can...I can *feel* you," I replied, stunned.

Riot's features softened slightly. "Yeah, I noticed that this morning."

"Oh." *Way to be observant, Grace.* "That's...unexpected. It seems sort of..."

"Soul bond-y?" Riot suggested, lips quirked. "It does, doesn't it?"

Riot resumed making the grilled cheese, remarkably unphased, while I walked to my room in a daze. He seemed to be taking this development better than I was. Perhaps because he'd had the day to consider it. I was only vaguely aware that I'd pulled out a blush-colored loungewear set from the drawer, and changed quickly before returning to the living area where Riot was sitting at the table waiting for me.

Was it soul bond-y, as he'd so eloquently put it? I shook off the thought, conflicted by the bubble of hope it caused in my chest.

"I'm sorry," I said as I sat down to join him. "I already feel like I've ripped you out of your life, and now you're *cooking* for me."

"I have a lot less going on in my life than you think," Riot replied wryly.

"I'm sure that's not true," I protested.

"Seriously," Riot deadpanned. "I was living with my dad, but he kicked me out due to an...*employment* disagreement. I was on my way to a friend's place last night."

I *almost* asked what kind of friend. The question was on the tip of my tongue, jealousy churning uncomfortably in my gut.

I'd never been the jealous type before, not really. I'd felt some envy that my friends had met their soul bonds and I hadn't, but I'd been more sad for my own future rather than begrudging *their* happiness.

Riot looked puzzled for a moment before grinning broadly at me. Sugar, that expression bordered on sinful.

"I felt that," he said, a teasing lilt to his voice.

"You felt what?" I asked, my voice a little too high to sound natural. *Please don't say jealousy.*

"You're jealous."

Fudge. Had I given out any luck today? Because I certainly felt like I was getting some bad luck back.

The amethyst in Riot's eyes seemed to sparkle with amusement, and I felt my face grow hot under his attention.

"That's absurd, isn't it?" I asked nervously, not having any experience with this kind of thing.

Riot scoffed. "I know you don't have any soul bonds, but I'm hoping you don't have a boyfriend. Or a girlfriend. Whatever. A little jealousy wouldn't even *begin* to cover it."

I almost shivered at the possessiveness in his tone. It *definitely* didn't frighten me the way it probably should have.

"I don't," I breathed. "Agathos don't date."

"Ever?" Riot replied, reeling back in his chair. "The soul bond things...that's it?"

"Well, there are four for most women," I replied, trying to understand his question.

"And you don't date before that? Casually? I guess if you can't feel attraction..." he trailed off, looking disturbed at the idea.

"No," I said instantly, feeling my eyes grow wide at the very concept. "It would be considered the height of disrespect to our future bonded to date. It...it *couldn't* happen, there'd be cleansing ceremonies at the temple and prayers to Anesidora..." I shook my head, finding it hard to even articulate how frowned upon it would be.

"Okay," Riot drawled, still looking vaguely unsettled. "So, you meet your soul bond and you're connected and that's it? No questions asked?"

"Yes." I blinked, trying in vain to see what the issue was. Perhaps I hadn't explained it properly?

"The Goddess herself assigns soul bonds," I added slowly. "They are a gift."

Riot laughed humorlessly and just the *sound of it* bordered on wickedness. *Everything* about him was so wicked, and it scared me how much that appealed to me. Not just the monstrous darkness in me, but all of me.

"Some gift, Gracie—"

Riot paused, the nickname taking us both by surprise. He looked like he was waiting for me to correct him, but I sort of liked the sound of it on his lips.

"A gift doesn't come with conditions," Riot continued eventually. "If someone gives you a...a *purse*, and you don't like it, you can just shove it in the back of your closet and forget about it."

I listened to his patient, judgment-free tone with increasing discomfort.

"You can't *gift* a person, Gracie. They have their own free will, goals, dreams that may be incompatible with yours."

"Anesidora doesn't make mistakes," I replied instantly, the words rolling off my tongue with practiced ease. After all, they'd been drilled into me from birth.

"Unless we do end up being soul bonds," Riot said wryly, sitting back and spreading his arms wide as if to say *look at me*. "That would seem like a pretty big mistake, since you'd never want a daimon for your bonded."

I nibbled nervously on the edge of my grilled cheese, wondering if I should tell him that I'd asked the Goddess of Night for help before I'd left the house last night. Maybe Anesidora hadn't been involved in this at all.

At the same time, I couldn't help feeling like this was out of the Goddess of Night's powers—I wasn't a daimon, surely she didn't have jurisdiction over me? Maybe Riot was different from other daimons, and Anesidora wanted me to draw him towards the light.

Or maybe...maybe I was just bad. I'd often struggled with thoughts less *pure* than I should have. But I'd always apologized to Anesidora for my failings, and strove to do better.

Surely, she wouldn't punish me when I was trying to do better?

I looked at Riot leaning back in his chair, the pain in his eyes impossible not to see no matter how much he tried to deflect, and I *loathed* myself.

How could I even entertain the idea that he was a punishment?

Hesitantly, I leaned forward, tentatively reaching out my hand to rest on top of his, half expecting him to push me away.

He didn't, and we both stared silently at our hands for a moment as the physical ache and exhaustion I'd been battling with all day slowly seeped away.

"I should have corrected the assumption that I don't want you right away," I said softly, my skin almost humming at how good it felt to *not* feel drained for a moment.

Riot snorted dismissively. "Don't lie on my account, Gracie. No agathos wants to be bonded to a daimon."

"I couldn't lie even if I wanted to. We don't have to think of ourselves as a daimon and an agathos right now. We can just be Riot and Grace."

He gave me a dubious smile that didn't reach his eyes, but flipped his hand over to give mine a quick squeeze before we resumed our dinner.

"So, uh, what did you do today?" I asked, internally cringing at the awkward question. Why did I always sound so dorky? Why couldn't I sound cool and unaffected?

Riot's lips twitched as he glanced up from his dinner, looking across the table at me like I was adorable. Which was kind of nice? I'd had some very *un-adorable* thoughts about him though, and I half wondered if they were one-sided.

Though he did say that thing about *kissing* last night. Kissing in... *other places.*

"A friend, I guess, asked me to help out at his tattoo studio for awhile, so that's what I'm doing at the moment," Riot replied, steering my thoughts in a more wholesome direction.

"You *guess* he's a friend?" I asked with a frown.

"We're not really designed to maintain friendships," Riot said cynically. "Everything is usually an exchange. A deal."

"That's kind of sad," I replied, thinking of my friendships with the girls I'd grown up with. Though they had mostly fallen by the wayside, hadn't they? They were busy with their families and couldn't relate to me. Plus, as much as I liked them, I couldn't exactly trust them the way friends were supposed to trust each other.

I could never tell them about this.

"It is what it is." Riot shrugged.

"So what did you do before?" I asked before taking an unladylike bite of my grilled cheese. Mother would faint.

"I'm not sure you really want the answer to that question," Riot chuckled. He was so easy to talk to, sometimes I found myself forgetting he was a daimon at all, even with the red and purple eyes. But I had the feeling whatever he was referring to would serve as a sharp reminder. Riot watched my face carefully, sighing in defeat when I didn't back down, then set down his sandwich.

"My dad sells drugs. It was assumed from birth that I'd go into the family business, like he had growing up."

"Oh."

Riot gave me a wry smile that didn't meet his eyes. "It wasn't something I ever wanted to do. A few months ago, I refused to sell anymore. It's been...a point of contention."

I was torn between feeling sympathy for Riot's plight—I knew what it was to not live up to a parent's expectations—and horror at the lives he'd potentially damaged. Ruined, even. I was a bad agathos, but I was still an agathos, and everything in me rejected the idea of human misery in any form.

Riot was watching me carefully, his eyes guarded, as he waited for a more substantial response than "*oh*". I wasn't quite sure what he was expecting—possibly for me to kick him out of my apartment? His expression certainly said that.

"But you don't do that anymore," I settled on eventually.

"I don't."

"Okay, well, that's...I mean, so long as you're not doing it anymore—"

"It would be a mistake to think of me as the good guy, Grace. I'm not," Riot said flatly. I could feel his self-loathing like blades against my skin, but even if I couldn't, it was written all over his face.

"We're more than the sum of our regrets, Riot," I told him softly.

Riot's eyes suddenly sparkled with amusement, and even though the rest of his features were unchanged, it transformed his entire face.

I thought that dark and brooding Riot was the most tempting, but the faintly amused Riot blew him out of the water.

If he smiled, really *smiled*, I might spontaneously combust.

"We're not really wired for regrets. I feel guilt, which is pretty undaimonic in itself, but I don't have that urge to do anything differently that I'm told comes with the sort of regret humans feel. If I got the chance to go back in time, I wouldn't change anything."

He looked momentarily frustrated, like he was struggling to conceptualize the idea, which I could understand. We both lived on the periphery of the human world, we used their terminology, their ideals, but we *weren't* entirely human and we physically couldn't process emotions the same way they did.

Apparently for daimons, it was emotions like remorse that were off limits. Agathos couldn't lie, cheat or steal, and we weren't meant to experience anger and bitterness the way I seemed to.

It definitely wasn't lost on me that Riot was an unusual daimon and I was unusual agathos. If this connection was the result of La Nuit's interference, she was a good matchmaker...

97

"What about you? Do you have regrets, Gracie?" Riot asked in a low voice, tilting his head to one side.

Did I have regrets? The chilling silence after my spur of the moment prayer to the Goddess of Night sprung to mind. The sudden darkness as the candle extinguished, and the realization that I may have bitten off more than I could chew.

"Not yet," I replied, the answer coming surprisingly easily.

I'd followed the rules my entire life no matter how miserable they'd made me, how wrong they'd felt, and I didn't regret that either. I'd *tried*. Whatever happened with Riot, whatever this was, it made me wonder how much longer I could walk the tightrope of my community's expectations of me and the darkness inside that urged me to seek something more.

There was a very good chance I would regret *that* choice.

I insisted on cleaning up since Riot had cooked, and left him in charge of picking a movie for us to watch. It all felt weirdly domestic, but I sensed we were both leaning on that domestic normalcy. Everything else was weird and unexplainable, but when we were sitting around watching television, we could pretend for a while that it wasn't.

By the time I came out to join him, the reprieve I'd gotten from being apart from him during the day seemed to be over. My body was back to feeling achy and restless, and it definitely seemed like this was the way soul bonds were pushed together. Right? What else could it be?

I wanted to cuddle him. I'd *felt* his emotions. *What else could it be?*

Instead of acting on my suspicion, I sat at the opposite end of the couch and hugged a pillow to my stomach.

"So..." I began, picking a loose thread on the cushion I was holding like a snuggly shield. "Do you do a lot of cocaine?"

Riot choked a little on his own spit, shooting me an incredulous look. His messy black hair had fallen forward over his eyebrows, and I squeezed the cushion tighter, resisting the urge to push it out of his face.

"Er, sometimes. I guess. Can't say I've been asked that question before," he muttered, though his mouth twitched like he was amused. I could *feel* his amusement, brushing against me like soft, ticklish feathers. "The daimons are descended from different lines. The original lines. Did you know that?"

I shook my head silently. It made sense, the agathos were descended from original lines too, but we were all mixed together now.

"I'm from the Moros line."

The hatred that Riot brought to that statement felt like shards of ice against my skin. It was the strongest emotion I'd felt from him yet, and even without the connection between us I would have been able to tell how much it affected him. It was like the light in his eyes had switched off.

"What does that mean?" I asked carefully.

"The Moros personify impending doom. We are designed to lead humans to their destruction. That's our job."

At that moment, I wished there wasn't a connection between us. I didn't want Riot to feel the way I was responding to his admission. The horrified nausea that churned in my gut that such a *job* existed. The pity and outrage warring in my mind that Riot had been given such a horrendous mission, and his goddess hadn't even had the compassion to remove his conscience. He was being eaten alive by guilt, that much was obvious.

"Most daimons are descendents of the Moros line," Riot continued in a monotone voice, not looking at me. "The Keres are the next most common. They like violence. The Philotes are rarer even though their thing is fucking. The Oneiroi are almost extinct. They do mystical dream shit. There are others, but those are the ones I'm most familiar with."

Death, violence, sex and dreams. That was...something.

If my mother had been present for this conversation, we would have needed the smelling salts. There wasn't a single doubt in my mind about that. While what Riot was saying was everything I'd been programmed to hate, that hungry darkness in me, my *monster,* was curious. It rose up at his words, like a beast sniffing out its dinner.

With more forcefulness than usual, I shoved it back down. *Be sweet.*

"We have lines of descent too," I replied, desperately scrambling for a response that wouldn't make Riot feel worse.

"Kindness, purity, and charity?" Riot asked drily, glancing at me.

"Close," I admitted with a grimace. "Intelligence, moral virtue, piety, self-restraint, mercy, and glory. Those are some of the prestigious ones anyway. All agathos can ease pain, but they inherit one special gift too. Since the lines are mixed, the ability we inherit can seem random. "

"Are you going to tell me yours?" Riot asked, seeming genuinely interested.

"It's not a glamorous one," I replied with a tight smile. "Eutychia. I can give humans good luck."

GRACE

CHAPTER 7

"That's *not* glamorous?" Riot asked incredulously. "How can good luck not be glamorous? Seems pretty fucking awesome to me."

"It's not as prestigious as, say, bestowing wisdom," I volunteered with a shrug. "Luck is fickle, and what they get depends on what they're trying to achieve. What if they were trying to do something terrible and I enabled them? I have to do more...*vetting* than other agathos to make sure I'm not doing more harm than good."

"If you only focus on the negatives, you'll only see negatives," Riot replied, cocking an eyebrow at me. "A chance encounter with a bit of good luck can change someone's life, Gracie. Don't undersell yourself."

I dropped my gaze to my hands, unsure how I should respond to that. No one in my life had ever been impressed by my gift. My parents had all hoped for something more prestigious at my emergence. That I had Eutychia only confirmed all of the worst thoughts my mother already had about me.

"I always talk to people first to understand their motives, and the more I give, the better their chances," I muttered awkwardly.

"How does that affect you?" Riot asked, brow furrowed. "Does it hurt you or anything?"

"Not immediately. Our gift comes with a cost. If I give someone good luck, I receive bad luck in return."

Riot blinked at me. "What the actual fuck?"

"Sorry?" I squeaked.

"So, your goddess put your people here specifically to play guardian angel, and yet you have to suffer to use the gifts she gave you? How is that fair?"

Riot pulled a lighter out of his pocket and I watched him for a moment to see what he was planning on doing with it, but he seemed content to just flick it on and off. Perhaps it was stress relief? He was definitely outraged and I knew it was genuine because I could *feel* it, like angry little tendrils that sprouted up and demanded action against a perceived injustice.

"Well..." I began to explain before trailing off.

How *was* that fair? I hadn't asked for this gift, or to be some kind of talisman for humans who didn't even know about our existence, but that's what it was. And I was forced to pay the price for using the gift that my instincts *demanded* I use.

103

"I guess it's not very fair," I said quietly, picking up the remote to scroll through movies.

Sugar, if he thought just the gift itself was bad, he'd hate to hear about the way Constance made me use it at the shelter. Bonded agathos shared the cost of their gift—if I was bonded, they would occasionally receive my bad luck in my place. Constance had always seen my lack of soul bonds as a reason to use my gifts *more* rather than *less*, since the only person it was hurting was me.

Riot gave me an assessing look, but didn't call me out on the blatant avoidance when I oh so subtly suggested we watch *Bring It On*. He was very nice, really—daimon or not—because I could tell by his face he didn't have the slightest interest in cheerleading.

The heavy, achy feeling that had eased off returned with a vengeance, and I found myself slumping back into the couch, my limbs too heavy to function within ten minutes of the movie starting.

"You should go get some sleep, Gracie," Riot suggested gently. "The past 24 hours have been a lot, and you look exhausted."

"Are you...will you stay?" I asked, feeling a little foolish. He looked as exhausted as I felt.

"I'll be right here," he assured me, stretching out and pulling the throw off the back of the couch to drape over his legs. "Besides, I'm already invested in Torrance's story," he added with a wink. "Can't leave now."

Shooting him an awkward smile, I stumbled to my bedroom, collapsing back against the closed door for a moment. What were we *doing*? It felt wrong to leave him out there, but it would be beyond inappropriate to sleep next to him, as tempting as the idea was. Everything about Riot was tempting. At the same time...I'd never been alone with a guy. I'd definitely never shared a bed with one.

I twisted the opal promise ring on my finger back and forth, feeling guilty that I'd even *contemplated* sharing a bed with him. That was definitely something reserved for soul bonds only.

Which he wasn't. Maybe.

I flopped down on my bed—for the first time not caring that I still had makeup on and my bedding was all white—and screamed quietly into my pillow.

I still hadn't worked up the courage to bring up the whole dark goddess prayer issue. Maybe the solution was another prayer to the Goddess of Night to see if the candle going out last night had been a fluke.

What I *should* do is pray to Anesidora like a good agathos, which I hadn't done out loud since yesterday. Before everything had changed.

Maybe I was a little bit scared.

My phone buzzed next to me and I latched onto the distraction, snatching it up instantly. Even that small movement highlighted the ache in my arm muscles. It felt like the one time I'd attempted lifting weights and had barely been able to move my upper body for a week.

Mercy:

Can we video call? Your mom is driving me crazy.

I smiled at my baby cousin's message, grabbing my earbuds so I wouldn't disturb Riot.

The call connected and Mercy beamed at me, lying on her front on her pale pink bed, earbuds in. In some ways we looked similar— we both had typical agathos eyes, golden brown skin and black hair, though hers was much curlier than mine. At 17, she hadn't quite lost the baby roundness of her face yet—much to her chagrin.

"Hi, baby cousin," I said quietly, hoping she wouldn't question why I was practically whispering in the apartment I lived in alone.

"Are you okay?" she asked instantly, the beaming smile she'd answered the phone with turning down. "You don't look well."

"Don't I?" I asked vaguely, switching the pictures on the screen so I could get a better look at my face. I grimaced a little at the dark shadows under my eyes and the sallowness of my skin visible even under my makeup. I wasn't feeling one hundred percent either, but I'd attributed that to the shock of the past couple of days and the meagre amount of sleep I'd had last night sitting half upright on the couch.

"Are you working too much? Is Constance being too hard on you?" Mercy asked, sounding concerned.

I flipped the pictures back around and gave her a smile I hoped was reassuring. "I'm not working any more than usual. Constance is Constance."

Mercy wrinkled her nose and I tutted quietly at her. I had to be careful with Mercy, she had the same negative predispositions as I did, and I didn't want to encourage her. Mom had less time to focus on Mercy's "training" the way she did when I was a teenager since she had my two little brothers to raise as well, and I wanted my little cousin to continue flying under the radar.

One of her fathers was my mother's brother, and they had given my parents free rein to train and discipline Mercy as they saw fit. They lived in Saskatoon, and had sent Mercy to live with us when she was 16 to finish her education at Auburn's more illustrious high school.

I'm sure they'd hoped she'd feel the call to a soul bond in Auburn too, but it hadn't happened yet.

"Did you hear that Joy's memorial is on Sunday?" Mercy asked, rolling over and holding the phone above her face.

"I didn't. But I'll be there, of course." Every member of the community was expected to turn out for that kind of thing, even the tragic singletons.

"You better get some industrial concealer before then," Mercy giggled. "Aunt Faith will flip if she sees those bags under your eyes."

I snorted at the accurate assessment. "How has she been frustrating you today?"

Mercy gave me a sheepish look. "The Basilinna of the Northeast is attending the memorial. You know, Harmony Daubney? Joy was her niece."

Apprehension skittered down my spine and I did my best not to let it show. Harmony Daubney was based in New York and rarely made it to events in Auburn even though it was one of the more old money, longstanding agathos communities in her jurisdiction. No one could find out about this strange connection between me and Riot, especially not the Basilinna. The agathos had no compunctions about hurting daimons, and just the idea of what they might do to Riot made panic swell in my chest.

"Why is that stressing out Mother?" I asked eventually, clearing my throat. My family may live among the elite, but we weren't high profile enough to register on the Basilinna's radar.

"Because of you," Mercy replied with an apologetic smile and I could have sworn my heart stopped beating for a moment. "Aunt Faith was at a knitting party with some of the older women this morning and the subject turned to you..."

"And why I haven't met any of my bonded yet," I finished flatly, not surprised in the least. "Mother never appreciates those conversations."

"They were pretty critical of her, apparently," Mercy relayed with typical teenage glibness. "More than usual. Talking about how it's your parents' fault that you are a single spinster."

"How could that possibly be their fault?" I laughed quietly, though the sound was a little too bright to be natural. It was the first I'd heard of anyone blaming my parents for my situation, usually it was all on me.

"Not praying enough or showing enough devotion to Anesidora, that kind of thing, or maybe not asking forgiveness for their own sins and you were being punished in their stead. Since Anesidora hasn't given you any direction on where to find them and all."

That's what I'd always assumed too, but when I thought about it, I'd felt strongly called to move to Milton, even though I knew no agathos lived here. At the time I'd attributed it to searching for a sense of purpose, since it seemed like I wouldn't be meeting my bonded any time soon. An adventure that was acceptable within the confines of what I was and what my community expected of me.

But now that I'd met Riot, I was questioning everything. Maybe what I'd felt was *the call*. That was a preferable explanation to this being a result of reaching out to the Goddess of Night. And it would mean Riot really was my soul bond, and I wouldn't have to fight all the feelings that arose when I was around him.

"Are you listening?" Mercy asked exasperatedly, and I gave her a tight smile, shaking my head.

"Sorry, I didn't sleep well last night. Something about the community center?"

"Just a regeneration project I'm taking part in over the weekend. You do look beat though," Mercy agreed. "Go sleep, I'll message you tomorrow. Love you."

"Love you too, M," I replied softly, hanging up and putting the phone and earbuds on the nightstand.

As much as I wanted to just collapse, I'd never be able to fall asleep with makeup on. I changed into a long-sleeve pajama top and shorts before quietly sneaking through the living room to the bathroom. Riot was lying on the couch with his arm thrown across his eyes in a restless sleep. He was fidgeting constantly, and I quickly let myself into the bathroom and took care of my business, hoping it wasn't because the couch was uncomfortable.

I was a terrible hostess.

I turned off the flickering television on my way back to my room and dug out another throw blanket to lay over top of him. It was a physical effort not to pull his arm away from his eyes so I could see his whole face. Riot's lips were parted slightly, his jaw lacking the tension it always had when he was awake. My fingers itched with the urge to touch him, and I forced myself to retreat to the safety of my own bed before I embarrassed myself.

I really wished there was some kind of guidebook for whatever this was, because I didn't feel like I was doing a good job navigating it on my own.

Usually sleep came easily to me once I was burrowed in my linen bedding, comforted by the faint smell of the lavender white tea wax melts I used in here, but not tonight.

Exhaustion was weighing heavily on me in a way I'd never experienced before. My limbs grew heavier and heavier, like I was under water and fighting to get back to the surface. It took an almost frightening level of effort just to roll to my side, silently begging for sleep to take me.

It never did.

The sharp ache began in my chest, but as the hours went by, it spread through every inch of my body. It wasn't so much a crippling pain as pangs of hollowness.

I felt like an empty husk, yet unbearably weighed down all at once. Trying to sleep through it was pointless, and my brain wouldn't let me forget about Riot sleeping fitfully on the couch.

Maybe he was uncomfortable too? Maybe he needed me? If I could just get to him, I felt like I could make it better...

If I was keeping a tally—which I didn't want to admit—this definitely seemed like a point in favor of soul bonds, because what was this feeling if not *overwhelming need*?

It wasn't whatever I had imagined the feeling would be—rampant, unquenchable desire perhaps?—it was worse. Cruel, even. Like Anesidora had concocted an increasingly painful slew of sensations for us to experience until we bent to her indomitable will.

Be sweet.

I didn't want to be sweet though. I wanted to scream. Because if that's what this was, I wanted to demand more time rather than be pushed towards a level of intimacy I had no experience with, with a man I'd never expected to be intimate with.

Was a few days of self-reflection really too much to ask for?

Eventually, I gave up on sleep, dragging my aching limbs out of bed.

Riot was now lying awake on the couch, face pinched in misery. He glanced over at me as I flicked on the lamplight, clearly too exhausted to be startled by my presence.

"Ignore me," he rasped. "I guess I'm having withdrawals. Maybe I'm more human than I thought," he added, sounding mildly amused by the idea.

"I don't think it's the kind of withdrawal you're thinking of," I murmured. "Come with me?"

Riot's eyebrows disappeared under his messy dark hair, and I felt my face heat.

"The pain," I explained hastily. "The achiness. I feel it too. It might be that overwhelming feeling people talk about."

Riot blinked slowly. "We're not having sex just to make the pain stop."

"No, definitely not," I agreed quickly, staring at the floorboards like I'd never seen anything so interesting, even as my inner monster preened at his suggestion. "When I came back from work, it felt like a huge weight off my shoulders to be near you again. Maybe we just need to be...closer."

In the course of my rambling, I hadn't noticed Riot get up and cross the short distance between us until his feet appeared right in front of mine. His large hands cupped either side of my jaw, lifting my head until I couldn't avoid eye contact any longer. Riot's usually impassive features were marred with a deep frown, and if my limbs had been obeying me, I might have reached up to smooth his furrowed brow without thinking about it.

"You think this *pain* is the overwhelming sensation your goddess pushes on your people to encourage them to consummate their bond?" he asked slowly, looking troubled.

"Yes?" I squeaked. Already the pain was easing just having his hands on my skin, his hot breath fanning over my hair when he spoke.

Riot shook his head slightly in disbelief. "Do you see how this isn't a gift, Gracie? A gift is meant to be free, to come without expectations. I don't regret whatever this is," he clarified as my heart twisted in on itself. "I don't understand it, but I can't bring myself to regret it. At the same time...it might be better described as a curse."

I scanned his face, looking for some sign of dishonesty or scorn, but found only genuine concern. The outrage I'd expected to feel at the insinuation that a soul bond was anything less than sacred never came. A loud voice in the back of my mind, the one I usually commanded to be sweet, agreed with Riot.

"Can we lie down?" I asked quietly, overwhelmed and exhausted. He nodded, a slight smile playing around his mouth. Riot's hands slid down from my jaw over my neck and along my shoulders, the contact sending a jolt of awareness through me. He didn't linger though, turning me gently by my shoulders and encouraging me back into my bedroom.

Fudge, why had I worn sleep shorts tonight? I would never show this much leg during the day, and I was feeling very...*exposed.*

We climbed on either side of the bed facing each other, and with some of the physical strain eased, my brain started going wild instead. Should I put some pillows between us? What if I snored? Or drooled? I'd know if I drooled, right? The last time I shared a room with anyone had been at the last sleepover I'd attended in high school.

"You're a noisy thinker," Riot mumbled, sounding vaguely amused by the idea. Before I had a chance to apologize, he'd tugged me towards him, one heavy, tattooed arm draped over my waist, our legs brushing lightly under the blankets. I sucked in a startled breath at the intimate position, mostly surprised at how much I liked it. At how right it felt.

I exhaled and forced my body to relax. The physical ache had gone, but that only highlighted the minute reactions happening in the rest of my body.

My heartbeat had picked up, my mouth was uncomfortably dry, and there was a fluttering, clenching sensation below my belly button that almost made me gasp. I almost rested my hands on my abdomen to see if I could feel the strange sensation under my palms, but I didn't want Riot to see.

It probably wasn't normal.

"Fuck," Riot exhaled. The quiet sound was enough to make me jump in the silent room.

"Everything okay?" I asked lamely. Riot chuckled darkly at the redundant question. Everything was very much not okay. He was silent for a long moment before he answered, and I found myself holding my breath as I waited for his reply.

"The Moros...when we encounter humans, we inherently know their downfall. We can sense weakness. That woman I dragged out of the club, the one who called you..."

"Rae?"

"Right. Hers is opioids. I've always hated that preternatural knowledge. It wasn't something I could shake off. It urged me to act against my wishes."

My heart sank with the realization of where he was going with this.

"Our connection makes you want to act against your wishes," I surmised, hating how small my voice sounded.

As much as the realization—the *rejection*—gutted me, there was no anger. The darkness in me didn't rise. I understood all too well what it was to resent a lack of choice.

"No," Riot growled, the rough intensity of his voice taking me by surprise. "It makes me want to do things I'm very confident I'd want to do anyway. It makes it feel impossible *not* to do them."

"But you won't," I whispered with absolute certainty.

"But I won't," he agreed. "Not until you're ready."

The band around my ring finger seemed to grow tighter, reminding me that I wasn't supposed to do any of the things I was almost sure I wanted to do.

"I wish I knew what you were to me," I murmured, tracking the sharp planes of Riot's face, the olive skin—seemingly the only part of him I'd seen that wasn't covered in colorful ink—his captivating amethyst and crimson eyes, the dark stubble on his jaw.

"Sometimes the right answer is the simplest one, Gracie," Riot rasped, cataloguing my features as thoroughly as I was cataloguing his. "What would be the simplest answer?"

"That you are my soul bond," I replied instantly. "Except there's nothing simple about that."

Riot tipped his chin slightly, conceding my point.

His desire brushed against my skin like gentle fingertips and I arched my back unconsciously.

"Gracie," Riot rasped, his grip flexing where he held me. "You're killing me."

But how was I supposed to find out if he was my soul bond without *experimenting* a little? Just a bit.

I'd never kissed anyone before. I'd been saving it, as was customary, for my soul bond. But even if that wasn't Riot, I still wanted to share this with him. I wanted more than almost anything to know what his lips felt like against mine, if kissing was really as magical as it seemed in the movies. I wanted to memorize the feeling so I could replay it over and over in my head for the rest of my life.

Just one kiss. For science.

"Maybe we could...have a goodnight kiss?" I suggested hesitantly, even as a deep hunger rose in me while I said them.

Riot exhaled slowly like he was steadying himself, and I briefly panicked that he was going to say no and I'd die of shame on the spot.

But then he pulled his arm out from under his head and his fingers were gripping my chin, guiding me back as he moved forward, his breath fanning over my lips. My heart pounded so loudly in my chest, I was sure he could hear it.

"You ever kissed anyone before, Gracie girl?" Riot asked, his voice low and seductive.

"Will you think less of me if I say no?" I replied, suddenly *acutely* aware of how my inexperience might be a dealbreaker for him. There was nothing sexy about not knowing what I was doing, was there?

"Hell no." His lips brushed lightly over mine, a teasing ghost of a kiss. "A caveman part of me I'm not entirely proud of might be pretty smug about it."

I smiled against his mouth and felt his lips tilt up in response. I didn't think many people got to see Riot's soft side, and I was honored that I did.

Then his lips moulded to mine, moving against each other, our breaths mingling, and I was pretty sure I would never have a soul bond, because my soul had left my body.

This was kissing? It was far more magical than it looked in movies. Messier, more energetic, less perfect but vastly *more* perfect at the same time.

Riot's tongue swept my lower lip, and I gasped in surprise as he pushed forward, boldly exploring my mouth, his grip on my chin tightening. His domineering hold was nothing like the sweet kisses in the movies I watched, but I *liked* it. I liked how safe I felt in Riot's confident care—like he would never steer me wrong.

I didn't try to suppress the darkness this time. It washed through me like a comforting friend and an invigorating rush all at once, electrifying my nerve endings.

Making me brave.

My tongue slid against his, my teeth scraped his lower lip, my leg crept over his thighs of its own volition, hips moving to a silent beat.

I felt *sexy*. Riot groaned into my mouth, one hand gripping my hip almost painfully, like he was forcing himself not to move higher or lower.

"You're playing with fire, Gracie girl," he rumbled before delivering a stinging nip to my lower lip that zinged through my entire body. "This is a lot less innocent than a simple goodnight kiss."

Reluctantly, I pulled myself back, struggling to catch my breath. My inner repressed seductress was fine with taking things further, but his words had reminded the logical part of my brain that I wasn't actually ready to rip my clothes off and find out what *other stuff* felt like yet.

Well, I sort of was, but the guilt I'd managed to suppress during the act was rising up with a vengeance.

What if Riot wasn't my soul bond? Had I given away something I was meant to be saving? Was I less pure now?

I rolled away from him, but Riot tucked me back against his body with one glorious bicep cradling my head. The warmth of his hard chest seeped into my skin through my thin pajama top, and I focused on how nice it felt to snuggle rather than how nice it *would* feel to do other things that I would probably regret. Eventually it worked, my eyelids grew heavy and Riot's breathing evened out behind me, his arm over my hip growing lax.

Maybe we were falling prey to one goddess or the other's plans for us, or maybe I'd meddled in something bigger than myself with my reckless prayer, but at that moment I couldn't bring myself to care about the machinations of the divine.

Just like I'd told him at dinner, we were just Riot and Grace.

RIOT

CHAPTER 8

Grace hadn't been wrong about the *closeness* easing the pain we'd apparently both been experiencing. Sunlight was filtering through her bedroom window, and I had no idea what time it was but at least I'd actually got a few hours sleep in the end and no longer felt like I was dying.

That was a bonus.

Plus, I'd tasted her sweet, eager mouth. That was *more* than a bonus.

Grace was still asleep in my arms, her cheek resting on my chest, hair pulled up messily on top of her head, one leg flung over mine, which meant the silky skin of her thigh was resting uncomfortably close to my dick. I felt like I'd popped fifteen boner pills, that's how fucking hard I was. The pain in my body had eased, but it had all migrated south instead.

If the pain was the result of her goddess pushing us together, then I never wanted to hear about the *Great Mother* being the *good* goddess ever again. The kind one. The one who *cared* about her creations, unlike the nasty old Goddess of Night. Fuck that for a joke. *My* goddess valued free will over almost everything.

I contemplated trying to extricate myself from Grace's grip—I was worried about how she would feel about *this* level of closeness when she woke up—but her bed wasn't big enough for me to go anywhere, anyway. She had a small bed in a small room, with layers of cream-colored bedding tangled everywhere now we'd both mostly kicked them off. There was a shelf directly above our heads with greenery dangling off it, and a large pot growing what looked like a small tree next to the window.

The amount of plant life in this tiny apartment had made me question my theory that agathos didn't care about nature, though they definitely didn't have the same aversion to eating meat that daimons had. Then again, Grace had some weird misconceptions about my kind, so my thought process was probably equally as wrong.

Grace stirred and my hand on her hip tightened reflexively, not wanting her to go anywhere.

The one daimonic trait I knew I had in spades was selfishness. We didn't share. So while I respected Grace's free will, I fucking *hated* sharing her time. Every second we'd been apart yesterday I spent wondering what she was doing and if she was okay, and if she obsessed about me as much as I obsessed about her.

Goddess, why was she even here? Grace wasn't meant for a dreary down-and-out town like Milton. She should be somewhere that didn't dull her shine.

"Oh, you're awake," Grace breathed, tipping her head back and blinking sleepily at me. I didn't think I'd ever get used to her eyes. They didn't have the red in them that mine had—the mark of the devil that was reflected back at me in the mirror each day. Grace's were a mixture of pale purple, aqua and gold, swirling and blending together in a way that no artist could replicate.

They were the color of the cosmos, and staring into them made me feel the same way as looking at a clear night sky did. Small. Insignificant in the grand scheme of things.

"How are you feeling?" I rasped, holding my breath as Grace suddenly pulled her leg back, realizing how close we were. *Please don't notice my boner.*

"Um..."

A flush spread across Grace's cheeks as she glanced away nervously, and I suppressed my chuckle at how fucking adorable she looked. Based on her reaction, I assumed Grace was experiencing a similar ache to me, but either couldn't or didn't want to articulate that.

It must be a pain in the ass not to be able to lie.

"I don't know what to make of any of this," Grace sighed, staring up at the ceiling. She made no move to roll away from me, which I was grateful for. "It feels so much like you are my soul bond, but if you are...I guess it's not how I thought any of this would go," she laughed quietly.

I hummed under my breath, staring at the top of her head, noticing how some strands of hair were more reddish than others in this light. "You thought you would have felt called to some nice, clean cut agathos boy by now with a 9-5 job and health insurance, and that would be it?"

"I mean, yes," Grace sputtered, ducking her head slightly. "But a more romantic version of that."

"Fair enough. Health insurance is really more of a second date conversation."

She nudged me with her shoulder, surprising us both with the affectionate gesture, and I guided her face back up so I could see her.

"None of this should shock me," Grace sighed. "I've never quite fit in with my community. Not even with my family."

"Now, *that*, I can relate to," I muttered.

Grace hummed, and I stayed quiet, giving her a chance to find her words. I got the impression she was used to filtering herself, which is why she often paused before speaking, but I couldn't tell if that was an agathos thing or a Grace thing.

I guessed that if I couldn't lie, I'd probably have to spend more time thinking about what came out of my mouth too.

"Do you think you're a good daimon?" she settled on eventually, her expression impossible to read.

"Good as in a good person? No. Good at being a daimon, also no. Why?"

"I've never thought I was a good agathos. I have thoughts that I don't think other agathos have..." Grace trailed off, chewing her lip nervously.

"What kind of thoughts?" I asked curiously. I didn't understand the agathos mentality. Was the mind really a place that needed policing? It seemed sort of totalitarian.

"Just things I shouldn't think. Mean things when I'm angry. Curiosity about things I have no right to be curious about. I think of it as my darkness or my monster. It lives inside me, making me reckless."

I *felt* Grace's guilt, which took me by surprise. Guilt was a feeling I had a lot of personal experience with, but wasn't used to seeing on someone else, since other daimons didn't seem to experience it.

I really hoped Grace wasn't feeling guilty for sometimes having angry or curious thoughts, because that was insanely fucked up.

"Listen to me," I commanded, cupping her jaw and running my thumb over her cheek. "Just because you feel something other than unadulterated joy sometimes doesn't mean it's bad, or that you're bad. You have nothing to feel guilty about, Grace."

Her hand covered mine, keeping my palm pressed to her jaw, and her eyes wide like she was marveling at the feel of my skin on hers.

There was a tension between us as we both forced our bodies to stay still, to not give in to the need between us. It was more than just being the horniest I'd ever been in my fucking life. It was like...like I could feel what Grace needed, and every atom in my body was urging me to provide her with it. What had been a faint whisper of emotion yesterday was a lot stronger and more urgent today.

Did that work both ways? Was there an on-off switch?

If this was the work of the Good Goddess, apparently she didn't give a fuck about privacy either.

Grace's fingers trailed lightly over my chest, tracing my pecs through my t-shirt like she was memorizing them. My breath caught in my throat at the gentle brush of her warm hand, the soft exploratory way she moved.

Her nail skated over my right nipple and Grace snatched her hand back with a surprised gasp as a jolt of pleasure ran through me. I almost groaned at how good it felt even through the fabric—Grace's touch was like nothing I'd ever experienced—but the alarmed look on her face kept my appreciative noises in check.

"I'm sorry," she whispered, pulling her other hand back from where it rested over mine and curling them both into fists, clutching them close to her body like she didn't trust her own limbs. "I didn't even realize what I was doing...Touching your..."

"Never touched a man's nipples before, Gracie?" I teased, exhaling slowly to try to relieve some of the sexual tension that was holding me hostage.

"I've barely touched my own nipples," she replied instantly, eyes wide.

Damn it. Thinking about Grace's nipples was not helping calm myself down. I felt the lust that *wasn't* mine like an echo of my own feelings. We were stoking each other's needs, driving each other higher, to the point of a whole new kind of pain. It wasn't sustainable to exist like this.

"We both need an orgasm," I gritted out. "Have you ever touched anywhere else on your body?" I asked tentatively, already feeling like I knew the answer.

"I've never..." Grace trailed off, giving me a pleading look. "We don't feel any kind of desire until we meet our soul bonds. It's meant to help us...save those things."

For fuck's sake. I was too horny to properly express the righteous anger that coursed through me at her words. Not at Grace, never at Grace, but at her goddess. What kind of fucked up game was she playing? They should have been calling her The Puppet Master, not the Great Mother.

"I have a lot of thoughts about that, but let's concentrate on getting you off right now. Neither of us are going to last the day like this," I said, attempting to keep my voice calm.

"Will you help me?"

There was so much vulnerability in her eyes, in her tone, that I wouldn't have been able to say no even if I tried. And a part of me *did* want to say no, to protest that this rampant sexual desire was being pushed on us by some unseen force who was playing with our lives.

"Clothes on, okay?" I told her solemnly. It was for both of our benefits that this didn't go too far until our heads were clearer. "Nothing further happens until we're completely ready for it."

I hadn't dry humped anyone since I was a teenager, but it seemed like the best way to *respectfully* eliminate the suffocating need between us. Right? Surely, that would be more comfortable for Grace than me directing her how to touch herself. *Shit, I was probably going to come in my boxers.*

"Tell me what to do," Grace whispered, and while she *sounded* innocent, there was a hungry glint in her eye that made me think she'd given this more thought than she was letting on. Or perhaps more than she was *supposed* to have thought about it.

Maybe this was the dark curiosity monster she'd alluded to. I wanted to see it.

"What do you want, Gracie?" I asked in a low voice, skimming my hand over the dip of her waist to rest on her hip. I wanted more than anything to slide my hand lower and grab a handful of that spectacular ass in those teeny shorts that had driven me crazy when I'd followed her into her room last night, but I managed to resist.

"What do you mean?" Grace asked, even as her hips rolled slightly— so, *so* close to grinding against my thigh.

"I mean," I began slowly, not wanting to spook her. "Tell me about those naughty things a good little agathos like you shouldn't have imagined trying," I murmured, my lips ghosting the shell of her ear.

Maybe I was imagining things, but it felt like her face warmed where her cheek rested on my chest.

I would have dropped the subject if she'd refused, but Grace tentatively moved closer, draping herself more completely over me.

Don't ask if she has dirty fantasies. Don't do it.

Wait a few days.

Her hips rolled experimentally again, her teeth sunk into her lower lip as she tested a slightly different angle. Part of me had known there was a burning curiosity underneath Grace's veneer of perfect politeness—I could *feel* it—but I was also a little surprised at how quickly she'd taken to the idea.

Maybe what Grace needed wasn't so much guidance as approval. That nod of go-ahead to just fucking *explore* and live, and not give a shit what anyone else had to say about it. And someone to tell her it was okay afterwards, when the inevitable guilt for feeling anything other than chaste positivity arose.

126

My hands found her hips and I gently guided her further up my body until she was straddling me, her palms flat on my chest to steady herself.

Don't come, I reminded myself silently. She was holding herself above me, hovering an inch away from where I wanted her, desire warring with indecision on her face.

"Your speed," I reminded her, loosening my hold on her hips. Grace scanned my face as though she was looking for a lie, and I resisted the urge to close my eyes. I wanted her to see the honesty in my face, even if I hated her seeing the red in my irises.

"I don't know what to do now," she breathed.

"Lower your hips. Just...listen to your body. When it feels good, you'll know," I instructed, wishing I was less useless. I knew how to make a woman feel good, but I wasn't clear on how to make a woman make *themself* feel good.

With a decisive nod, Grace lowered her hips until we were pressed together. I exhaled slowly, feeling her heat between the two thin layers of fabric. How did this feel so intense? As far as sexual encounters went, it wasn't my most daring, but it felt like *everything*.

Grace rolled her hips again, a quiet surprised moan escaping her. She was definitely hitting my piercing, but I didn't want to mention *that* yet. I doubted Grace even knew you could *get* piercings there.

Fuck, she felt good.

I scrunched my eyes shut for a moment, trying to regain some semblance of control over my own fucking body.

"Why does this feel so nice?" Grace whispered, grinding against me, her nails digging into my chest. Shit, I was kind of hoping for better than *nice*.

I forced my eyes open and found genuine confusion on her face. Oh, that had been a real question.

Who the fuck was giving agathos sex ed?

"Er, that's your clit," I replied, stumbling slightly over my words. There was no universe in which I was equipped to talk about this. "It's sensitive."

Fucking hell, Riot. *It's sensitive.* Yeah, pretty sure she'd figured that out just fine.

"And this, it's, um...It's meant to feel this good?" Grace asked shyly.

"Fuck yeah, it is," I growled, feeling echoes of the shame she was trying to suppress. "It's meant to feel fucking *great*, and it'll feel even better when it's my tongue rather than your sleep shorts."

Ah, there was that adorable squeak noise again.

"You've really never touched yourself here before, Grace?" I asked, my thumbs stroking close to her inner thighs.

"It's not allowed," Grace replied instantly, digging her nails in a little harder.

"People do things they're not allowed to do all the time."

"I tried sometimes. It didn't feel like this," she said quietly, tipping her head back. Most of her long hair had fallen out of its tie and was brushing the sheets covering my legs, and I cursed every bit of fabric in this room that stopped me feeling her skin on mine.

"Naughty," I teased, slipping my hands underneath her shorts so I could at least feel the smooth skin of her legs.

Grace leaned forward, draping herself over my chest and I swelled a little with pride that she was angling herself to find a better position, chasing her own pleasure. The shift forced me to move my hands so I cupped the back of her thighs, feeling the edge of her panties under my thumbs. Not moving my hands any higher was a fucking marathon effort. Grace scooped her hair over one shoulder and leaned in close, her lips brushing against my jaw.

"I don't think I'm as good as you think I am," she whispered, sending a shot of lust directly to my balls. "And I don't think you're as bad as you think you are."

"I'm not so sure about that," I murmured, running my thumbs over the edge of her cotton panties again. "I'm having some very bad thoughts right now."

Grace leaned back, biting her lower lip for a moment before reaching back with one hand to grab my wrist, encouraging my hands higher. There was definitely a goddess involved in the creation of this ass. Maybe multiple goddesses. I grabbed both cheeks with enough pressure to make her gasp, grinding her down harder on my painfully hard dick.

"Give me your mouth, Gracie," I commanded. I wasn't going to let her overthink this. This was about pure enjoyment.

Soft lips brushed tentatively against mine, and I snagged her lower lip between my teeth, drawing back slowly, coaxing her to relax. To let me give her this pleasure that she hadn't been able to find on her own.

Mine. Fucking mine. I'd fight the goddesses myself if they tried to take Grace away from me.

"Something is happening," Grace breathed. "I can't, I don't know what to do."

There was a plea in her voice I would have understood even without the vague brushes of helplessness against my skin. I rolled us both easily, and Grace landed on her back with a gasp of surprise, looking up at me with complete trust in her eyes that I absolutely hadn't earned.

I hitched her leg up over my hip, bracing one arm next to her head and gripping the back of her knee while I took over, rolling my hips until I found the rhythm that made her eyes roll back into her head.

"Right there?" I confirmed, barely recognizing my husky voice.

"Right there," Grace sighed, arching her back.

The movement highlighted the points of her nipples and I moved my head down slowly, giving her time to see what I was doing, to stop me. Grace's eyes met mine, her breathing labored, but she didn't protest. If anything, her back arched higher off the bed, and I wasn't about to say no to that invitation. I closed my mouth around her nipple through the thin fabric of her t-shirt, soaking through the material before scraping my teeth over the sensitive bud.

Grace cried out, a breathy, whiny sound that I wanted to fall asleep and wake up to for the rest of my life, as her inner thighs clamped around my hips, body writhing underneath mine. I rocked against her, drawing out her pleasure as long as possible, as I found my own release, acutely aware that I was coming harder than I ever had, and my thin cotton boxers were not going to hide anything.

As Grace came down from her orgasm high, I rolled us again so she was draped over me, just like she was when she'd woken up, and gathered her close. She was breathing hard, clinging to me for a moment before shifting her head back against my bicep to look at me.

I really needed to go clean up, but the last thing I wanted to do was rush off when I knew Grace's thoughts would probably be all over the place.

"That was..." she began, trailing off like she couldn't think of the right words to articulate an orgasm via dry humping.

"Life changing?" I teased.

"A little, actually," Grace admitted worriedly, one of her hands was fidgeting restlessly, and I glanced down to find her nervously pushing the ring on her finger in circles with her thumb.

"It doesn't have to lead anywhere else, Gracie. We can do that again, or never do it again. There's no pressure here," I assured her. Had I moved too quickly? Corrupting innocent maidens was the domain of the Philotes line. I didn't have experience with anyone as *inexperienced* as Grace.

"I'm worried about how much I want to do that again. And how I'm going to survive all day at work knowing we could be doing that instead," Grace muttered, frowning.

My lips twitched. "The anticipation is half the fun. If it makes you feel any better, I'll be suffering too."

"It's probably a bad thing that does make me feel better," Grace mused.

"You little sadist." I patted the side of her hip before extricating myself, needing to get in the shower before I freaked her out.

She followed my movements with wide eyes. "You're going to come back tonight, aren't you?"

"Of course, I'll come back if you want me here," I told her easily. *Good luck getting rid of me.*

"I would like you here please," Grace replied shyly.

I was halfway to the door before she spoke again, her nervousness skittering over my skin. "Um, do you want me to, you know, return the favor?"

"Trust me, that was very mutually beneficial. Which is why I need to go clean up," I added with a wink over my shoulder, enjoying the shy, almost proud look on Grace's face.

Patience had never been my strong suit, but I had no problem waiting for Grace. I didn't just want her firsts, I wanted her to *ask* me for them. I wanted her *excitement*. And I'd wait however long she needed to get there.

What was Grace doing right now?

The question had been circling in my brain on a loop all fucking day, which was a little embarrassing because I doubted she was thinking even half as much about me. Well, maybe she was wondering where I was, since it was already after dark.

I had too much time on my hands here. Working for Dare meant mostly spending the day on my own while he focused on his endless stream of clients. There was only a half wall separating us so it wasn't like I was excluded from their conversations, but I didn't want to distract him either.

His books had been a mess, but I'd begun tidying them up as best I could considering I had no idea what the fuck I was doing. I'd updated his social media pages. I'd even caved and got him dinner, even though I'd grumbled the entire time about him making me his bitch. Dare worked fucking hard, and he was doing me a solid by hiring me, so it was really the least I could do.

If I'd rebelled by not selling drugs for my dad, Dare was the original rebel. Most of the Philotes got into sex work—they were driven by lust in the same way I was driven by doom—but Dare had never had any interest in that life. He'd gotten into tattooing as an alternative way of appreciating the human form.

Really, the only downsides to working for Dare were long as hell days because he was booked solid and had no idea there was somewhere else I wanted to be, and that I used my downtime fantasizing about Grace making those breathy little moans again, and time could not have gone any slower.

Was she thinking about me that way? Probably not. Most of the staff at Hope House were agathos—everyone I knew avoided that place like the plague. If anything, Grace was probably feeling guilty again about what we'd done this morning.

The sun had well and truly set and I was still hanging around because Dare's last client was running seriously fucking late—I wouldn't be surprised if Grace was asleep by the time I got back. Hopefully she didn't think I'd changed my mind. It would be a lot easier if we could just message each other without her having to worry about her parents monitoring her phone like she was a teenager.

I grimaced as I took another swig of my now cold coffee, filing away the backlog of receipts that still needed to be dealt with for tomorrow. That lethargic feeling that seemed to come with being away from Grace had already crept back into my muscles over the course of the day, although the pain hadn't set in yet, and I wondered if it was taking longer to crop up because of what we'd done this morning.

If that was the reason, well...that was really fucked up. I hadn't given much thought to how fucked up the agathos really were until I'd met Grace, but I definitely had some thoughts on it now.

Dare's last client emerged—an enormous bald human man who was wincing slightly as his impractical pants rubbed against the new ink on his leg—and I forced myself not to snap at him for taking so fucking long while I reminded him about aftercare and processed his payment. I could see Dare moving around behind the partial wall, cleaning the equipment and packing it away, and he was probably as desperate to get out of here after a long day as I was.

For very different reasons.

"Hey, do you wanna hit the gym?" Dare asked, leaning against the half wall as his client walked out. He rolled his neck a few times, probably stiff from working in the same position for the past couple of hours.

"I've got plans," I replied, already grabbing my jacket and forcing my heavy arms into them. Fuck it, I was rushing back for snuggles and I had zero regrets about it.

"Your version of plans is finding the corner of a bar to get loaded in, then sitting around moping about your life choices," Dare scoffed.

"Maybe I'm a changed man?"

"Mm, something has changed, that's for sure," Dare replied, eyes narrowed on me. "You fucking someone?"

It wasn't an unreasonable question—daimon didn't *do* relationships—but even if I was fucking Grace, that wouldn't even begin to describe what was happening between us.

"It's not always just about fucking," I said lightly as I let myself out of the studio onto the dark street.

"Since when?" Dare called after me.

Since Grace.

It took about half an hour to get back to her place, and I didn't fuck around since it was after dark and most daimons were up and about. I didn't need anyone getting curious about where I was going. There was no doubt in my mind that my dad had told everyone who'd listen that he'd kicked me out.

I tipped my chin at Rogue as I passed her ground-level apartment, and she returned the gesture tiredly, patting a screaming baby repeatedly on the back in front of the window. We'd gone to school together, and it blew my mind that she was someone's *mother* now. She looked miserable, honestly. Since we were incapable of maintaining relationships, daimon kids were always raised by just one of our parents. Usually the human while we were young, but not always.

When our abilities manifested, our daimonic parents had to step in and take over, and explain to us what we were and why the humans in our lives could never find out.

It didn't always work out. Some kids were abandoned by their daimonic parents. Without anyone to guide them, they usually ended up institutionalized.

I pulled my lighter out of my pocket, absently flicking it as I remembered my own mom. She was a human woman who'd had me at 19, barely kept me alive until I was 17 when she'd overdosed, then I'd been forced to move in with my dad. It was one of the few events in my life I didn't *feel* guilty about.

I'd been trying to help her get clean before I even fully understood what that meant. I *knew* how she'd meet her end, and I'd tried to prevent it, but I had long since accepted she needed more help than a kid could give her.

I sighed heavily as I saw the devil himself walk out of the corner store, shoving his graying hair out of his face. I could have hidden, but I'd rather get this confrontation over and done with.

"Riot," Dad growled, suddenly animated as he stalked towards me.

"I know, I know," I drawled, holding up my hands. "I'll give it back."

"You little shit bag," Dad snapped. "Why can't you just work for a fucking living like everyone else? You're always making my life so fucking difficult."

"I've *been* working," I replied. "I just don't want to work *for you.* I'll drop the stuff at your place."

"You're not welcome in my house," he muttered, looking surly. "You expect me to believe you've got any of it left? You were always an ungrateful asshole of a kid."

"I learned from the best." I shrugged, shooting him a smirk as he scoffed loudly, but the tension leached out of his shoulders. He was a dick, but as long as I gave him back the drugs I skimmed and maybe a little cash for housing me for the last six months when I wasn't bringing in any income, he'd leave me alone.

Daimons were pretty civil to one another, so long as deals were honored and debts were repaid. Respect was our only moral code.

"You got somewhere to stay?" he asked begrudgingly.

"I'm good," I assured him, clapping him on the back as I moved past him. "Gotta run. Take care of yourself, old man."

"Fucking softie," he muttered as I walked away. He'd always complained that I was too soft for a daimon, and he wasn't even wrong.

I just didn't care anymore that he was right.

CHAPTER 9

We were at the beach.

My upper body was resting on a blanket on my stomach, but my legs were on the powdery white sand, sun beating down on my exposed back. Was I wearing a bikini? It definitely felt like I was, but that couldn't be right. I'd never worn a bikini in my life. Mother would have a stroke.

There were voices around me—masculine ones that I didn't recognize—but my head was turned away from them, looking out at the expanse of ocean in front of me. Whoever they were, I must have trusted them because I felt completely relaxed.

A rich, deep laugh filled the air and I knew instantly it was Riot's. I'd never heard him so happy, and the sound warmed me even more than the sun did. He was talking to someone, and whoever it was, he obviously got along well with them.

"You need lotion, Grace," a low voice murmured from above me, sending a tremor of desire through my body. It was a deep, rumbly baritone sound I didn't recognize, and it almost sounded raspy from lack of use.

"Any excuse," someone else teased affectionately.

"Avoiding sunburn is a reasonable excuse," the deep voice replied wryly. I should tell him I could put it on myself, it was entirely inappropriate for someone else to do it—where was Riot? Was he okay with this?—but the man's enormous hands began massaging lotion on the back of my thighs and I forgot how to speak.

His fingertips were so high up, it was just shy of being indecent, and the thumbs that began rubbing circles on my inner thighs were unquestionably *indecent.*

I still didn't tell him to stop.

A breathy sigh escaped me, and Riot chuckled. "Careful, Gracie. This is a public beach."

That should bother me, yet I couldn't have cared less who was watching at that moment. Let them watch. Let them see the trust and happiness and love *that was here. How could anything so wonderful be something to feel ashamed of?*

I tried to turn my head back to see whose hands were on me, but it felt like an invisible weight was keeping it pressed to the blanket, forcing me to stay still. The more I tried to push my head up, the harder the invisible force pushed back.

"You can't see their faces yet because I can't see their faces yet," a musical voice said. He sounded different from the others—like he'd pulled himself out of the vision to speak into my ear. The hands massaging lotion down the back of my legs continued to move as though the man hadn't heard anything.

At that moment, Riot walked around the front of the blanket, shooting me a cocksure smile as he passed. I wanted to giggle at the sight of him in a tank top and shorts, the colorful tattoos all down his legs on display.

"Except him," the disembodied voice chuckled. "Him, I can see now."

"Why can't I see you?" I breathed. Surely the mysterious voice could envision himself.

"You always ask me that question," he replied affectionately. "Every time I show you one of these visions. And the answer is always the same."

"What's the answer?"

"I don't know if I'll be part of this future," he replied wistfully. I could feel his sorrow—it was so powerful that the whole vision began to change. Dark clouds rolled in over the blue sky, the gentle lap of the waves turned into crashes like thunder.

"It's time to go, Amazing Grace," the voice said softly. "Riot is home."

"Wait," I breathed, thrashing on the blanket as the wind whipped up the sand. Every part of the dream scattered into nothingness, slipping faster through my fingers the harder I tried to grasp it.

"Grace. Gracie, wake up," Riot murmured softly, his breath fanning over my face.

I woke and sat up with a start, gripping the thin throw from the couch to my chest and panting like I'd run a marathon, just barely missing headbutting Riot because he flung himself backwards.

"Sorry!" I squeaked.

"That's okay," he replied, huffing a quiet laugh. "I didn't mean to scare you. Were you having a bad dream?"

"I don't think so," I replied, frowning. "I don't really have bad dreams, but I never remember what they're about."

Though I had this strange sensation that I *should*. It had felt important somehow. It had felt so *real*. There was a beach. I definitely recalled a beach. I discreetly rubbed my calves together, half expecting to feel the grit of sand on my skin, and felt almost disappointed when I didn't.

I gasped in surprise as strong arms scooped me into the air, my hands grabbing aimlessly to stop myself from falling, eventually settling on a cotton shirt pulled taut over solid muscles.

"Sorry," Riot said, not sounding very sorry at all as he bundled me in closer. "You'll be more comfortable in your bed, and I was going to die if I didn't get my hands on you."

"Well, we wouldn't want that," I sighed, my body relaxing instantly and my head falling to his shoulder.

The logical part of my brain told me I barely knew this guy and I shouldn't feel so comfortable, but the heaviness that had plagued me all day dissipated like it had never been there and I felt like I could finally *breathe* again after hours apart. All logic went out the window.

"I wondered if you were coming back," I said quietly as Riot carefully laid me down on the bed and tucked me under the blankets. It was technically true—I *had* wondered—but even then, I had felt strangely calm about it. Like even if Riot had panicked and ran, it wouldn't have been the end of us anyway, just a little breather. Whatever this was, it definitely didn't feel done yet.

I'd still kept myself busy until I'd collapsed with exhaustion on the couch while I waited though. The apartment was spotless, my plants were happy, my nails were now pearlescent pink instead of ballet blush pink, and the whole place smelled like vanilla wax melts. There had been something quite cathartic about tidying and getting the house in order after being so thoroughly thrown off my routine these past couple of days.

My heart stopped for a second as Riot straightened and I thought he was going to leave, but he began undoing his jeans instead and my heart reacted for a whole different reason.

I wondered if he usually kept his shirt on to sleep or if he was just doing that to make me more comfortable. There was definitely part of me—the dark, bad part—that would have been more comfortable with him sans shirt. Sans all clothes, really.

The ring on my finger seemed to dig into my skin at that impure thought.

"I was later at the studio than I'd planned," Riot explained, and I could hear the grimace in his voice. "Did you really think I'd just bail on you, Gracie?"

"I wouldn't blame you if you did," I told him as he moved around the bed and climbed in next to me. "Or if you at least wanted some space. I have sort of upended your whole life."

I wasn't entirely confident space was an option—the physical discomfort would be unbearable—but I'd try if that's what Riot wanted.

"Nope," Riot replied confidently, pulling me into his side like it was the most natural thing in the world. "Not that I had a whole lot going on anyway, but I guarantee you there's nowhere I'd rather be. I'm not sure I can be so generous. You might be stuck with me, Gracie."

I snuggled in closer, not wanting to admit how happy that idea made me. It had felt like a million years since I'd seen him, yet also like we'd never been apart.

Riot exhaled quietly, and I wondered if he was feeling the same rush of physical relief that I was feeling at being together again. *We barely knew each other*, a small voice in the back of my head reminded me. How did I know which feelings belonged to me, and which were being pushed upon us by the outside force that had brought us together?

Had my parents felt this way when they met? Surely, anyone would feel a little overwhelmed at such a sudden influx of intense emotions. Why didn't they ever talk about it though? If this was a soul bond, if it really was such a coveted gift, why was it so shrouded in secrecy?

If I had learned anything from the past few days with Riot, it was that I had let too much go by unquestioned. My mother had worked hard to train my questioning nature out of me when I was a kid, but I wasn't a kid anymore, and I was annoyed at myself for accepting so many things, even when they'd made me unhappy. Especially when I knew now that there was more waiting for me if I'd just reach out and grab it.

I couldn't shake the feeling that I dreamed of exactly that.

Considering how awake I'd been, I was surprised that I fell back asleep at some point and didn't rouse until my alarm went off. Riot was lying on his back, one arm bent behind his head in a way that really showed off his bulging arm muscles to maximum effect. Unsurprisingly, I was sprawled all over him again like he was my personal pillow, but I forced myself not to get embarrassed about it this time. He'd been very clear that he didn't mind me snuggling up to him, and it provided a welcome reprieve from the discomfort of being away from him during the day.

Just like a soul bond would experience.

I wasn't even sure why I was fighting the idea of us being soul bonds. Even if it were inconvenient for that to be the case, it wasn't like me to deny the truth that was right in front of my face just because it was inconvenient. Usually, I was good at confronting uncomfortable realities, at least in my own head, even if I didn't vocalize them.

My entire life was a series of uncomfortable realities.

Maybe it was because I wasn't the only one affected this time. Riot's whole life would change too, and it was quite possibly my fault considering I'd been the one who'd asked the Goddess of Night for help. Something which I had yet to casually work into conversation, but definitely would. At some point.

Carefully, I extracted my limbs from Riot's and slid out of the bed, grabbing my workout gear so I could get ready in the bathroom. His ability to sleep through my alarm going off and the sunlight filtering through the window blew my mind, but I guessed daimons tended to be more active at night.

I took care of my business and dressed in matching lavender leggings and a fitted singlet, pulling on a thin gray hooded sweatshirt but leaving it unzipped, then securing my hair in a tight ponytail. By the time I emerged, I could hear Riot moving around the kitchen, making coffee.

"Hi," I said shyly, leaning against the door jamb. Sugar, it was so much easier to be confident under the cover of darkness.

"Hey," he replied drowsily. He glanced at me, sleep rumpled hair falling into his eyes, before doing a double take and turning to face me more fully, coffee cup in hand. "You going for a run?"

Riot's eyes traveled up from my socks over my legging-clad legs, pausing at my tight top, before continuing up to my burning face.

It wasn't the most modest of outfits given how fitted it was, but really the only time we were allowed to be even a *little* immodest was when we were working out or swimming. Even then, we were pretty covered up by most human standards.

I'd almost bought a crop top once, just out of sheer curiosity, but I knew I'd never have the courage to wear it. I still felt like if I ever wore something that exposed my midriff, my mother would sprout bat wings and fly here all the way from Auburn to punish me.

"Yes," I squeaked, before clearing my throat. "Yes, I'm going for a run."

Riot pursed his lips, tilting his head to the side thoughtfully.

"Do...Do you want me to change?" I asked, plucking at the lavender singlet. I'd never had a boyfriend before, and while I didn't want to say that word out loud and freak us both out, I should probably consider his opinion on things like this, right? Wasn't that how relationships worked?

The corner of Riot's mouth tipped up in an amused smirk as he shook his head, his black hair flopping with the movement. "Fuck no, Gracie. Wear whatever you want. You look incredible."

"Oh. I was worried it might be too form-fitting, and you might be uncomfortable with it, and I know daimons can be possessive..." *Sugar, stop talking, Grace.*

I slammed my mouth shut, barely resisting the urge to hide behind my hands. I appreciated that Riot never outright laughed at my awkward moments. His lip just twitched a little while he looked at me like I was endearing and not socially stunted.

Riot set the cup down on the counter with an ominous *thud* before closing the short distance between us. He stood close enough that I could feel his breath fan over my face as he gently grabbed the two sides of my hoodie, lightly tugging me towards him.

I went willingly, closing the tiny gap until my breasts brushed against his hard chest. Heat exploded across my skin at the barest hint of touch, even though it was only *yesterday* that I'd had that life changing moment grinding all over his lap.

Would I need that every day now I'd had it once?

I was inclined to think the answer was yes.

"I am very possessive," Riot murmured in a low voice, dripping with sin. "That doesn't mean I want to tell you how to dress. It means I want you to wear my clothes just because you want to. It means I want my name tattooed on your skin. It means I want to run next you and tell anyone who looks at you to fuck off. Unfortunately, those aren't options for us," he added irritably, though it sort of sounded like he said *for now* under his breath.

"I wish they were," I whispered as my hands found their way to his abs, surprising myself with the words. How nice would it be to call Riot my boyfriend? To go for a run with him in the morning, or grab some lunch together during the day?

To not worry that if we were seen together, my community would lock me in the temple and attack him. I didn't even know how the daimons would react.

Riot's eyes flashed with hunger and I felt my breath catch in my throat as I saw the desire on his face a second before I felt it curling around my skin. That was it, I was done for.

How did he do that? It was so subtle—a flash in his eyes, the way his chin dipped slightly, the subtle movement of his tongue running along the inside of his lower lip. That was all it took and my body responded like it was hardwired to his.

That fluttery clenching feeling below my belly button was back with a vengeance.

"Better start running now," Riot said, his grip tightening around my hoodie, pulling me close enough to feel his hardness against my stomach. "You stand there looking like that much longer and you won't make it out the door."

I opened my mouth to argue because surely there were more fun ways to burn calories than jogging, but Riot's lips brushed over mine before I could speak.

"Go," he insisted, mouth still moving against mine. "My self control is weak this morning."

I appreciated the sentiment—I didn't even know what I wanted or how far I wanted to go, and I'd really relied on him setting the boundaries yesterday. But I didn't think I could walk out of this room without at least a kiss.

I pushed Riot gently, encouraging him backwards, and he relented with just a cautionary look. I guided him until his back hit the fridge and pressed both his wrists back next to him. The darkness inside me seemed to swell in victory, a rush of adrenaline running through my veins, making me brave.

"Grace..." he warned as the red in his eyes darkened with desire.

"Let me have the self control for both of us this time," I said in a throaty voice I barely recognized as my own, going up on my tiptoes to reach his mouth.

Riot groaned even as he parted his lips willingly, hands plastered back against the fridge, flexing slightly in my grip but never trying to break it.

For all my bravado in taking control of the situation, I was a little lost now that I had Riot at my mercy. I could count the number of kisses I'd had on one hand, and they'd all happened with him.

Letting instinct guide me, I brushed my lips, *once, twice,* against his, testing how it felt, how he responded. *Good,* I decided. I went in again, using slightly more pressure, nibbling lightly on his lower lip experimentally before running my tongue over it. My thumbs pressed into the pulse points at his wrists and I couldn't tell whose heartbeat was pounding out of control, or if it was both of ours.

The desire definitely belonged to both of us. Mine was coiled low in my belly like a spring, ready to explode. Riot's wrapped around my skin like tendrils of the softest silk.

Plus, his *erection* was digging incessantly into my belly, which seemed like a giveaway. I may not have a lot of experience with that particular organ, but I'd seen enough movies and heard enough innuendo to get the gist.

"Gracie," Riot rasped, tipping his head back against the fridge with a thud, his expression pinched. "You're playing with fire."

"I'm sorry," I whispered, forcing myself back on the flats of my feet to put a couple of much needed inches between us. "I've never experienced this before. *Lust,*" I clarified, face heating again.

Riot's eyes darkened dangerously. "I know, and I hate that. While I selfishly enjoy having your firsts, I would never want them at the expense of your freedom to choose things for yourself."

"That's kind of a mood killer," I teased lightly as I took a step back, never sure how to respond when Riot made very valid points about the agathos way of life and the gifts bestowed on us.

"Maybe for you," he countered with an amused smirk, blatantly adjusting himself through his jeans. Sugar. "But now you *really* should go."

"Okay," I agreed, backing away slowly, very aware that I was prey locked in the sights of a predator in that moment, and not feeling remotely frightened about that. As tempting as it was to stay and explore the promise in Riot's words, we both knew I'd pushed the limits enough already this morning. Both his and mine.

I wanted him, but my stomach churned with guilt every time I thought of all the things we'd done already.

I shoved my feet into my white running shoes quickly, tucking my key into the pocket of my leggings before letting myself out the door and jogging down the stairs, grateful for the cool fall air on my overheated cheeks, though an ice cold shower would have been more effective.

Had I really pinned him to my fridge like some sort of seductress? Who did I think I was? I was going to overthink every minute of that and dissect it for the rest of my life.

What would happen if I did accept that Riot was what he appeared to me? My soul bond, all mine, mine to give myself to? Theoretically, I could be with him freely, without guilt, yet I already knew it wouldn't be that simple. I'd been conditioned my whole life to believe intimacy was something that would just occur between myself and my agathos bonded. Would I ever be able to have a physical relationship with Riot without feeling like I was doing something illicit?

My fingers itched with the urge to rip off my opal ring and throw it in the nearest bush. I'd made a vow when I put this on that I'd keep myself and my thoughts pure for my soul bonds, and I couldn't even tell if I was breaking that vow or not, which made the guilt all the more suffocating.

I should at least *know* if I was committing the crime.

I wished I had someone to talk to about this, or that it was talked about at all. Did Verity Mae ever feel guilty about being with her partners? We'd both been raised on the same diet of chasteness and purity, but she'd met her first bonded before we even finished high school, so I guessed she wasn't as conditioned as I was.

I did some quick warm up stretches next to the building, hoping I was far enough away from Riot that he wouldn't feel my guilt from inside the apartment, but also not really understanding how far this connection between us actually stretched. I hadn't ever felt his emotions while I was at work, so I assumed it was distance related, and I tried to focus on happy things until I was further away from the apartment just in case. It wasn't his fault that I was struggling with this, and I didn't ever want him to feel like he'd done something wrong.

Sugar, what would my parents say if they found out about Riot? If they knew what I'd been doing? Rae had left Hope House again, and I doubted she was close enough with anyone else there to talk about me anyway, but still. She *knew*, which always meant someone else could find out. Knowing my track record, I was one bad luck away from my mother barging into my apartment when Riot and I were mid-makeout. That was *exactly* the kind of thing that would happen to me.

She'd be so humiliated. Everything she'd done to prove herself within the upper crust agathos community would be for nothing. At least two of my fathers would be furious.

I ran faster and pushed myself harder than I ever had, determined to fight off the surge of unwelcome what-ifs. Those thoughts belonged to a different Grace from a different time. Last week, but still. Whatever this thing between Riot and I was, it was clear that I couldn't afford to think like the lonely agathos girl with the forbidden angry tendencies I'd been my whole life. She was gone.

This Grace had mysteries to unravel and secrets to keep. If every agathos gift came at a price, the gift of Riot came at the cost of my innocence about the world I'd grown up in. Or perhaps my *ignorance*.

It was a price I was more than willing to pay.

GRACE

CHAPTER 10

Riot had left by the time I got back to the apartment and I showered and dressed for work quickly, frowning a little as I pulled on my agathos-approved tan pleated skirt, white sweater, and light denim jacket. Would it really be so bad if I wanted to dress a little differently sometimes? Would Anesidora *really* care if I wore ripped skinny jeans instead of knee-length skirts?

I couldn't quite suppress the blasphemous thought that if she cared that much about my clothes, she could be focusing on more important things instead. Maybe later, I'd feel guilty about not silently apologizing for that thought. For not redirecting it in a more grateful, kind direction, but the self-censoring was just so *exhausting*.

Riot's pessimism was rubbing off on me.

It was an overcast day, and the orange brick facade of Hope House looked particularly grim and foreboding as I made my way up the concrete stairs to the entrance, my heeled ankle boots clicking loudly with each step. How could I feel so fulfilled by my job and so wary at the same time?

The answer made itself known the moment I entered the foyer.

"Ah, finally," Constance snapped, wrapping a bony hand around my upper arm and practically dragging me past the reception desk towards the common room.

"What is it?" I asked, stumbling slightly in my bid to keep up with her. Sugar, this woman walked fast.

"New guest. They're down on their *luck*."

My heart dropped as we paused at the entrance to the common room and Constance tipped her chin at a young man slumped in the bright blue armchair in the corner, looking desolate and more than a little hungover.

It wasn't unusual for Constance to seek me out to use my gift. If I'd come across him in the waiting room, I'd have felt compelled to help him anyway, but I had been hoping to avoid any bad luck while I was harboring a daimon in my house.

The grumpy monster in my head reminded me that I was never good enough to work with the guests until someone needed a lot of help. Then, suddenly, I was the best option for the job because no one wanted to pay the price themselves by using their gifts, even if their skills were better suited to the situation than mine.

I could taste the bitterness of my own thoughts on my tongue.

"Jordan," Constance cooed, using the voice she saved especially for Hope House's guests. It never failed to grate on my nerves. "This is Grace, who I was telling you about. She's just going to sit with you for a while. Why don't you tell her about your art?"

A little of Anesidora's magic threaded through her voice, relaxing Jordan and making him more open to accepting my help.

Constance angled me into the chair next to his and practically shoved me into it, shooting me a tight smile before excusing herself. I awkwardly pulled off my jacket and set my bag down next to me, trying to hide my irritation that Constance hadn't even given me a moment to put my things away.

I startled as I noticed two other people across the room who hadn't been visible from the doorway. It wasn't unusual to see people in the common room, even non guests sometimes when we were trying to find somewhere else that could take them. It was strange to see a child here though. Hope House only housed adults.

The woman's misery was so tangible, I could feel it thick in the air like smoke. This was someone who *needed* luck, but I couldn't walk away from Jordan either. I could feel his sadness too, and this is where Constance had instructed me to be.

Jordan shoved his dirty blonde hair out of his eyes before tugging his oversized gray sweater back down over his hands, and I reluctantly gave him my full attention. He fidgeted with a frayed hole in his dark jeans, staring unseeing at the floor between his feet.

He would talk. Perhaps he would take some time to open up—naturally reserved humans took longer—but eventually his woes would come spilling out, because that's what we were here for. I existed to listen to their problems, to take their pain, to give them a leg up.

"My parents kicked me out," Jordan said eventually, still looking at the floor. "They don't respect my art," he added with a sneer.

I nodded silently. That was unfortunate.

"They just blacklisted me from my own fucking life, just like that. My friends can't hang out with me because their parents are friends with my parents. I was supposed to start college this month, but they're not going to pay for my housing anymore. I mean, I have a scholarship, but how am I supposed to live, you know?"

I listened quietly as Jordan went on to tell me about how he'd just taken some pills to dull the pain, and how he'd fallen asleep in the park and had been mugged in his sleep, and my heart did go out to this poor *kid* who had been thrown out with nothing, and had never existed in the real world on his own before.

At the same time, he'd come from the kind of privileged life that I'd come from, and usually I tried to bestow large quantities of luck on those who hadn't had the kinds of advantages he'd had. It was one of the many reasons Constance didn't like me—she was an elitist, no matter if it was human or agathos she was speaking to. Her version of who was *deserving* was very different from my own.

She barely used her gift anymore anyway. Hers was wisdom—the most common agathos trait, two of my fathers held it too. She had a way of *knowing* things that she could impart on humans, giving them advice that could change their life, though it was at the cost of her own knowledge. Things would just disappear from her memory each time she imparted help.

Constance would have felt the same urge to help Jordan that I felt, but she seemed to justify denying that urge by delegating to other agathos instead of taking the burden on herself.

The woman opposite me shushed the girl who was getting excited watching whatever was on the television, climbing out of her chair to jump around on the floor. It was a rare spark of joy in this place.

I forced myself to pay attention to Jordan again, my palms itching, ready to reach out and give him a little luck. He was so young, and so lost. He had his whole life ahead of him if only he got on the right path now.

But the little girl opposite me was even younger—perhaps around eight years old—her hair braided into elaborate twists around her head, and matching unicorn jumper and leggings a little worse for wear. Her mother looked exhausted, slumped in the chair with her eyes fluttering closed occasionally before she caught herself, blinking rapidly to wake herself up.

I could help them all, I resolved. I had to. I doubted I'd be able to walk away even if I wanted to. Constance had probably known that when she left me in here with all of them.

Barely aware of how little I could afford bad luck right now, I took Jordan's hand and rested my other one on top, and began reciting my generic speech of feel good platitudes I'd had memorized since I'd learned to talk, distracting him with words to keep his hand in place as the magic passed from my hands to his.

Tapping into this well of luck was the only time I truly felt connected to Anesidora. Eutychia felt like liquid sunshine flowing through my veins, and in those all too brief moments, I really felt like a child of the Sender of Gifts.

I cut it off while I still felt like I had plenty to spare, finishing up my speech about finding hope in dark places before tapping the back of Jordan's hand awkwardly and pulling my hands away.

He blinked slowly, pushing himself to standing, brow furrowed. "I think I'm going to go for a walk."

"That's a great idea," I encouraged gently. He had a little luck, now he just needed to follow his instincts. Perhaps he'd find a job while on his walk, or bump into an old friend willing to let him crash at their place for a while.

"Thanks," he muttered absently, already halfway out the door with luck running through his veins.

One down, one to go.

I glanced nervously at the door, not hearing Constance's thundering footsteps yet, and hoped my bad luck could hold off until I'd finished this.

"Hello," I said softly, sitting next to the mother who glanced up at me in surprise, totally lost in her own world. "My name is Grace, I work here at Hope House. I just wanted to check on you, see if you needed anything."

"I'm Angel," the little girl said confidently, shooting me a beaming smile. "Can you find us somewhere to stay? The mean lady said we can't stay here. I don't like her."

"Angel," her mother sighed, gently chastising her. I bit down my urge to agree with Angel. I didn't like Constance either. Which was not at all a gracious thought. *Bad, internal monster.*

"I will check on how they're doing out front finding you somewhere," I replied diplomatically. "Are you doing okay?" I asked the mother, using the Anesidora-infused tone that made humans more amenable to help as I rested my hand over hers, but I probably didn't need to. The woman looked like she really needed someone to talk to who wasn't her child.

She looked at me with wide eyes for a moment, like nobody had ever asked her that question, then the words started to spill out. I lowered the walls around my well of magic and let it drain completely into the woman sitting in front of me while she talked.

Her name was Jasmine, and she'd been working two to three jobs for years to support her family while her husband gambled away almost all the money she brought in. I wanted to offer her words of support and encouragement while she told me about how she'd bundled Angel up a few weeks ago and walked out on him, but my head was starting to spin as it always did when I gave people a lot of luck. My *veins* seemed to hurt from channeling the magic through them, and my senses were dull and hazy, like I'd been holding my breath too long.

159

I forced myself to take a deep breath, hoping it would ease the dizzy sensation before I slid off the chair.

"I feel so much better just from talking to you," Jasmine said, sounding surprised as I pulled my hand away. "You are...wow. I've never met someone with such a calming presence."

"That's very kind of you," I managed to reply with a soft smile in her general direction. My vision was blurring around the edges, and I really hoped I didn't faint at work. Constance would probably put it as a strike on my record.

"Angel, honey, we need to go," Jasmine called, voice full of excitement. I was vaguely aware of her thanking me again, and Angel's protests as she was dragged away from the television, but I could barely summon the energy to lift my head.

They must have gone at some point. My head cleared slightly, and I registered the hum of the television as fear snaked through my system. It was always like this. The moment I was finished transferring large amounts of luck to someone who desperately needed it, my head cleared like I'd been underwater for too long and was finally breaking the surface for air, and the weight of what I'd just done hit me. I *couldn't* be objective in the moment, because I was designed by Anesidora to serve and being around those who needed me turned me into a mindless serving robot.

Now that the haze had cleared, I was again acutely aware of how little I could afford a huge dose of bad luck.

I schooled my panicked features a moment before Constance's thundering steps preceded her entrance. I was staring at the floor when her dark red low heels appeared, her foot tapping impatiently as she waited for me to look up and show her proper deference.

I wasn't really in the mood.

I wished Riot was here.

What would he say when he found out what I'd done? Would he be disappointed in me? This thing between us wasn't just my secret. It wasn't just my life I was putting at risk.

With marathon effort, I tipped my head back as Constance's severe features came into focus. She couldn't get angry at me for helping Jasmine—not when I'd helped Jordan as she'd asked, and Jasmine was obviously in need of some good luck—but I was confident she'd find another reason to be angry with me.

"You took too long to complete your task. You have overused your abilities and made yourself useless to myself and your colleagues." *There it was.* "Go to the break room and compose yourself. You have ten minutes and then I expect to see you doing rounds. Are we clear, Grace?"

"We are clear," I replied with a tight smile, forcing myself up onto wobbly legs, biting back a complaint at the unfairness of it all.

Riot had mentioned fairness multiple times—whether the things that were expected of us were fair, and whether our "gifts" were actually gifts. I hadn't argued particularly hard against him because he'd brought up some valid points, but in that moment I was feeling the kind of outrage that Riot seemed to feel.

I had given, and given, and given. I'd acted almost before I realized what I was doing, because my instincts had commanded it. I'd always thought I'd made a choice to help the people I'd helped, but had I really? Or was the choice to give everything I had to both Jordan and Jasmine made for me before I even stepped foot in this room by virtue of *what* I was?

I stumbled into the empty break room and managed to pour myself a glass of water before collapsing on one of the uncomfortable plastic chairs at the dining table in the center of the room to catch my breath.

The rest of my shift passed in a blur of exhaustion, while contemplating what I'd just done and all the ways it might come back to haunt us.

In addition to the ball of dread that had taken up residence in my stomach, I'd felt drained all day—more than just the drained I got from missing Riot—and I wanted nothing more than to get home, eat my body weight in chocolate and snuggle the very unsnuggly-looking daimon who was currently living in my house. Despite how rotten I felt, I was determined to cook a nice dinner tonight. Maybe it would soften the blow of my bad luck news? Besides, I hadn't managed to cook for him yet, which was just atrocious manners considering he was staying with me. *He'd* cooked for *me* that first night.

That was just awful hostessing. Mother would faint.

I was already feeling guilty about ripping him out of his life, plus there was the whole prayer-to-the-dark-goddess thing that I was *definitely* going to mention...soon. The least I could do is cook us a meal.

What did vegetarians even eat? I wondered as I climbed into my car. Not meat, obviously, but how did I even create a dish without meat as the centerpiece? Agathos *loved* meat. The Elders even used the animal's blood for rites. *Nothing* went to waste.

Mother had not prepared me for this kind of scenario. I was almost disappointed I had to keep Riot a secret so I couldn't point out this flaw in her homemaking training.

I shook my head slightly as though I could shake off the snarky thoughts. I was feeling more vulnerable than usual, and it made my dark thoughts harder to control.

Think kind thoughts, Grace.

I had all the ingredients at home for my homemade pasta sauce, I just needed to grab some pasta to go with it. I could just leave the meat out, right? It'd probably be fine. I pulled into a spot in front of the store around the corner from my apartment, feeling resolved as I climbed out of my car, wishing I'd put my jacket back on the second the cold air hit. I'd buy pasta and maybe some dessert. It would be like a date, kind of.

Guilt churned in my gut at that thought. We weren't supposed to date anyone other than our soul bonds, but I was already breaking the rules, so what was one more? A slightly more romantic setting for dinner was the least egregious of my crimes.

My face heated just thinking of the other *things* we'd done. The kissing, the *rubbing* all over him, our moment against the fridge this morning...it was all stuff that was meant to be reserved for my bonded, and there was a good chance he wasn't, because it shouldn't be possible. Worse still, would I be able to give him up, even if he wasn't mine? It didn't *feel* like I'd be able to just walk away from Riot, even if I wanted to.

"Nobody move."

I froze, standing in front of the shelf of dry goods I'd been perusing, my hand hovering over the pack of pasta I'd been about to pick up.

I'd only vaguely registered the guy entering the store just behind me, head bent down with his hood pulled up. I had *not* noticed the gun he was concealing in his front pocket, because of course I hadn't. Because I was due some bad luck.

He strode up the middle of the three aisles, shouldering past a woman who stumbled into the shelving with a pained wheeze, his gun outstretched.

How could this be happening? In the months I'd been living in Milton, I'd never experienced anything like this.

The store was mostly empty—the cashier and owner, Dev, was frozen behind the register, eyes wide and panicked. He was a human and a nice man. A family man. I'd met his wife and son here a few times. There was an older human man closer to the register, shaking like a leaf, and the young woman in the aisle opposite, her face obscured by her long blonde hair.

"Come on, man," Dev pleaded, the color rapidly leaching from his face as his eyes zeroed in on the gun pointed directly at him. "Don't do this. You can take all the money, I don't care. Just don't shoot."

The guy's hood fell back a little when he straightened his head, and I could see just from his profile that he was beyond desperate, even if I hadn't been able to feel the misery pouring off him.

He was so young, perhaps even a teenager judging by the wispy hair around his jaw and acne on his cheeks. Too young to be doing something this level of life ruining, but he was also feeling the kind of all consuming agony that made reasoning impossible. What he needed was a reprieve.

I could give him that. I *had* to give him that. My limbs shook with the need to act, to *help*. It was what I was designed by Anesidora specifically to do.

The blonde woman glanced back at me and I startled at the purple and red eyes that met mine. Not that I hadn't seen daimons in this store before, but usually I was aware enough of my surroundings to at least wait in my car until they'd left.

That was probably part of my bad luck too.

There was no enmity in her eyes though. We were both scared at that moment, and I was the only one who could do anything about it.

Well, anything *good*. I didn't know exactly what she could do, but it probably wouldn't help the situation.

I just had to get close enough to the gunman to touch him, which seemed...*risky*. Given the gun and all.

"Distract him?" I mouthed hopefully at the daimon woman. Sugar, she was supernaturally beautiful. It was almost absurd seeing her in the middle of a dingy store in Milton. Her blonde hair hung completely straight, and her makeup was so chic yet definitely edgy enough that my mother would have a stroke on the spot if I tried it. Ugh, she even had a *nose ring*. Impossibly cool. She looked like she should be on a stage somewhere, half hidden in shadows as she played the bass, all cool and aloof.

She had an incredibly apathetic face, and I sort of admired how cool and detached she appeared in her gray knit jumper with the sleeves pushed up to her elbows, showcasing the flower tattoos that covered both of her arms. Given the situation, she should probably look a little less relaxed, right? I definitely was not feeling relaxed.

I didn't know how I expected her to react to my request. An outright refusal, probably. Since I'd met Riot, I'd felt uniquely connected to the daimon community, even though I knew I appeared like a regular agathos nobody to them.

To my surprise, she gave me an exasperated nod, rolling her purple and red eyes dramatically. Maybe she was just desperate enough to roll with it in the hopes I could get us all out of here alive. Or maybe she thought I had a better plan than I actually had.

"Your father died," she said to the gunman in a flat voice, her stare boring into the side of his head.

"What?!" he gasped, swinging around to point the gun at her chest. *Sugar.* His back was fully turned to me now, and I crept along the aisle on my tiptoes, cursing my decision to wear heeled boots that morning. "How do you know that?"

How did she know that?

"Suicide," the woman continued, in that same terrifyingly monotone voice. "A terrible way to go. This won't fix things though. It won't solve your mom's financial problems. You'll go to jail. She'll be all alone."

"Stop talking!" the gunman ordered, looking shaken. I rounded the end of the aisle, only two feet away from him. Dev was standing as still as a statue behind the register, shooting me an alarmed warning look with his eyes. "I don't know you, lady. How do you know all this stuff? Stop talking," he said again, shaking his head so violently that his hoodie slipped off, revealing short brown hair underneath.

"I'm a psychic," she deadpanned, barely sparing a glance at the gun pointed at her heart. "I see nothing but sorrow in your future if you continue down this path."

Were there psychic daimons? Riot had mentioned something about dreams, but this woman was very much awake, and seemed to be coming up with her speech on the spot.

Her eyes slid to mine over his shoulder in a very clear *hurry up* signal, so perhaps she wasn't as relaxed as she appeared. Understandably so.

Steeling myself and hoping I didn't pee my pants out of fright, I rushed across the short distance between myself and the gunman and slapped my hand on the back of his neck, the only exposed skin I could find, before changing the angle slightly so at least to the humans watching us, it would look like I was pressing on his carotid artery.

Luck wouldn't help this situation, even if I had any left to give. Instead, I sucked all of his emotional pain into me, draining him as fast as I could. Fast enough to knock him out. To knock both of us out probably, judging by the agony he was carrying around.

Even hearing a small fraction of what he'd been through from the daimon woman, I didn't think I could have prepared myself for the agony I was jumping head first into.

His mind was a dark mire, full of gaping pits of hollowness framed by sharp, jagged edges. It was a terrible place, and this man—this *young man*—had been residing in it for a long time, because this kind of pain didn't arise overnight.

It was the kind of dark misery that was so thick, it seemed impossible for any light to get through. The kind that made hope seem like a thing of the past, rather than an option for the future. I couldn't give him hope, that wasn't my gift, but I could clear some of the murkiness so he could find it for himself.

Since I hadn't verbally eased him into accepting my help, the man startled at the sudden contact, struggling for half a second to shake me off even though the feeling was probably quite pleasant on his end. That half second was all it took for me to catch an elbow to the eye, and my grip tightened on his neck as I sucked in a pained breath, forcing myself not to let go.

Freaking ouch! That was definitely going to bruise.

This is why we don't just grab people, Grace.

Wincing at the injury, I pulled harder on his anguish and the man stopped struggling, probably feeling as dizzy as I was beginning to feel. His would be a good dizzy though. A brief reprieve from all the hurt.

The daimon woman smacked the weapon out of his hand the moment the gunman began to slacken and Dev moved quickly, rushing around the counter to grab him as his legs started to buckle beneath him.

I was vaguely offended that he hadn't come to my aid instead, but I supposed to him it didn't look like I was doing anything particularly strenuous. On the inside, my head felt like it was exploding—my vision was fading around the edges and I watched my hand drop from his neck like I was watching someone else's limb.

My head hurt, but my body felt numb. Too numb to hold me upright.

Oh dear.

I was going to collapse, and that would definitely raise questions. I shouldn't have left Auburn. I didn't want to be unconscious and all alone here. If someone called the authorities, they'd probably get hold of my parents.

Hadn't I had enough bad luck already?

Purple eyes rimmed in red met mine, but they weren't the right eyes. There was too much purple. Too much eyeliner.

"You're not Riot," I murmured as spots filled my vision. It almost looked like the eyes in front of me widened.

And then there was nothing.

CHAPTER 11

"My dick is going to fall off if I don't get laid soon," Dare sighed, slumping dramatically onto the bench chair in the waiting area, flexing his cramped hand. He'd been working for hours straight, and I felt like his mother, reminding him to take breaks all day.

"If it were anyone else, I'd say you're exaggerating," I chuckled, shutting down the laptop at the front desk. Even that movement felt hard. Everything was sore and tired again from being away from Grace. "But given your lineage..."

"Shut up, it's not actually going to fall off. I don't think," he added, frowning a little at his lap like he was checking it was still there. Ha, sucker.

My phone vibrated in my pocket and I pulled it out unenthusiastically, not expecting a call from anyone worth hearing from since Dare was already here. Maybe Bullet, but only if he was willing to be more helpful than he had been last time we'd talked.

"Who put that look on your face?" Dare asked, sounding amused.

"Rogue is calling me. That's weird," I muttered, staring at the screen. I couldn't even remember the last time I'd actually spoken to her.

"Maybe she thinks you're still selling?"

"She just had a kid," I scoffed.

"You know firsthand that moms can get high," Dare pointed out casually. I rolled my eyes as I swiped to answer the call.

"Riot?" Rogue asked, her usually flat, unaffected voice sounding a smidgen more emotive today.

"What's up?" I asked, already standing from the desk, eager to get out of here and see Grace. I was glad I'd had the full day to calm down after she'd pinned me to the fridge this morning, but now I was more than ready to see her again.

"I don't suppose you're friendly with a sweet-as-pie little agathos, are you?" Rogue drawled, stopping me in my tracks.

"What are you talking about?" I growled, even as my stomach flipped nervously. Surely she couldn't be talking about Grace?

Fuck. She had to be talking about Grace.

"No judgment, but this chick just passed out and she looked at my eyes and said I'm not Riot, sooooo..."

"Where are you? Where is she?"

I forced my feet to move, rushing past Dare and letting myself onto the street, already jogging towards Grace's apartment. Every step felt like an ordeal as I pushed through the lethargy, and I could hear Dare behind me, calling my name, but panic had me singly focused in my attention.

I needed to get to Grace.

"The mini market on Springdale. She's still out cold."

Fuck. Why was she unconscious? My chest felt so tight I thought I might be having a heart attack, and I forced myself to focus. To keep my feet moving. To formulate words.

Springdale. Mini market. That was right by her apartment, it'd take me thirty minutes to get there on foot.

"What happened?" I managed to ask, the words feeling like they'd been ripped out of my chest.

"She's fine," Rogue said as tonelessly as usual. "She just needs to *recuperate.* I'll wait with her, but hurry the fuck up, I have shit to do."

The call cut off and I cursed Rogue's name to every deity that might be listening.

"Hey!" Dare yelled out the window of his truck, crawling up the street beside me. "Get in, you fucking madman. Where do you need to go?"

I jogged into the street, climbing into the passenger side and gave Dare instructions before I'd even closed the door. She'd be fine. She just needed to recuperate, that's what Rogue said. Maybe she'd worked too hard today, or hadn't eaten enough for lunch. People fainted when they didn't eat, right? It was probably that.

Fuck, I was the wrong person on every level to be relied on for help. I had no idea how to handle this.

"What is going on?" Dare asked, stepping on the gas and looking at me out of the corner of his eye like I'd lost my mind.

I opened my mouth to answer, to confess what was going on and hope that Dare would have a better idea of what to do than me, but my phone buzzed as we turned a corner, distracting me. I glanced down in case it was Rogue, finding a message from Bullet instead.

Bullet:

Don't let anyone else find out about her. It isn't time.

What the fuck?

Why couldn't he have used his psychic bullshit to tell me *before* she fainted? *Weasly little fucker.*

"A...*friend* of mine is in trouble," I replied hesitantly.

"The girl you've been fucking?" Dare asked, raising an eyebrow at me.

That would be the obvious answer. I could say yes, and he wouldn't question it. We may not be built for monogamy, but we were possessive of shiny new things, including bedmates.

I opened my mouth to agree, but all I could see in my mind was Grace's soft smile, her multicolored eyes that looked at me like I wasn't a fucking monster, the gentle way she touched me until lust clouded her mind and those soft touches turned greedy and desperate.

Even if we *had* been having sex, I could never reduce her to just a girl I'd been fucking. She was so much more than that.

"You don't have to answer that," Dare said quietly, looking straight ahead.

"I don't have an answer for that," I admitted. "You can't stick around though. I wish I could explain more..."

Dare sighed heavily, turning the corner onto Springdale. "You sure you're not in trouble, Riot?"

"Not the kind you're probably thinking of," I replied absently, my eyes scanning the street for any signs of, well, *anything*. Fucking Rogue, she couldn't have given me a little more to go on? Her and Bullet were both on my shit list now.

"I have no idea what to make of you lately," Dare muttered. "I guess I just have to trust that you know what you're doing though. You do know what you're doing, right?" he asked dubiously when I didn't respond.

"Sure," I replied hurriedly, jumping out of the truck the second it slowed near the convenience store.

"Riot!" Dare yelled exasperatedly out the passenger window, but I waved him off and with an irritated rev of his engine, he drove away. He was a good dude. Not just for a daimon, but in general. I should really give him more credit.

I barged into the almost empty store, trying to ignore the assault on my eyes from the fluorescent lighting, and made a beeline for the front. Grace was lying on the ground off to the side, still as a corpse, Rogue kneeling next to her head. One of her eyes was swelling up, and a hot rush of anger ran through me at the obvious sign of injury, mingling with the ice cold panic that seemed to have seized my lungs.

She was so still.

"Finally," Rogue muttered petulantly. "There are *people* everywhere," she added, glancing pointedly at the human man pacing behind her. Everywhere was a bit of an overstatement—the only other human here was a terrified looking middle aged woman behind the register.

"What happened?" I demanded. Rogue's irritation had at least broken the grip that fear had on me. This wasn't the time for me to freak out. I had to step up to the plate and make this right, even though I was the least qualified person ever to do it.

Could I pick Grace up? What if she had a spinal injury?

"She overdid it," Rogue said quietly. *Okay.* Okay, she overused her agathos gifts, probably. "You need to get her out of here, that guy is itching to call an ambulance and I can't get him to fuck off."

I scooped my limp girl up in my arms, heart stuttering at the way her head lolled backwards. *Come on, Gracie. Wake up for me.*

The human guy behind me made a noise of protest, but I shot him a glare that clearly told him to fuck off before I *made* him fuck off, and he relented.

"Grab her keys from her purse," I instructed Rogue unnecessarily. She was already fishing through Grace's bag. She followed me out and unlocked the vehicle, and I carefully maneuvered Grace into the back seat, sitting on the edge of the seat, half out the doorway so I could rest Grace's head in my lap.

Should I take her to the hospital? If she'd just overused her abilities, then rest was probably the best thing for her, but then again, I didn't know shit about how agathos abilities worked.

I couldn't just drive off either because fucking *Rogue* knew about us, and I had to deal with that first. She stood in front of the open door, blocking the view of Grace and I from the street.

"What happened?" I gritted out. "Why was she using her ability?"

"Armed robbery," Rogue replied, sounding bored. "She went all super agathos on me and I don't know. Touched his neck and it did something? They both passed out."

"And her eye?" It didn't look terrible, but it was definitely swelling.

"He clipped her in the face with his elbow, I think. I couldn't really see. She held her own," Rogue added. If I didn't know better, I'd think she was impressed.

"Where is *he*?" I asked coolly, entirely ready to work out my anger on his face.

Rogue snorted. "Out back. Dev, the guy who owns the store, called his brothers to come beat the shit out of him. I get the feeling they don't want cops involved. That was his wife at the counter. Anyway, who's the girl?"

"None of your fucking business," I snarled, curling an arm protectively around Grace's head. I could have sworn she made the tiniest groan under her breath. That was a good sign, right? Shit, I knew nothing about taking care of people. I didn't even know how to *worry* about someone. It kind of made me want to puke.

"I think it's a little my business," Rogue protested as I pulled out my phone, shooting off a text to Bullet. I still didn't know what he'd *seen* about Grace, if he'd seen her at all, but he had said *her* in his last message.

Me:

Consult your cards.

Bullet:

You get a short answer because you're a heathen who doesn't understand the cards anyway. Four of Swords. Rest and recuperation. She will be fine.

"Hello. Still standing here," Rogue huffed while I set my phone down to stroke Grace's hair.

"I'm not telling you shit, Rogue," I sighed, giving a warning look. "And you're not going to tell anyone else shit."

"Or?"

"Or I'll ruin your fucking life," I replied easily. "I don't care if you're someone's mom."

"So, this is the thanks I get for calling you? Aren't you a peach," Rogue remarked snarkily, though she looked more puzzled than angry.

"Riot," Grace whispered, her voice hoarse.

"I'm here, beautiful," I said, leaning over her face, the nickname rolling easily off my tongue. She *was* beautiful, but I also didn't want to tell Rogue her name.

Grace's eyes blinked open slowly, and she scrunched them tight as though she was looking directly into the sun instead of the dark inside of her car.

"How are you feeling?"

"So, so bad," Grace groaned.

"What do you need? Should we go to the hospital? You scared the shit out of me," I admitted as I traced the edge of the swelling around her eye, forgetting for a minute that Rogue was still standing there, watching our interaction.

Grace seemed to notice her at that moment too, her surprise brushing at my skin like little sparks. I'd never been so grateful to feel her emotions before. It was a reminder that she was very much *awake* and here with me.

"No hospital," she breathed, attempting to push herself up on weak arms. I lifted Grace into a sitting position, and she gripped my thigh for a moment while she steadied herself. "I just need sleep. And carbs."

"Fascinating. Well, I gotta go," Rogue announced. "I left Quinn with my brother and I need to make sure they're both still alive. Shall we ensure your secret is safe with me?"

"Name your price," I replied resentfully, tightening my grip on Grace like I could shield her from Rogue's curiosity. No daimon ever did anything for free. Except maybe Dare.

"A favor."

"To be determined at a future date, I'm guessing," I deadpanned.

"It's not like you have a choice," Rogue sang, extending her hand. For fuck's sake.

"Fine," I gritted out, taking her hand. "In exchange for your *complete silence* about what happened here tonight, I will grant you a favor to be determined at a later date."

"Deal," she replied with a self-satisfied smirk as a ripple of La Nuit's magic passed between us. Grace was silent throughout the exchange, but I could feel her curiosity reaching out to me like tendrils searching for something.

"See you around, lovebirds," Rogue announced, flipping me off over her shoulder as she strode away, and I grimaced at the promise I'd just made. Maybe Bullet could give me some guidance on her, since he'd decided to be helpful with his cards this time around.

"I need to get you home, Gracie," I murmured. "We're too exposed out here, and you need to eat. I'll make you grilled cheese."

"I was so looking forward to making you dinner this time," Grace sighed heavily, looking oddly disappointed considering the hellish ordeal she'd just been through. "And not only have I still not made you dinner, now at least one person knows about us."

"You don't sound as upset about that as I thought you would," I said, helping her buckle in. Hopefully it was dark enough that no one recognized me driving her car. As the only agathos in town, everything about Grace was pretty notable, including her silver SUV.

"Well, it's kind of my fault," Grace replied with a wan smile.

"It's no one's fault. I'm just glad you're okay." I pressed my lips against her forehead as Grace made a noise of disagreement, staying there a beat longer than necessary just to appreciate how fucking great it was that she wasn't unconscious, before I climbed out and let myself in the driver's seat.

"Shouldn't we have stayed?" Grace asked as we rounded the corner to her building. I was driving like an old lady, but I was worried if I went any faster I'd jostle her and she'd faint again. "Won't the police want to speak to me?"

I snorted. "Apparently the owner and his brothers are dealing with the guy himself."

"That sounds terrible," Grace replied, alarmed.

"Oh, I don't know," I said absently as I parked across from the apartment. "They'll probably rough him up a bit and tell him to fuck off."

Sounded better than a criminal record to me, but I also didn't really give a fuck about the guy who could have shot my girlfriend.

Well, not my girlfriend.

Was she my girlfriend?

I glanced back in the rearview, suddenly worried that Grace could somehow hear my embarrassing train of thought, but she seemed totally lost in her own world, chewing nervously on her lower lip and glancing over her shoulder like she wanted to go back.

Shit, she *did* want to go back. A human in trouble was like a siren call to her, even when she had exhausted her abilities. I'd always thought being an agathos would be easier than being a daimon, but now I wasn't so sure. We were both bombarded with human misery, but they were actually expected to *fix* it.

I climbed out of the car, taking a quick look around to make sure we hadn't been followed before making my way around to her side of the vehicle. Grace startled when I opened her door, so lost in her thoughts she hadn't even realized I'd gotten out of the car.

"It's not your job to save everyone," I told her gently, reaching across her to undo her seatbelt. Her breath hitched at my nearness, and I brushed my lips across hers as I pulled away.

"It is though," she whispered, licking her lips. "Helping humans is literally what I was created for."

I couldn't stop the disgruntled noise that came out of me as I helped Grace out of the car. I was called to human doom, but I had free will as well. I *could* walk away without doing my "duty" and not feel a smidgen of guilt for letting the goddess down. The *Great Mother* hadn't been so generous with her creations.

I wrapped an arm around Grace's waist, shrugging her purse over my other arm, and led her across the street to her building. She was walking, which was positive, but definitely leaning pretty heavily on me.

I wanted to know exactly what she'd done that made her feel this exhausted so I could make sure it never happened again, but getting food in her first was more important.

As soon as I got her in the house, I kneeled on the floor to tug off Grace's boots while she blushed profusely, before removing her coat and guiding her to the couch. In the very recesses of my memory, I remembered my mom setting me up on the couch with the TV remote and snacks when I'd broken my leg in fourth grade. It was one of the few memories I had of her actively taking care of me.

With a tight smile, I handed Grace the remote and went to the kitchen to grab peas from the freezer for her swollen eye, wrapping it in a kitchen towel as I brought it back to her. She'd settled into the corner of the couch with a throw over her legs and gave me a bemused look as I handed her the peas.

"For your eye," I explained, feeling like an idiot. I wouldn't know how to take care of a goldfish, much less a person.

"Thank you," Grace replied with a gentle smile, wincing as she brought it up to her face. "It's not so bad," she assured me.

"It shouldn't have happened," I muttered, heading back to the kitchen to make grilled cheese again. I should probably learn to cook something else. My phone buzzed in my pocket while the food was cooking and I pulled it out to find another message from Bullet.

Bullet:

Everything okay?

Fuck, I was going to have to tell Grace about him. He obviously knew about her, and I wasn't going to keep that information from her.

Me:

Fine. I have plenty of questions for you though.

Bullet:

All will become clear in time, mon chéri. Go look after your patient, Nurse Riot.

He really was the worst.

I brought a tray of food out for me and Grace, who instantly tried to push herself up.

"Woah there, where are you going?" I asked, setting the tray down on the coffee table.

"We're eating here?" Grace asked, looking at me like I'd just sprouted horns.

"Uh, yeah? Is that okay?"

"Oh. I've never eaten dinner on the couch before," she replied, looking bemused. "This is fun."

I really needed to up my game if Grace's version of fun was eating dinner on the couch. Too bad I couldn't take her on a proper date. This secrecy thing was bullshit.

"Okay," I announced, handing her a plate. "I'd like to hear what happened today, but first I need to talk to you about Bullet."

"Bullet?" she replied, blinking at me. "Is that a name?"

"Hm? Oh, yeah. He got shot when he was a kid and wears the bullet that almost killed him around his neck, hence the nickname."

"Right," Grace replied faintly.

"He's from the Oneiroi line so he has prophetic dreams, plus some other methods of communicating with the Goddess of Night," I continued, surprised when Grace suddenly straightened, giving me her undivided attention. "Anyway, I'm pretty sure he's been having visions about you. He knew something had happened tonight, and even though he didn't mention you by name, he said he couldn't do a reading on me alone if I wanted answers." I scratched the back of my neck sheepishly. "I haven't told him anything about you specifically, but I thought you'd want to know that you're on his radar."

"I assume agathos don't usually appear in daimon visions," Grace replied, looking resigned rather than upset.

"I assume not," I agreed. "Anyway, he seems to be on your side—*our* side—and I guess meeting him is an option if you want to turn to the darkness for answers. I should warn you, I knew him growing up. He's a pain in the ass, speaks in riddles, and loves show tunes."

183

"He sounds kind of fun," Grace replied with a fond smile. "Obviously, I haven't met him before because I didn't know any daimons before you and I'd *definitely* remember someone named Bullet, but when you talk about him...I don't know. He sounds familiar to me."

I frowned as I took a bite of my grilled cheese. Surely, Bullet would have mentioned something if they'd met? No, they couldn't have met. Bullet barely left his house these days.

"Speaking of other daimons...Rogue, was it?" Grace asked casually, her curiosity burning against my skin. I froze with my food halfway to my mouth, suddenly realizing this could become a very uncomfortable conversation, very quickly.

"Uh, yeah. Rogue. She won't say anything. A deal between us is binding with the goddess, backing out is a direct invitation to get your life ruined. Besides, an unspecified favor from a daimon is too good to throw away, it's basically a blank check," I added with a shrug. The Goddess of Night was big on honor.

"She said she was a psychic."

I snorted. "No. That's just her devastating sense of humor." There was a sort of slimy, unpleasant crawl across my skin and it took me a moment to realize the emotion was coming from Grace. Was that jealousy I was sensing? *Interesting.* "Rogue is from the Oizys line. She can sense a person's misery. More than sense it, she knows the details of it, and can twist it into something worse."

"That's...yikes." Grace swallowed thickly. "She seemed so nice too."

"When?" I asked, baffled.

Grace's lips twitched. "She distracted the guy when I asked her to. And she called you, right? That was pretty nice of her."

Thank the goddess Rogue called me, I couldn't even think about what would have happened if she hadn't. I'm guessing Grace's parents were her emergency contacts, and she'd have been whisked back to Auburn before I'd even known something was wrong. That thought was...unsettling. Just another reason to hate the secrecy we had to maintain.

"It was my bad luck," Grace added, brushing the nonexistent crumbs off her fingers onto her plate. "I exhausted my gift at work today. I knew something bad would happen at some point."

I got the sense that what had happened in that store had shaken her more than she was willing to let on, but Grace was used to smiling through her pain. Maybe one day she'd feel comfortable taking off that mask around me, but I guessed we weren't there yet.

It was a strangely disappointing realization, considering we'd only met a few days ago.

"I'm not sure you can afford bad luck right now, Gracie," I murmured worriedly. I didn't want to criticize her, especially after the day she'd had, but we both needed to be smart right now.

"I can't walk away if someone needs me, Riot. It's like instinct takes over, I'm barely aware of what I'm doing." Grace's eyes pleaded with me to understand, and I managed a strained nod, trying to tamp down my frustration before Grace sensed it, but not really understanding how this emotion sharing thing worked.

"What did you do to the guy in the store?"

"All agathos can absorb suffering—mental and physical. I took a lot of his mental anguish at once, which is why he fainted. And why my head hurts," she added as an afterthought.

185

"Shit, you probably need Tylenol or something," I muttered, setting my plate aside and jumping up to head to the bathroom cabinet. Why hadn't I thought of that?

I returned with water and medicine, and Grace shot me a bemused smile. "You don't need to worry, usually I just hole up in bed and sleep it off when I overdo it. I'll be fine by tomorrow, off to work as usual."

"Not happening," I replied, appalled that she'd even suggested it. "You exhausted two different abilities—one of them *at work*—and caught an elbow to the face. You need a day off."

Grace looked at me like the concept was completely foreign to her. Surely, if her boss expected her to use her gifts at work, she was given time to recover? It's not like I'd worked a regular job to know how these things worked, but if they didn't give her time to recuperate...it seemed a little exploitative.

"I guess I could," Grace hedged. "It would be nice to rest before dinner at my parents' house tomorrow night. I have to go every Friday," she added, giving me an apologetic look.

"I'll take the day off too," I decided. It would be a convenient way to avoid Dare's questions as well. "I'm going to be the sexiest nurse you've ever seen."

"Without question," Grace laughed, wincing slightly as the movement pulled the sensitive skin around her eye.

I took the empty plate off her lap and scooped her into my arms with a squeak of surprise. "Come on, Superwoman. You've had your carbs, now you're going to sleep."

186

As desperate as I'd been for a little morning makeout session, possibly resulting in Grace writhing all over me again, she definitely hadn't been game for that this morning. She'd slept like the dead—which meant I'd spent hours awake just staring at her like a lunatic to make sure she was still breathing—and when she'd woken up, she'd still seemed pretty groggy.

Plus, her eye was still all purple and swollen, which didn't help. Maybe I'd ask through the grapevine how thoroughly that little worm was punished because I wouldn't mind taking a few cracks at him myself, and I generally wasn't a violent guy. Not my bloodline.

I could hear Grace on the phone in the living room with her boss while I attempted to silently make coffee in the kitchen. I wasn't eavesdropping *per se*, but it was a small house...

"I know it's very inconvenient for you—" Grace stopped abruptly again, as she had the entire five-minute conversation. I already hated her boss. Grace had been hesitant to talk about her, and I was pretty sure this was why. They definitely weren't treating her right.

Contemplating a future with Grace seemed like a smart way to torture myself, but if I could really keep her, if we could find a way to live a normal life together... Firstly, I'd do whatever I had to do to make that happen. Secondly, I'd encourage her to find an employer that actually valued her.

Thirdly, I'd give her an orgasm last thing each night and first thing each morning.

"I absolutely will be there on Monday—"

I padded out of the kitchen silently, only to find Grace frowning down at the phone in her hand. "She hung up on me."

"Does she always act like that when you take a day off?" I asked, handing Grace a coffee that was ninety percent hazelnut creamer.

"I've never taken a day off," Grace replied, shooting me a grateful smile. "We don't get sick. Overusing my gift would be the only reason to take a personal day."

"Overusing your gift is a great reason for a personal day."

"I highly doubt my mother will agree," Grace replied wryly. "Family dinner is going to be a nightmare."

"It's a few hours away," I said with a shrug. "I vote we see how many of your favorite teen romance movies we can watch until then."

GRACE

CHAPTER 12

"So, you're really into this Troy Bolton guy, huh?" Riot teased as I hummed along to the final number from *High School Musical 3*. We'd binged all three movies—basically living on the couch all day—but evening was approaching and I had to get ready for family dinner.

"He was *everything* back in high school. That long side swept fringe..." I set down my makeup sponge to fan my face dramatically. I'd set my makeup and a hand mirror out on the coffee table and was sitting cross-legged on the floor so I could maximize my time with Riot before I left instead of getting ready in the bathroom alone.

Even this felt like a small act of rebellion. Even if Riot were my soul bond, Mother would be appalled at the *casualness* between us.

Riot tugged his messy black hair all the way forward before shoving it to the side, flicking it back out of his eyes in a move that I honestly would have found quite cool a decade ago, and I couldn't suppress my laugh.

"Does this do it for you, Gracie?" he asked in a mock seductive voice.

I swatted him on the arm before returning to my meticulous concealer work, too worried about what truth might slip out if I replied. Riot didn't have to do a single thing to *do it for me*. He *did it* for me by just existing.

I lifted my compact mirror up and dabbed concealer lightly over the purplish bruise that had formed around my swollen eye, just barely suppressing my wince. Riot raised a disbelieving eyebrow at me as he pushed his hair back into place, and I knew he was trying to hold in his disapproval of me covering up the bruise at all since the process was obviously causing me pain.

He pulled his engraved lighter out of his pocket, fiddling with it mindlessly the way I'd noticed he did when he was feeling agitated.

Mother would hate a visible bruise though. She'd see it as a sign of laziness if I didn't at least attempt to conceal it, and that was without her knowing I'd taken the day off work. That would *definitely* be noted as a sign of laziness.

I couldn't bring myself to regret it, though. It might have been the best day of my life. Riot and I had gorged on snacks, watched all three *High School Musical* movies and snuggled on the couch the entire time. It hadn't gone any further than that—for which I was grateful because my eye really hurt and I was still feeling rundown, but the snuggling had helped a lot with the recovery. I felt like I'd somehow absorbed some of Riot's energy and it had soaked into my skin.

I finished doing my makeup and ducked into my room to change, selecting one of Mother's favorite dresses to try to stay on her good side. It was a pale pink dress with a high neckline, three-quarter length sleeves, and a scalloped hem. My mother loved this dress. It was...not my favorite. It made me feel like a porcelain doll.

"Alright," I announced, walking back into the living room with my purse in one hand, the other smoothing down my hair. "I'll be a couple of hours. Three, tops."

Riot's eyes ran slowly over my outfit and I felt my face heat at the small smile playing around his mouth.

"Do I look ridiculous?" I sighed. I felt so much more ridiculous, having seen him talking to Rogue with her cool monochromatic outfit and tattoos and piercings. That was the kind of woman Riot had grown up around. He probably thought I looked like a cupcake.

"You look adorable," he replied, sounding completely genuine, which made it worse. I didn't want to be adorable around him. I wanted that *sexy* empowered feeling back that I'd had when I'd pushed him up against the fridge in a moment of insanity.

"Thanks," I muttered. "Are you going to be okay here?"

"I need to swing by my dad's place, but I'll be here when you get back," Riot said, standing up and crossing the short distance to me. His hands skimmed lightly over my hips and I marveled at the colorful ink on his skin next to the soft ballerina pink of my stiff dress. "You sure you're going to be okay?"

No.

"I'm sure it'll be a routine family dinner," I replied instead. I hesitated for a moment before leaning up to kiss the underside of Riot's jaw. Before I could step back, his hands had tightened around my waist and he captured my lips in a proper kiss that had probably wrecked my nude lipstick.

"I know it goes against your instincts, but *please* try not to give anyone good luck," he said quietly, holding me close. "I don't know how this shit works, but I *hate* seeing you suffer."

He didn't ask me to make him any promises, which I was grateful for because I knew I couldn't keep them. Right now, my head was clear and I had no desire to put myself or him at risk.

If I encountered someone in need though...

"I'll try," I replied softly, meaning it with every fiber in my body. There was enough gas in my tank to get to and from Auburn without stopping, and that is what I planned to do.

"I'll be here when you get back," Riot said, dropping a kiss on my forehead as my hands dug into his shirt. I nodded silently, forcing myself to let him go.

His reassurance that he'd be here meant so much more than he could possibly know.

No one had ever stuck around just for me before.

I shot Riot a tremulous smile before making a dash for my car before my courage ran out.

I pulled into my parents' circular driveway, light spilling out from what seemed like every single window of the house.

Their house was an enormous colonial mansion in suburban Auburn. The walls and columns around the front entry painted an almost blinding shade of white, while the shutters on the second-story were done in a tasteful shade of navy, and the whole thing was surrounded by lush sloping lawns and unsettlingly symmetrical landscaping.

Having spent the whole day with Riot, I felt both buoyed by his energy, and more than a little terrified that it was somehow visible. When I'd stopped at the lights, I'd even checked in the rearview that my eyes weren't somehow turning red. Logically, I knew that wouldn't happen—probably—but the paranoia was making me act irrationally.

I checked my reflection again in the dim light, making sure my lipstick was firmly back in place. Did my lips look more swollen than normal? *No*, I was imagining things. From the outside, I was fairly certain I looked the same as I had last week.

Mother's face appeared in the dining room window, similar to mine yet so much harsher, glaring at me impatiently. Apparently my pre-dinner panic time had come to an end.

Nerves churned in my gut as I let myself out of the car. Every Friday night was an exercise in patience, and that had been back in the simpler time of a week ago when I hadn't been hiding anything.

Well, I hadn't been hiding anything like Riot. Just the usual array of un-agathos thoughts that I'd kept hidden my entire life.

"What were you doing out there?" Mother snapped the moment I walked through the enormous white double doors. Sugar, she was dressed like the first lady in a matching sage pencil skirt and blazer set, nude high heels on just to walk around her own house. She'd pulled her long black hair, thicker and curlier than mine, back into a low chignon, and her makeup was impeccable as always. She hated her skin tanning any more than necessary and avoided the sun like the plague, which probably explained how we looked more like sisters than mother and daughter.

No one would guess she'd had three kids, aged 25, 8, and 5, though she'd only been 20 when she had me which helped. Most agathos women would have had at least ten children in that time—one girl and a litter of boys usually, but Anesidora hadn't been generous to my parents on that front.

"Do you have any idea how rude it is to just *sit in your vehicle* while your host is waiting inside for you? Six months away and it's like you've forgotten everything I ever taught you," Mother added while I floundered for a suitable reply.

No matter how much independence I achieved, my mother had the ability to make me feel like a child again.

"She was probably just on her phone," Chance said as he passed me, dropping a kiss on the top of my head. He was the tallest of all my fathers and had always been the lankiest, with a shock of red hair that he diligently tamed before attending his job in the Planning and Zoning Department. He had been raised here, and there had been no question that when my mother found him, this was where they'd settle.

"I'm more worried about your eye," he added, doubling back and gently lifting my chin up to inspect my black eye. Not for the first time, I catalogued the features we had in common—mostly our noses and jawline. It was never spoken of, but I always assumed Chance was my biological dad, just like Tobin was Earnest's, and Leon had an uncanny number of Valor's mannerisms.

"I used a lot of luck yesterday and ended up in the middle of an armed robbery," I said, self consciously pulling my hair forward to cover the injured side of my face.

"We know," Mother said coolly, giving me a scathing look. "Constance already called to tell me you'd taken the day off."

"Which seems entirely reasonable," Chance added softly, though Mother's face said she strongly disagreed. "Did you have a relaxing day today?"

"Very relaxing, thank you," I said with a tight smile. Could they tell I was hiding something? Oh gosh, they would totally be able to tell.

So long as their questions weren't too pointed, I'd be fine. Surely, Mother would be too aggravated about me taking the day off and making her look bad to ask about anything else.

"I'm going to get Mercy and the boys," she huffed, spinning on her heel and marching up the sweeping staircase that dominated the foyer, her stilettos clicking ominously against the wood with each step.

I followed Chance into the kitchen. Earnest, one of my other dads, was preparing dinner and I assumed Valor was in his study, and the fourth, Creed, was upstairs with the boys.

When I was growing up, Mother had been the most hands-on parent, but apparently I'd burned her out as Creed had mostly taken over with Leon and Tobin.

"Grace," Earnest said, giving me an unusually guarded look. His skin was a deeper brown than mine, partially covered by the silvery gray beard he'd only grown in recent years, his hair shaved short. Like many agathos, he worked among humans. He and Creed were both attorneys.

Earnest, Valor, and Mother were quite similar. They were all strict, legalistic, and agreed on most things. Creed was gentler, and Chance had a mostly well-hidden rebellious streak that supported my theory that he was my biological father.

"Where did your mother go?" he asked, looking past me into the foyer. "And what happened to your eye?"

"She's getting Mercy and the boys. And bad luck," I replied, immediately going to the sink to wash my hands so I could do salad prep.

Valor strode into the kitchen, his gaze sweeping imperiously over the dinner preparations. He was a very serious-looking man—tall and wiry, with salt and pepper hair slicked to the side and heavy rimmed glasses. He taught science at the small agathos private school in Auburn that myself and everyone I'd grown up with attended, and was always dressed like a science teacher in his slacks, collared shirts, and wool jumpers.

"Grace," he said sharply. "Your mother is very distressed that you were sitting in the car outside, being so inconsiderate of your hosts."

I tried to force out an apology, but I couldn't lie and I wasn't sorry. I'd been sitting there three minutes tops, and it was my *parents' house*.

196

"You really should be more conscious of your mother's feelings," Valor continued. "Your situation is so hard for her. It's been worse since you moved away."

"Are you still happy in Milton?" Earnest asked dubiously, pulling the garlic bread out of the oven.

"Very much so."

All three of them looked at me with matching stunned expressions. It was definitely my most effusive answer to that question since I'd moved to Milton. *Sugar*, I needed to work on my poker face.

"Well," Chance said with a clap, pulling out wine glasses. "Your happiness is what matters most."

Valor huffed like he didn't agree with that assessment, but said nothing.

Mother swept in with Mercy's arm linked through hers in a vice-like grip, my grimacing cousin rushing to keep pace. Tobin and Leon were still on the stairs, Creed's gentle voice cajoling them down.

Sometimes I wondered if I'd have turned out differently if my fathers had been more hands on raising me, and if that's *why* they were more involved with Tobin and Leon. To avoid another *me*.

"Mercy," I greeted her, pulling her gently out of Mother's hold. We weren't an overly affectionate family—I had almost shoved Mercy away in a panic the first time she'd launched herself at me. Now, I'd grown grateful for her hugs.

"Cousin," she exhaled gratefully, wrapping her arms around my waist. "I have *missed* you," she whispered dramatically, which was code for she'd been having a tough time at the house recently.

"I missed you too," I replied quietly, squeezing her shoulders as I pushed her unruly curls out of my face.

"Dinner," Mother commanded curtly. I'd wondered before if the hugs between Mercy and I made her uncomfortable because that wasn't how our family was, but I was beginning to think she was envious. Mother didn't have that kind of easy affection outside of her soul bonds, not even with her own children.

Leon and Tobin waved as they skipped past me to the table, and I followed them feeling a little sad that I didn't feel particularly close to my much younger brothers. They looked at me like a fun aunt who dropped in occasionally. They'd looked at me like that even when I'd lived here.

At least the food was good at family dinners—I could endure almost anything for lasagna.

I almost regretted the amount of snacks I'd consumed today, but then I remembered how fun it had been to have Riot hand-feeding me popcorn while I bopped along to *We're All In This Together* and decided I had no regrets at all.

"So, about Constance," Mother began as we all sat down at the more informal dining table in the kitchen. My lasagna-fuelled balloon of hope sank like lead.

"I asked if there was any hope for you moving up from a Monitor role sometime soon," Earnest volunteered, finishing Mother's train of thought. "She didn't seem optimistic. We've been wondering for a long time if this job is the right fit for you."

My hands tightened around my cutlery to the point of pain, and I forced myself to relax before Mother noticed. Was it too much for someone to say '*Grace, how are you?*' or perhaps ask what I'd been doing lately, or how the changes I'd been making to the apartment were coming along, or any open-ended question that demonstrated a genuine interest in my life?

They didn't even seem that concerned about the black eye, and honestly it stung. Agathos women were meant to be cherished, and they *were*. Just not me. I'd been a weird, difficult kid who'd emerged with a gift no one respected, and then never felt the call to my soul bonds like I should have.

My mother had worked so hard to raise our reputations when people in Auburn had looked down on her as tacky and nouveau riche, and I was the black mark against the name she'd been trying to build.

Creed and Chance shot me sympathetic smiles, but I wasn't surprised when they didn't speak up. Their passive natures seemed to be designed by Anesidora to balance out the three more domineering ones.

"I enjoy my work," I said evenly. "Of course, it would be nice to move up to a role with more responsibility, but everyone at the shelter is helping the people who stay there, no matter what role they are in."

"Hear, hear," Chance replied, winking at me from across the table.

For a while, we ate in awkward silence. My parents seemed to be having a silent conversation with their eyes, and I bit my tongue so I didn't make the situation worse for myself. Even Tobin and Leon were quietly eating their dinner, sensing the tension in the room. I got the feeling my parents had never worked out what to do with me when I didn't immediately comply with their wishes, because it was such an un-agathos thing to do. My friends certainly didn't push back on their parents' wishes.

I couldn't tell if my parents were unduly harsh, or if I was unduly rebellious.

Mercy discreetly gave me a supportive nudge from her spot next to me, and I shot her a grateful smile in return. She was the one person who made me feel like I wasn't a total alien within my own family or the community as a whole.

Mercy wasn't very good at being sweet either.

I dropped my napkin on the floor so I'd have a reason to bend down and discreetly rub my aching chest. The aching hollowness that came with being apart from Riot was creeping up faster than usual. Probably because I was wishing more than anything that he was here with me, offering me his unending support like he always did.

I never felt judged or unworthy with him, even when I was doing things that I judged myself for.

"The Elders have proposed a new outreach trip, leaving in a month," Valor said with forced casualness. I glanced up to find all of my parents wearing matching expressions of grim determination. There was a heavy sense of resignation at the table, with the exception of my oblivious brothers and a suddenly alert Mercy.

This was definitely not a spontaneous choice of topic.

"Oh?" I managed to ask, bumping my elbow hard on the edge of the table and trying to hide my wince as foreboding creeped like spiders up my spine. I'd never been fond of outreach trips. Agathos were all over the world, but we were drawn to densely populated areas where we were best able to serve. Outreach trips were always in rural areas that agathos didn't want to live in, designed to give the humans there a chance to experience our gifts. They sweetened the deal by choosing beautiful locations, which most agathos would never get to see because we mostly only traveled to find our soul bonds in other cities.

Those were the official lines, at least.

I'd always thought of them as a convenient way to put single agathos men somewhere. Those whose soul bond hadn't made it to adulthood and had never felt the call. There weren't a lot of them, but when it happened, they were inevitably moved along. The structure of our society, the social events, even the housing in agathos communities was all designed around a specific type of family unit, and singles were surplus to requirements.

It was exile by a prettier name.

"To Indonesia," Valor continued. "A small community in Sumatra where you can see orangutans right across the river. Wouldn't that be something?" he asked as if he'd ever had an interest in animal life before now.

I looked between him and my tight-lipped mother, trying to figure out if I risked their wrath by just demanding they tell me where they were going with this.

Be sweet. Think about chubby babies and rainbows and happy things.

"The Elders would like you to go, Grace," Mother said eventually, lifting one shoulder like I wasn't being essentially banished from my community.

"What?" Mercy interjected. "No. Girls don't go on outreach trips. What about her soul bonds—"

"If Grace hasn't felt the call by now, the Elders do not believe she ever will," Valor cut in, giving Mercy a warning look. "If she were a man, she would have already been assigned somewhere."

I already knew that, but I'd never considered that *I* would go, given that women were never sent on outreach trips.

"The Elders believe this is what Anesidora wants for Grace," Valor responded, speaking to Mercy rather than me, which only drove my irritation higher. "That this is a rare opportunity to bring the Eutychia gift to areas where agathos do not usually live. You would not stay in one place forever, Grace. The Elders would be happy to move you around to different locations—"

"—I don't want to leave—" I protested, but Valor continued on as though I hadn't spoken.

"—and you would have the opportunity to travel far more than most agathos get in their lifetimes. They are being tremendously generous with you," he added with a pointed look.

"By taking away my choice?" I asked, baffled.

"*Choice?*" Mother hissed. "They are *choosing* to see your defects as a potential blessing rather than the curse it is. Your choices are irrelevant. We live to *serve.*"

I blinked rapidly, forcing back the hot rush of tears. It wasn't anything Mother hadn't said before, and I knew my single status caused her a lot of embarrassment in the community, but it was difficult to swallow that she'd rather I just be sent away.

"Of course, if you *do* feel the call in future, that would be respected," Earnest said with unusual gentleness, considering how formal he normally was. "Think of it as a way for you to spend your time in the interim."

I could feel myself panicking, my mouth opening and closing like a fish, as I tried to think of a legitimate way out of this that didn't involve me shouting that I may have already found a soul bond.

Just the idea of being sent half a world away from Riot made my throat constrict, the ache in my muscles intensifying to the point I thought I might gasp out loud from pain.

I couldn't leave him. I wouldn't.

In the past, despite whatever questions or concerns I may have had, I'd always conceded in the end. I was afraid of being ostracized. Afraid of drawing even more negative attention to myself than I already had. Just *afraid*.

I'd met plenty of people at the shelter whose decisions were motivated by fear—fear of leaving, fear of staying—and I'd never judged them for it. Fear was a legitimate motivator, and one that I knew firsthand.

But I'd judge myself forever if I let fear of speaking up drive me away from Riot. I'd never forgive myself if I did nothing to stop it.

"My answer is no," I said firmly, startling Creed and Earnest. My heart pounded triple time in my chest, and my palms were getting grossly sweaty as I fought to stop the tremble in my hands. Valor and Mother frowned, while Chance's mouth twitched in what may have been a suppressed smile. "I have bought an apartment in Milton, I have a job I care about, a life there. It isn't reasonable to uproot me on a whim—"

"This isn't about *fair*," Mother spat. "This is about serving where you are needed, selfish girl."

"I am needed where I am," I replied with absolute confidence, impressed that I kept the shake out of my voice. "I will not leave."

Chance's smile became strained, eyes filled with sympathy. "You know we are all at the Elders' beck and call, Grace. If they believe Anesidora wants you elsewhere, they are within their rights to move you."

I'd defended the agathos' way when Riot had criticized our lack of choice. I'd told him it was a gift, and that Anesidora didn't make mistakes. I didn't think I'd ever regretted something so much in my life. They were really ready to just rip me out of my own life, just like that.

"That being said, I'm sure we can request an extension for you," Chance added, giving Valor a hard look. "You'll have things here that need to be sorted out. Selling the apartment, wrapping things up at the shelter..."

"So it's just a done deal then," I said weakly, looking between them. "It's been decided."

"The Elders asked Constance today to give her recommendation." Mother's voice rang with finality, and a chill spread through me from the inside. Today? Of course they asked her today, the first time I'd ever taken a day off work. It was all just so...*unfair*. More than unfair, but my brain was running through too many worst case scenarios to find the words to articulate my anger.

Mostly, I just wanted to cry, which annoyed me. I wasn't sad, I was *furious*, but my anger often manifested in the form of tears just to be extra humiliating.

Mercy grabbed my hand under the table, and I vaguely registered that she was squeezing it, but I mostly felt numb.

"We'll ask for an extension," Valor replied eventually, his voice gruff. A lesser man would have withered under the glare my mother sent him at the smallest of accommodations he'd made for me. "But the Elders have already voted, Grace. They feel your place is in outreach. They are giving you a future."

I was pretty sure I'd found my future all on my own, and the words burned on the tip of my tongue, desperate to get out, but I held them back, reminding myself the risk was too great.

I wouldn't insist on the future I'd discovered for myself if it meant putting Riot's in jeopardy.

RIOT
CHAPTER 13

I felt the moment Grace got back from her family's house. I'd been growing increasingly impatient waiting for her, I was about to run out of fluid from fidgeting with my lighter so much. I felt like she *needed* me tonight, and I wasn't there for her, and it was driving me fucking insane.

Almost insane enough to go after her. I hadn't known exactly where she was—one of the obnoxious mansions in Auburn, presumably—but I almost felt like I could follow the panic I was feeling all the way to the source.

Grace shoved the door open and practically fell inside, kicking off her shoes and leaving them on the floor instead of putting them neatly on the shelf like she usually would, and threw her purse down on the side table. I was surprised she didn't rip the buttons of her jacket with how aggressively she tore it off as I hovered by the couch, debating what to do.

I really wished I knew more about women. Or just people in general. Just like last night, when I'd gotten the call from Rogue, I wished I was more *alpha male* and *take charge* when shit went south.

Grace's anger felt hot and painful against my skin, but there was an undercurrent of something else too. Resignation, maybe.

Had her family found out about us? Would she even be here if they had?

She stepped into the living area, stopping next to the couch in her stiff pink dress that she seemed to hate, chest rising and falling rapidly, but her expression was totally unreadable.

For a moment, neither of us moved. The air crackled with more than just the unspent sexual chemistry that seemed to hang around us like a permanent cloud. There was a new intensity between us that I'd never experienced before, and I forced myself to stay in place when all I wanted to do was throw Grace over my shoulder and take her to bed.

But then she burst into tears, and I came to my fucking senses.

"Shit, Gracie. What's wrong?" I asked, crossing the room and scooping her into my arms.

She shuddered in relief and *goddess*, I could relate to that. Everything felt better having her close.

"The Elders," she sniffed, the sound muffled as she turned her face into my t-shirt. *Elders?* Had *they* found out about us? What else would upset her this much? Then again, I assumed they had some kind of agathos jail where they chucked people who didn't fit their restrictive mold. If they did, that's definitely where Grace would end up for fraternizing with a daimon.

Well, they could try. I would never let that happen.

207

"Come here," I murmured, dragging her down to the couch on my lap and wrapping my arms around her waist. For a moment, she kept her head buried against the crook of my neck, silently sobbing as I ran my hand up and down her spine, letting her compose herself.

I knew fuck all about comforting people, but I'd gathered that Grace didn't like to let anyone to see her in a state any less than perfectly put together. Last night in the car when she'd been freaking out, wanting to go back and help that asshole who'd given her a black eye and could have *shot* her, her emotions had been all over the place, but she'd fought hard to keep her mask of calm in place.

After a few minutes, Grace's hiccuping sobs slowed, and I listened to her take deep, steadying breaths before she lifted her head to look at me.

"My makeup is a mess, isn't it?" she sniffled, blinking rapidly and looking up at the ceiling which seemed to be some sort of magic girl hack for stopping tears.

"It's...fine," I hedged. Grace would probably disagree, but messed up mascara and the concealer that had rubbed off her bruised eye wasn't the biggest priority here. "What happened at dinner? What's this about Elders?"

Even their title was creepy. Agathos made everything so weird.

Grace dabbed under her good eye with the heel of her hand for a moment, looking like she was trying to figure out how to answer my question.

"There are these things called outreach trips," she began slowly. "There aren't a lot of single agathos—and no women until me, apparently—but the ones who exist are assigned outreach trips by the Elders to remote locations where agathos don't usually live."

"They're exiled," I replied flatly.

"Yes," Grace sighed. "That's exactly what it is. I'm next. In a month."

"Fuck no," I growled, arms tensing around her like I could keep her with me purely by force of will. I felt like I could. Like whatever this was between us was strong enough to bend the universe to my will, even though I'd only just met her.

Grace looked back up at the ceiling, rapidly blinking again. "I don't want to go. I told my parents no, but the Elders have already decided on it."

I bit back the avalanche of criticism of the agathos that was threatening to spill out. It was obviously a subject that made Grace uncomfortable, and now wasn't the time anyway.

Even if I thought they were fucking dictators and all of the agathos were prisoners to a system they'd been born into and never given the tools to question.

"I'm not going to go," Grace whispered, opal-colored eyes catching mine. "I'm *not* going to go," she repeated more forcefully.

"Damn straight, you're not going to go," I agreed, leaning forward to press a kiss against her shoulder. I didn't know what her *disobedience* would mean for her or for us going forwards. I doubted the Elders or her parents were going to accept that news lying down, but it wasn't fucking negotiable. "You're not going anywhere."

If they wanted to fight her on it, they'd find out exactly what happened when someone tried to rob a daimon, because Grace was mine.

And no one took what was mine.

"Do you..." I hesitated for a moment, not sure how my question would be received, but needing to ask. "Would you consider running? Moving out of their reach?"

Grace sniffed, looking contemplative. "I sort of am out of their reach, it's why I moved to Milton. They're not going to snatch me off the street or anything, it's not how they operate."

I wanted to argue, but Grace knew her people better than I did. At the same time...I was worried her trust in the agathos to do the right thing was misplaced. Grace reached up, smoothing away my frown with her thumb, giving *me* a sympathetic smile like *I* was the one suffering.

She was too compassionate for her own good.

Her sadness retreated the longer we sat together, seemingly incapable of keeping our hands off each other, and that intense sexual energy that always simmered below the surface flared to life between us again.

It was frustrating that I didn't know if it was our chemistry or her interfering goddess' magic. I'd never experienced anything like this with anyone before—this constant hum of sexual heat that seemed to turn into something crackling and alive the moment we let it. And suddenly I was all too aware of Grace sitting in my lap, the way her breath fanned over my collarbone, the feel of her soft curves in my arms.

I'd been so good all day while we were snuggling under the blankets. I'd given my dick at least six internal pep talks when Grace's limbs got a little too close, or when she laughed all husky, or looked at me like I was the most attractive guy she'd ever seen.

Daimons weren't designed to be good.

I cupped Grace's face with my hand, rubbing away the evidence of her smudged makeup with my thumb. Grace leaned in to my touch and I marveled at the way being near her always felt like exhaling after holding my breath for too long.

"I missed you tonight," Grace whispered. "Like a lot. Like more than what is probably healthy considering I met you less than a week ago."

"Oh, I definitely missed you more than any sane person would consider healthy," I teased, guiding her face closer to brush my lips against hers. "I find I'm not very sane when it comes to you."

"I don't know what it says about me that I find that attractive," Grace replied softly, looking up at me through thick black lashes, still wet from her tears.

"I guess we're just as twisted as each other." I slanted my mouth over hers, brushing my lips softly against hers and pulling away, teasing her a little. Grace always started off shy, but it never took long for her desire to overrule her inhibitions. Surely enough, Grace's mouth chased mine, her grip on my shirt tightening.

Every time I kissed Grace, it felt like the first and the last time. There was a thrill that never stopped feeling new, but the edge of fear that this might be it. That whatever this tenuous thing between us was would disappear from under me, or she'd realize that I was a daimon who probably had blood on my hands, and run as far as she could in the other direction.

I slid my hand up Grace's smooth leg before gripping the back of her knee and guiding it towards me, encouraging her to straddle me. Her hands slid experimentally down my chest before working their way under my t-shirt, stroking the abs that I was definitely clenching for maximum impact.

"You're so hard here," Grace murmured innocently, running her fingers over my stomach.

I grunted in agreement, definitely able to think of one place I was *harder* at that moment. Not wanting to terrify her with that organ, I discreetly adjusted myself as my mouth moved down her neck, drawing out those soft needy noises I loved so much.

"I want to touch you," I murmured against Grace's collarbone, my thumb rubbing the crease of her hip and thigh. That was a tremendous understatement. I wanted to rip her clothes off, spread her out in front of me and feast on her pussy until I could say for certain if it tasted as sweet as the rest of her.

She probably wasn't ready for that.

"Where? Under my panties?" Grace whispered, eyes adorably wide. This woman would be the death of me.

"Only if you're comfortable with that," I assured her. "We can stop right here, Gracie. I'll never take anything from you that you're not willing to give."

From what I'd seen, Grace's whole life had been an exercise in giving up parts of herself for other people.

"And what if I want to?" Grace asked shyly before frowning to herself, her eyes flitting to the opal ring on her finger. "I shouldn't want to, I don't think."

"Unless we're soul bonds," I supplied, because I was pretty sure we were, even if she wasn't ready to admit it.

"But even if we're not," Grace continued breathily, wriggling in my lap in a way that made me consider giving my dick another talk. "I...I don't think it matters. Touch me, Riot. I want you to touch me because it's *you*."

I captured her lower lip between my teeth, sucking it into my mouth as my hand moved under her skirt, my thumb brushing over her slit through her cotton panties. I doubted those words had come easily, and I wanted to reward her for them.

"Is this pussy wet for me?" I asked against her mouth, smiling against her lips as she sucked in a surprised breath. I was testing her a little, seeing where exactly her boundaries were and what got her hot.

For all her bashful blushing, she'd pinned me against the fridge and slid her tongue in my mouth just fine.

"I think so," she replied shyly. "And I am very much hoping that's normal."

"So fucking cute," I murmured, encouraging her to lift her hips so I could tug her panties down her legs. I didn't rush my movements, just in case this was getting a little too real for her and she changed her mind, but Grace obligingly lifted her knees to peel them off.

There was a saucy little temptress underneath that good girl exterior, waiting to come out whenever Grace let it.

I traced her lip with my thumb, tipping my chin up as I observed her, learning what she liked. She seemed to want me to take charge, at least for now, while she was figuring out what felt good.

213

Grace mimicked my movements, her own chin tilting up before her lips parted slightly, tongue darting out to lick the tip of my finger. Her eyes dilated at my groan of approval and she repeated the movement with more confidence, swirling her tongue around my thumb with impressive muscle control that I would *love* to see demonstrated on other parts of my body.

When she was ready.

I slipped one hand underneath her dress behind her, giving her bare ass an approving squeeze as I pulled my thumb away from her mouth. *Fuck*, what an ass. As adorable as all her matching sweatpants and jumpers were, it was a crime she wore clothes at home.

Grace held her breath as I slipped my hand between us and ran my thumb slowly through her folds, brushing her clit with the softest touch. Grace's head fell back as she let out one of those breathy moans that gave me a better high than any drug ever had.

"Tell me how you feel, Gracie," I demanded in a low voice. My dick was so hard, I felt like it was about to tear through my jeans.

"I...*Sugar*. That is...wow."

I smiled to myself as she wriggled in my lap, seeking more friction. "If you've lost the ability to form sentences, then I'd say I'm doing an okay job," I said wryly.

She hummed, biting down on her lower lip as I circled her sensitive nerves teasingly, wanting to build her up until she felt like she would *burst* with the need to come. We found a slow rhythm as Grace's movements gained confidence, but I wanted a better angle. I wanted *more*.

214

"On your back," I commanded, maneuvering her onto the couch. Grace went willingly, her body pliant as she all but melted into the cushions. She was in the perfect position for me to throw her legs over my shoulder and devour her pussy, but I felt like that would be a step too far for her today.

Maybe tomorrow.

Instead, I planted one hand by her head and stroked my fingers between her thighs again, leaning down to capture her lips in a filthy kiss that was all teeth and tongue, and none of the usual gentleness I'd shown her so far. Grace mewled into my mouth and the noise shot directly to my dick. My hand moved without conscious thought, one finger sliding into her pussy.

"Riot!" Grace gasped, breaking our kiss as she arched her back.

"Fuck," I gritted out. It was probably a good thing Grace wasn't ready for anything more. I wasn't sure how I'd ever keep my dick *out* of her once I had a taste of how good she felt wrapped around me. "Are you okay?"

"It feels...weird. Good. Kind of uncomfortable, but it's getting better," Grace whispered, but her desire-tinged curiosity brushed against my skin and I exhaled a quiet breath of relief that she wasn't feeling concerned or scared. I never wanted that for her.

"Relax," I murmured, leaning down to capture her lips again. "Kiss me. Just focus on that."

Proving my hunch correct that Grace enjoyed me taking the lead, she relaxed almost the instant my lips touched hers, and my movements grew bolder, more deliberate.

215

I grinned against her mouth, enjoying the soft whines she couldn't quite suppress as I added a second finger, curling them upwards until I found that sensitive spot that made her gasp, and she bucked her hips reflexively against my hand.

"Are you going to come for me?" I asked, changing my angle slightly to rub the heel of my hand against her clit, feeling her inner walls flutter around me.

"Um, yes. I think so," Grace stuttered, wrapping her hand around my bicep and digging her nails into my flesh as she tightened around my fingers, finding her release with a husky little moan.

I wasn't sure there was a sight more beautiful on this entire planet than Grace lost in the throes of pleasure. She was always exquisite, but seeing her unguarded, vulnerable, lost to pleasure was indescribable.

"Did I tell you to stop, Gracie?" I purred in her ear, pulling my fingers out of her to circle her clit. "Keep going. I want you to come so hard you see the goddess herself."

To my surprise, Grace *bit* down on the inside of my forearm to muffle her moans as one orgasm rolled into another, and I filed that incredibly attractive fact away for later.

Her teeth released my muscle as her head fell back and I admired the two curved lines of indents they'd left behind. Pity they'd fade. Maybe I could get her to bite harder next time and ask Dare to tattoo over the lines.

"Is it normal to feel like this? Is it meant to be this good?" Grace panted, her long hair fanning out over the couch, breasts rising and falling quickly as she tried to catch her breath.

"For us? Fuck yeah," I growled, bracing my forearms on either side of her head so I could lean down to trail soft kisses up her neck. She turned her head to the side, giving me better access as I left a small love bite on the sensitive spot behind her ear. "I will always make you feel that good."

"But I'm not really doing anything for you," Grace protested, the hint of a whine in her voice that made me smile.

"You can't even imagine what you're doing for me, Gracie," I chuckled against her neck. *I could barely comprehend what she was doing for me.* I propped myself up so I could look at her face, her pastel eyes hazy with desire, parted lips swollen from kissing, face flushed.

Sometimes, I struggled to believe she was real.

"You're everything I don't deserve," I whispered against her lips. "You're light and goodness, and so fucking sweet I don't know what to do with myself."

There was a sliver of guilt Grace wasn't quick enough to suppress, and I pulled her back up into my lap, keeping my arms tight around her to try to chase the misplaced feeling away. I hated that any kind of intimacy made her doubt herself.

"Riot," Grace breathed, looking up at me with wide eyes, her head resting against my shoulder.

"Yeah?"

"I don't know how it's possible—it *shouldn't* be possible—but I just think you should know, I believe you're my soul bond."

I smiled against her hair, a weight lifting off my shoulders that she'd arrived at the same conclusion I had.

"I think so too, but it wouldn't matter if I wasn't, Gracie. I'm still keeping you.

When I'd woken up this morning, I'd wanted nothing more than to roll her over and give her the kind of wakeup call she deserved, but I didn't want to wake her on her day off. So here I was, spending my Saturday staring at the top of Dare's head over the half wall in his studio as he bent over his client.

I'd agreed to give him a hand, even though I'm pretty sure he only wanted me here so he could bug me for details about what had happened at the store the other night. Fortunately his client had arrived first thing, so he hadn't had an opportunity to question me yet, but I knew it was coming.

And I'd have to lie to him, which was bullshit. I didn't want Grace to be my dirty little secret, and I didn't want to be hers.

Was she awake yet?

I'd swung by my dad's empty apartment last night to drop off the merchandise I'd swiped and the cash Dare had paid me, and while I was glad he'd be off my back now, I wished I'd saved some money to get a burner phone for Grace. I wanted to be able to talk to her during the day more than ever. She'd admitted she felt we were soul bonds.

Soul bonds.

While I definitely didn't reject any part of that idea, and I felt in my bones it was the truth, I did feel more than a little guilty for inflicting myself on Grace. She obviously deserved far better than me. Someone with clean hands and an intact soul for starters. Someone with a real job and a place to live too. Maybe a car.

None of those clean cut agathos boys would appreciate Grace for who she was the way I would, though. Maybe that's what this was about. Some goddess or another had decided that Grace deserved a soul bond who embraced the things that made her unique, and they'd somehow settled on me.

It definitely couldn't be a reward for me. I hadn't done a single thing in my life to deserve her.

I never thought I'd even have a *girlfriend*, let alone this, but I was determined to be the best fucking soul bond in the history of ever. Starting with morning orgasms, as soon as I had a morning off.

I glanced up as something out the window of Dare's studio caught my attention. Blonde hair, dark clothes, and a slightly maniacal smile.

It could only be Bullet.

"I'll be back in five," I called to Dare, letting myself out the front door. I didn't need Bullet coming inside and scaring away the customer with his cryptic psychic talk.

"Bullet," I greeted him, pulling the door shut behind me. "I thought you had imprisoned yourself in your country manor, content to spend your days with just your cards and musicals for company."

Bullet tilted his head to the side, his pale blonde hair flopping over as he did so, grinning like a lunatic. "Firstly, it's a temporary imprisonment. Secondly, you say that like it's a bad thing. Obviously, you've never experienced the life changing event that is the *Hamilton* soundtrack."

"I prefer my music more-"

"Emotionally tortured? Dripping with angst? Esoteric?"

"I was going to say *subtle*," I groused, crossing my arms. "Are you here to book an appointment?"

Despite my teasing, I knew Bullet did leave his house sometimes. Dare had inked multiple tarot cards into him over the years, ones that Bullet felt strongly connected to. None of them were on display today. As always, Bullet was dressed like he was going to strut down a catwalk—today it was a dark navy suit, but with a gray knit jumper instead of a shirt, and black kicks. The gold bullet he always wore on a thin chain hung around his neck.

It all highlighted how pale his skin and blonde hair were. If he wasn't an Oneiroi and tortured by his dreams, he'd probably be a model with his angular features. *Grace would probably find him pretty,* I mused, startling myself with the bizarre thought.

"Not today," Bullet answered breezily, tapping his foot to a beat only he could hear. "I'm here to see you."

"To explain how you know all the shit you somehow know?" I asked hopefully. I still didn't know how I felt about his preternatural knowledge when it came to Grace. We needed allies, but Bullet was yet another unknown factor.

"Nope." He popped the 'p' obnoxiously and I rolled my eyes. "That conversation involves more people."

I glanced around the street, not wanting anyone to overhear this conversation, but there was no one close by and Dare's client hadn't emerged yet.

"Then what do you want?"

"You should really work on your customer service skills," Bullet said cheerfully.

"You're not a fucking customer," I snarled.

"Well, not at this exact moment—"

"Bullet," I hissed impatiently. "To what do I owe the *pleasure* of this visit?"

"Fiiiiine." He gave me a mischievous smirk that I wanted to punch right off his face. If he knew something about Grace, then I needed to hear it *now*.

"The paths have diverged again."

"What does that mean?" I asked as unease slithered through me.

"Exactly what it sounds like," Bullet said casually. "The path she was traveling has split again. There is a new option that wasn't there before."

"This is about what the Elders decided?" I asked in a low voice. "Should we run?"

Bullet gave me a look that was almost sympathetic, which was a bizarrely normal reaction for him.

"No. Running will delay the inevitable, and do more harm than good."

I opened my mouth to argue with him, but Bullet shook his head slightly, cutting me off.

"I know you don't want to believe me, and I get it. Trust me, I get it a lot more than you think I do. But don't run."

Fuck.

Fuck, fuck, fuck, fuck.

So, what were we supposed to do? Just hang around and hope for the best? Why couldn't Bullet provide a step-by-step guide on how best to stay ahead of the interfering agathos? What was even the point of being psychic if he couldn't do that?

I glanced back through the window as Dare led his client out, a young blonde woman who was inspecting the elaborate saran-wrapped mandala tattoo on her upper arm.

"Hold on, I need to deal with this," I instructed Bullet, not surprised in the least when he followed me inside. Dare's client did a double take when the two of us walked in, looking between Bullet, Dare and I with surprise.

"This must be the most attractive tattoo parlor in the Northeast," she said, blinking slowly.

"Probably," Dare replied with his most charming grin. "What brings you here, Bullet?" he asked, leading the customer over to the desk to pay, waving me away when I tried to take over.

"I just needed a word with my old buddy, Riot," Bullet replied, draping an arm over my shoulders. He grunted as I elbowed him in the gut and shrugged him off, grinning the entire time.

I grabbed his upper arm and steered him back out while Dare finished up, my mood already souring from spending hours away from Grace. It probably wouldn't help the situation to go off on Bullet, but he was doing jumping jacks on my last fucking nerve.

Couldn't he have put this in a text message?

"You wouldn't be so grumpy if you'd bonded," Bullet muttered under his breath, stopping me in my tracks.

"What are you talking about?" I hissed, glancing back to make sure Dare was still occupied.

"You know exactly what I'm talking about," Bullet replied easily. "I'm glad you've finally worked out the answer to the question you were asking yourself all along, the question you both already *knew* the answer to, but this thing between you is bigger than just you two," he added, confirming what was possibly my worst fear.

Bullet gave me an appraising look, scanning my face. "The cards are clear."

"I would never push her to *bond* with me," I spat, disgusted at the concept. I would be no better than Grace's oh-so benevolent goddess if I did that.

"No, you won't," he replied with a tight smile that seemed less maniacal than normal. "Time is no longer on your side. As I was saying, my vision changed last night. The pathway that was once relatively clear now diverges."

"Into what?"

"Into a path you can walk together, and a path she would walk alone."

Unacceptable.

"She'll never walk alone while I walk this earth," I replied in a low voice, feeling the conviction of those words deep in my bones.

"Well we're in agreement on that then," Bullet said cheerfully, grinning even wider when I narrowed my eyes at him.

"How do you know all this? What aren't you telling me?" I asked, even though there were probably a million things he wasn't telling me.

"Nothing you won't find out when the time is right for you to learn it." Vaguely, I wondered if all people with prophetic abilities were insufferable, or if it was just a Bullet thing.

"You could just tell me now," I pointed out. Bullet's eyes darkened for a moment before his usual grin was fixed back in place.

"It's not a future I'm willing to risk changing by divulging it too early. You'll know when the time is right. In the meantime, you'll have to *wait for it, wait for it,*" he sang while I stared blankly at him.

"*Hamilton.* No? You are such a philistine."

I frowned as I examined Bullet, remembering the time he'd gotten revenge on Viper back when we'd hung out in high school. Viper, noted asshole, had shoved Bullet in the hall in front of everyone, and as payback, Bullet claimed he'd visited Viper's dreams that night, giving him a nightmare so fucking twisted he'd made Viper wet the bed.

"Can't you dreamwalk?"

"I can," Bullet replied, his face completely serene, and not giving anything away. The tricky bastard. "Time is no longer on your side," he repeated, stepping around me and moving to the side as Dare's customer exited. "Be ready to act, Riot."

How the fuck was I supposed to be ready for anything if he wouldn't tell me what I was meant to be getting ready for? Asshole.

Dare joined us outside, leaning back against the door with his arms crossed, looking intrigued, and Bullet paused for a moment, tilting his head to the side as he examined Dare like he'd never seen him before.

"You'd look good in a purple toga," he observed, like he was considering something. Dare's eyebrows raised slowly as he looked from Bullet to me, like I knew what the fuck he was rambling about. "Interesting. I'll be seeing you, Riot. You know I always enjoy getting visitors."

He gave us a half-assed salute before shoving his hands in his coat pockets and striding confidently down the street, radiating a borderline psychotic level of cheerfulness as always.

"Is he whistling *Amazing Grace*?" Dare laughed, making me freeze. Even hearing Grace's name come out of his mouth was bizarre. "Bullet is something else."

"Ain't that the truth," I murmured.

Time is no longer on your side.

I pulled my lighter out of my pocket, running my thumb over the grooves of the dragon before flicking it to life. He could only be referring to that outreach thing Grace had mentioned, but the agathos Elders were out of their fucking minds if they thought they were taking Grace. I'd burn Auburn to the ground before I let that happen.

"What was that all about?" Dare asked from behind me.

Time is no longer on your side.

"Riot," Dare sighed. "You were being weird as *fuck* the other night, and now Bullet is visiting you? Give me something, man. Is this about your dad? Are you in trouble?"

"No. And maybe," I admitted, still staring at Bullet's back as he disappeared down the street.

Dare's hand landed on my shoulder and he pulled me around to face him, looking more concerned than I'd ever seen him. "I don't know what to make of you lately. You're somehow the most chilled out I've ever seen you, and the most stressed at the same time."

My lips twitched at his eerily accurate description of my mental state.

"Talk to me," Dare commanded, unusually solemn. "What do you need?"

"Have I told you lately that I appreciate you?" I asked.

"Not once in the whole time we've known each other," Dare deadpanned.

"I wish I could tell you more," I assured him. "But Bullet's visions are involved and he seems to think things need to happen on a certain timeline."

Dare looked frustrated, but eventually gave me a terse nod. "Who am I to interfere in the goddess' plans? Just...don't do anything stupid. I've gotten used to having you as my errand boy, you're good at fetching my coffee. It'd be a real shame if you got killed."

"Aw, I love you too, buddy," I teased, bumping him with my shoulder. I had no intention of getting killed, but I was beginning to worry that it was a genuine possibility.

Bullet had seen a path where Grace was alone, and there was no way I'd ever let her go willingly.

GRACE

CHAPTER 14

I tapped my fingers impatiently on the steering wheel, waiting for the car in front of me to parallel park so I could get around them.

I doubted they'd be able to do it.

That was an uncharitable thought, I chastised internally, albeit weakly. It felt increasingly difficult to remind myself to be sweet all the time. Maybe because Riot was making me question everything about who I was meant to be. Whether or not it mattered if the thoughts in my head were sweet or not.

Maybe in asking La Nuit for guidance, I had fundamentally changed my makeup. Or maybe I had always been this way, but was feeling less uninhibited about it now. Everything in my life felt like a series of unanswered questions.

Or maybe it was because my parents and my boss had conspired with the Elders to send me away with zero regard for my wishes.

Sighing in irritation at the car in front of me, I quickly hit 'call' next to Mercy's name on the dashboard. We usually spoke every day, but I hadn't been great about it this past week, and she'd been so supportive last night at dinner. Guilt churned uneasily in my stomach at that realization. I should make more of an effort. Mercy was still a kid—for a couple of months at least.

"Hi," she greeted, sounding far less peppy than usual.

"Hi. Everything okay?" I asked cautiously.

"I'm tired," she laughed, though it didn't have that carefree, airy quality that Mercy's laugh normally had. "I had that regeneration project at the community center today, remember?"

"Of course," I replied, annoyed with myself for forgetting. "How did it go?"

I remembered doing hundreds of such community projects when I was a teenager. They were often weak excuses to bring in young agathos women from other cities who may have been feeling the call to that area. I'd never felt the call to travel to one, and so far neither had Mercy.

Anesidora, please don't let Mercy be alone for as long as I was.

I couldn't quite bring myself to pray that she meet four nice agathos soul bonds, though. Because I loved Mercy, and I wanted her to have the kind of meaningful connection I had with Riot, even though it was a lot more complicated than what a *normal* soul bond would be.

I felt like he and I were happier than my parents had ever been, but maybe that was just the stress of time and raising children, rather than the fact that they were all agathos.

"We had to work extra hard to finish it today because the memorial is tomorrow. It would usually be a two-day project," Mercy replied eventually and I frowned at the dashboard. That wasn't really an answer to my question.

"Was everyone nice to you?" I pressed. Sometimes her peers looked down on Mercy because she'd basically been shipped to her family in Auburn to raise her prospects like a Regency-era young woman.

"I'm stressed because my emergence is in a couple of weeks," Mercy deflected again, though it was a reasonable excuse.

"Of course," I murmured sympathetically. All agathos were required to take a test with the Elders when they turned 18, before being led down to the basement altar in the temple for the emergence rites that awakened their gift.

Hopefully hers wouldn't end in Eutychia like mine had. It had been a very quiet drive home.

"I remember how stressful that day was," I volunteered.

"I'm sure you passed with flying colors," Mercy muttered, an unexpected hint of bitterness in her tone. The car in front of me finally gave up on the parking spot, and I began moving slowly down the street towards home again.

"Not at all," I assured her, frowning to myself. Maybe she was angry that I was being sent away? She hadn't brought it up, and I wasn't particularly willing to talk about it. "I aced Knowledge and Wisdom, passed Self-Restraint and Justice, but barely scraped through Moral Virtue and Piety. Mother didn't tell you that?"

"No," Mercy replied after a long pause. It wasn't like Mother would brag about my dismal results, but I thought she would have used it as motivational material for Mercy.

Get low results on your Moral Virtue test, be alone forever, or something along those inspiring lines.

"That should make me feel better..." Mercy said nervously.

"But it doesn't," I finished with a grim smile she couldn't see.

"I admire everything you've accomplished in your life," she said hurriedly. "Getting your degree, moving out, buying your own place..."

"But you don't want to end up like me. That's understandable, Mercy. You don't need to explain."

The words hung in the air in the ensuing silence, and I tried not to let the hurt and failure burrow in like it usually did. I had my bond with Riot. I wasn't alone. Maybe no one else would ever understand what we had, maybe they would never be able to know about it, but it meant everything to me. I could *feel* his emotions when he was around me—his desire, his concern for me, his awe and admiration for me— and I felt all those things and more for him.

That tether to him, knowing what I *meant* to him meant the sting of not meeting everyone else's expectations hadn't been as sharp as usual lately.

Mercy wasn't *everyone* though. She was the one person in my family who I felt like I hadn't disappointed yet.

"I'll leave you to study," I said softly, blinking back the uncomfortable rush of tears threatening to fall. "See you tomorrow, Mercy."

I pressed the disconnect button before she could reply, and for once I didn't care if I was being rude. It wasn't like I ever expected to be anyone's role model, but it was still disheartening to realize I was the exact opposite. A cautionary tale, even.

Of course she didn't want to end up like me. She'd sat there at dinner and watched my parents explain that my future was in exile. *No one would want to end up like me.*

Usually Mercy and I had a great relationship, and a pain shot through my chest at the idea those days were behind us. *She was in a bad mood,* I reminded myself. *She's been painting all day and she's worried about her emergence. Don't take it personally.*

I'd see her tomorrow at Joy's memorial anyway. We could talk about it then and try to get back on steadier ground.

Riot wasn't back yet when I let myself into the apartment, making multiple trips to transport bags of groceries up from my car, finally able to restock the pantry properly after a chaotic week.

For a while, I pretended that I wasn't going to have to defy the will of my parents and the Elders and every other agathos I knew. I pulled out the unfamiliar ingredients I'd purchased so I could try some vegetarian dishes—I still wasn't a hundred percent sure what I was supposed to do with tempeh, but I'd give it a shot—and pretended that Riot and I were just a normal couple, newly living together and merging our lives.

We hadn't talked about the future at all, but we'd both admitted we thought we were soul bonds, so I was sort of hoping that meant he wasn't planning on going anywhere. I liked him living here.

I paused in the middle of refilling the soap dispenser, frowning to myself. *What if he wanted to leave?*

It wasn't something I'd ever contemplated. In my mind, when I'd eventually meet my soul bonds, we wouldn't need to have conversations like that because they'd already know what to expect. Still, even now my body was growing exhausted and achy from the distance between Riot and I. I doubted either of us would *survive* living apart.

Just consummate the bond, a dark voice in the back of my mind whispered almost gleefully. The thought was almost immediately followed by a crippling level of guilt. It was easy in the moment to let go and just *feel* with Riot, but if I actually *thought* about it...

My entire life, I'd had the importance of purity and chaste thoughts pushed on me, and I'd always struggled with the latter more than other agathos seemed to. I'd *tried* to do things that I knew were forbidden, and punished myself by using my gift as much as possible to help others, hoping it would balance the scales for my bad actions.

Would I always feel guilty when it came to intimacy? Would I always feel like I was impure now? I couldn't imagine sex would improve *those* feelings.

Mood thoroughly ruined by my own thoughts, I let myself outside to give my roses some much needed attention. Gardening wasn't a usual agathos hobby beyond having an impeccably manicured lawn, and even that was usually outsourced to humans. I'd managed to get away with a few houseplants in my parents' house, but I couldn't properly indulge my fascination with botany until six months ago when I moved here.

I rearranged the pots, cutting back the longer stems to protect them from the wind and adding a layer of mulch around the base of each plant to protect them from cold snaps. I was relying on the internet for instructions, but I hadn't killed anything yet.

By the time I was done and showered to get the smell of mulch off me, I was missing Riot too much to get up and cook. Instead, I poured myself a glass of sparkling grape juice and went back out on the deck with a blanket to sit and admire my hard work while I ordered vegetarian Chinese food on my phone.

It wasn't until I was sitting down with all my jobs out of the way that the conversation with my parents snuck back into my mind again. I had been doing my best to avoid thinking about it because I wasn't going to go on the ridiculous outreach trip anyway, no matter what they'd decided, but I hadn't actually given any thought as to *how*.

Serenity, one of my agathos friends growing up, had a brother who was sent on an outreach trip, but she never talked about him. It was announced at a temple gathering that he was going, and all of a sudden, he was *gone*.

Had he protested? Did anyone ask him what he wanted?

Would they physically restrain me if I refused to go?

No, I couldn't believe they'd do that. Agathos weren't violent by nature, and maintaining civility was of the utmost importance. That was why I hadn't considered it when Riot suggested running away. It would be difficult, and I'd have to argue my case, but I didn't think I was in actual danger from the Elders.

I was still outside ruminating on that and my conversation with Mercy when Riot got back, his concern scratching insistently at my skin. I'd take it though. It was preferable to the pain of missing him.

He moved up silently behind my chair, pausing for a moment before his hands cupped either side of my neck, smoothing down towards my shoulders. He stopped right at the juncture of my neck and shoulders, his long fingers spread over the bare skin of my collarbone, just barely nudging my shirt aside.

"Pretty roses," Riot remarked quietly. "Unusual hobby for an agathos, gardening."

I hummed in agreement, staring unseeing beyond the pots into the neighbor's barren backyard. "It never used to be. Nature is Anesidora's creation, after all. Most agathos seem to have forgotten that."

"You're definitely not most agathos."

I'd heard similar statements my whole life, but they were usually a lot less reverent in tone. Riot was incredibly good and incredibly bad for my ego.

"It's cold," he murmured, thumbs brushing softly up and down my neck. "Come inside."

I didn't think the goosebumps that erupted over my skin had anything to do with the temperature, but I managed to nod my head silently in agreement.

"Are you okay?" Riot asked, guiding me to the couch and plucking the empty glass out of my fingers.

Why couldn't I lie? What benefit was there to not being able to tell a little white lie to stop other people from worrying? He'd be able to sense the truth anyway, but it would be nice to at least pretend I was putting his mind at ease.

"I will be," I replied with a tight smile.

"Talk to me." It was a casual command, but Riot seemed to have a gift for demanding just enough control that I could just relax and stop overthinking for a moment.

Usually, I wouldn't have elaborated, but when it came to him, I wanted to. I wanted to tell him all the thoughts I'd always been forced to keep to myself.

"I was thinking about the outreach thing," I admitted. "But also my cousin, Mercy, has her emergence coming up."

Riot dropped onto the couch next to me, close enough that our sides pressed together, and I leaned in against him, soaking up his warmth.

"What's an emergence?" he asked, pushing his dark hair out of his face.

I probably should feel bad even saying that much. The rites are sacred, and revealing them to a daimon would be seen as the height of treason. At the same time, the more I question things in my head, the more I want an outsider's perspective to make sure I'm not being crazy. The more I want *Riot's* perspective, specifically.

"It starts with an oral exam," I explained, shuddering a little at the memory. I'd been so nervous, I was convinced I was going to vomit on the Elders who were administering the test. "They ask questions based on all the agathos' virtues."

"What kind of questions?" Riot asked, already looking vaguely appalled at the whole concept.

"Mostly they come up with scenarios where an agathos would need to assist a human and we explain what we would do or what kind of abilities would be best suited for particular situations. I didn't do so well on some of the sections," I laughed hollowly.

"What happens if you fail? It's not like you can *not* be an agathos anymore," Riot scoffed.

"Well, no," I conceded. "It does impact your standing in the community though, and the kinds of positions you're eligible for. I'm sure it's one of the reasons my boss has never liked me. Even if I lived until 120, I would never be eligible to be an Elder because I tested poorly."

Riot muttered something that sounded suspiciously like *"what the fudge"* under his breath. Except he probably didn't say *fudge*.

"After the exam, they take the initiates into the altar in the basement for the rites, and Anesidora unveils our gift."

"That sounds..." He struggled for words and I almost laughed at how polite he was trying to be when I could feel his horror brushing against my skin.

"Don't hold back now," I teased, poking him in the ribs.

"Archaic," Riot said eventually, pulling my hand onto his thigh and linking our fingers. "Archaic, and culty, and creepy as fuck."

"Well it is an ancient tradition, so archaic isn't the worst descriptor," I agreed, staring at our joined hands. My opal ring seemed to glint angrily at me in the low light, and for the first time since I'd been given it over a decade ago, I contemplated not wearing it.

Unfortunately, any agathos would spot its absence instantly, so that probably wasn't an option.

"What does all this have to do with your cousin?" Riot asked.

I made an exasperated noise in the back of my throat, annoyed with myself for being annoyed with Mercy.

"Mercy's emergence is coming up. She sort of said my poor results aren't any comfort to her because she doesn't want to be like me anyway," I sighed, tipping my head back against the couch and closing my eyes. "Well, she inferred it and I confirmed it. Which is a totally reasonable response to have, so I don't know why I'm being all sullen about it."

"Because it's total bullshit, that's why," Riot growled, startling my eyes open with the vehemence in his tone. "You are magnificent, and those test scores don't say shit about who you are as a person. She'd be lucky to be like you."

"You're biased," I replied, leaning up to kiss his cheek. He *was* biased, and I'd probably just made him hate my cousin which hadn't at all been my intention, but his words had made me feel better.

Maybe I hadn't tested well as an agathos, but I still tried to be a good one. There were many times I'd felt like I was a better agathos than Constance was—more generous with my gift, less elitist about who I helped—but none of that mattered in the eyes of my community.

Maybe their opinion wasn't worth coveting.

Riot startled when the doorbell rang, and I patted his thigh as I stood. "I ordered in, hope that's okay."

He hovered discreetly in the background while I answered the door, and we worked together to get bowls and utensils and lay out the food on the small dining table. I was definitely pretending again that we were just a regular couple and this was our normal life, but I couldn't help myself. It was a nice vacation from the inside of my head.

"So," Riot began, loading up his bowl. "There was something I wanted to ask you about."

Sugar, I really needed to tell him about my prayer to La Nuit. I doubted he was going to ask me about that, but that information felt like a guillotine blade hanging precipitously over my neck.

"Sure," I replied weakly, picking at my vegetable chow mein.

"When you fell asleep on the couch the other night, and I carried you to bed, you told me you never remembered what you dreamed about."

I blinked at him, startled by the random topic.

"That's right," I replied slowly. "I don't think I remember a single dream I've had in my life."

Riot hummed thoughtfully as he chewed his food, looking contemplative.

"I know that's unusual," I continued, a little unnerved by his silence. "I don't have bad dreams either, I don't think. My parents brought it up a lot when my brothers were born, in a joking way. They said they'd never learned how to deal with kids having nightmares because I never had any." I smiled a little at the memory of Creed telling me that.

"Why do you ask?" I said eventually, curiosity getting the better of me. Riot had been quiet for a while, seemingly lost in his thoughts.

"You remember I mentioned a daimon named Bullet?" he asked, watching my face carefully.

"I'm unlikely to forget that name," I replied, raising an eyebrow at him.

Riot's lips quirked. "True. So, the Oneiroi line are probably the most powerful daimons, but they're sort of cursed. He is gifted visions of the future from the Goddess of Night—about himself and other daimons—plus he can use tarot cards to gain insight from the divine. They're sort of the closest thing we have to priests."

"That is powerful," I replied, slightly awed. I couldn't imagine having such a strong connection with Anesidora.

"He has one other ability," Riot continued, frowning a little. "One I'd forgotten about until recently."

"What's that?"

"Dreamwalking," he replied with a grim smile. "He can visit a person's mind when they are sleeping and create a dream of his choosing. It'd be a more powerful gift, if the person could remember the details when they woke up."

Riot was watching me closely and I fought to suppress the shiver of apprehension that ran down my spine.

"But he wouldn't be able to visit an agathos, right? Our gifts don't work on each other."

"My Moros ability doesn't flare to life around other daimons," Riot pointed out. "But Bullet's gifts work *best* on other daimons. The Oneiroi's abilities are sort of the inverse of how most daimons work. Theoretically, he wouldn't be able to visit an agathos, but...well, you're not a regular agathos, Gracie."

Well, that was true, but surely I would know if someone had been popping into my dreams each night? The idea that I *wouldn't* know, that I just couldn't access those memories, was a little terrifying.

"I've always liked falling asleep," I said quietly, pushing my food around my plate. "Whenever things were hard or I felt alone, sleep gave me comfort. I always woke up feeling...settled. Sometimes a little sad too, but mostly settled."

I glanced up to find that Riot's expression had softened. "I think that's probably as good as confirmation, Gracie. Viper didn't remember the nightmare, but he woke up terrified. And covered in piss," he added as an afterthought, not looking terribly bothered by that idea. I guessed he wasn't the biggest fan of *Viper*.

"Why would Bullet visit my dreams?" I asked, perplexed.

Riot gave me an incredulous look. "You've got more experience with this whole polyamory thing than I do."

"Oh."

Oh.

He thought Bullet was...mine. My second soul bond. Could that be? I hadn't given much thought to the idea of having *more* soul bonds because I still hadn't felt *the call*. Then again, I hadn't felt the call to seek Riot out either.

"What are you thinking?" Riot asked, tipping the rest of the chow mein onto his plate. I made a mental note that he liked that dish. "I can feel your confusion."

"I'm thinking I haven't felt the call to anyone else, but I never felt called to you either."

There was a little rush of insecurity from Riot before he pushed it down, and I chastised myself for not wording it a little more considerately.

"That kind of makes sense. A call implies we're signalling you or whatever, right? Like we're lighthouses and you're the boat. But we don't have that built-in signalling function because we're not agathos."

He shrugged and continued eating his dinner while I stared at him in stunned silence, feeling like an idiot for not considering that before. *Of course* the call would come from them. Why had I always thought it would come from me?

I really was a terrible agathos if I was getting schooled on the inner workings of soul bonds by a daimon.

"If he was," I began slowly, not entirely sure how to approach this conversation. I'd always assumed my soul bonds would be aware of what they were and accustomed to the idea of...sharing. "How would you feel about that?"

Riot chewed slowly and I set my chopsticks down, suddenly too nervous to contemplate eating. What if he was totally against the idea?

"I'm not going to lie, I've grown accustomed to having you all to myself," Riot replied thoughtfully while my heart sank like a stone into my stomach. "Though it would be nice to have someone else who was unequivocally on our side."

"You already know Bullet, wouldn't that make it easier?"

Riot's lips twitched. "He's fucking infuriating most of the time, but you'd probably like him. You could do *High School Musical* duets together."

My face heated up instantly, even though that sounded kind of fun.

"Well, I guess we won't know until I meet him," I replied eventually. "I'm not entirely sure how I feel about him visiting me when I sleep... That seems a little creepy."

"I don't know how he does it," Riot said absently. "If I saw you every single day and each time you forgot who I was, I'd lose my fucking mind."

Sugar. Who was the real agathos and the real daimon here? Riot was far more empathetic than I was.

"Do you want to go meet him?" Riot asked, glancing up at me. "He lives in Devil's Den," he added with an understandable grimace. Milton was surrounded by agathos communities on three sides and the Long Island Sound on the fourth. Getting to Devil's Den was probably a stressful experience for a daimon.

Yes? No? Accepting Riot and I were soul bonds was one thing. In my mind, it was an anomaly, but a good anomaly. One that I was grateful for, because it was him.

Two daimon soul bonds meant it was a *thing*, and I wasn't sure I was ready for it to be a thing yet. But that was more than a little selfish of me if Bullet already knew about us, about what I was to him.

"Gracie," Riot said in a way that made me think it wasn't the first time he'd called my name. He reached across the table and tangled our fingers together. "Your emotions are giving me whiplash."

"I feel...I feel like going to see him, that would change everything." Riot gave me an understanding look even as I struggled to articulate what I meant.

I hadn't sought Riot out, it had just happened. I'd continued on with my life basically as normal, knowing that nothing was *actually* normal, but not needing to make any urgent decisions about that either.

242

Deliberately seeking out a daimon that I believed could be my soul bond felt like I was walking away from my life as I knew it and entering the unknown. It felt irreversible, and that was terrifying.

"You don't have to decide anything right now, Grace. You should probably just focus on getting through the memorial tomorrow without raging at your parents and the Elders in front of everyone," Riot said, quirking a smile as he gave my hands a squeeze.

"But if Bullet is waiting—"

"You'll probably see him in your dreams tonight anyway. You might not remember what you talk about, but he will. Besides, he's psychic. He knows when you'll meet him better than you do."

I nodded silently. Hopefully when I woke up in the morning, I'd feel a sense of reassurance that whatever happened in my dreams, I'd made the right decision.

GRACE

CHAPTER 15

"Riot's been talking," a musical voice sang cheerfully from somewhere behind me. *"You've never invited me into your dream scene before."*

Oh. Well, that explained why we were in my apartment. I was sitting on my navy blue couch, the voice coming from the doorway to my bedroom behind me.

I glanced down, surprised by my outfit. I never wore jeans—Mother hated them—let alone tight jeans like this with rips that exposed my thighs. And my top! I tugged it down self-consciously, shocked to see it even on my body. It was a sweater that was the shade of bubblegum, which Mother would hate, and cropped—cropped!—exposing the high waist of the jeans.

If I invited him here, had I picked this outfit as well?

Focus, Grace. You invited him to your dream. That is the more pressing concern here.

"If it's my dream, why can't I see you?" I asked, craning my neck.

"Because I am all powerful," the voice said in a low, dramatic tone, suddenly right next to my ear, and I jumped in surprise. "Would you like to see me, Amazing Grace?"

"Yes," I said instantly, hesitating for a moment before I continued. "Please, Bullet."

He appeared out of thin air, sitting next to me on the couch, not looking surprised in the least that I knew his name.

Oh my.

I'd thought Riot was exactly my type, but I guess I had more than one type because Bullet was definitely stirring up those same fluttery feelings in my tummy, even though he and Riot looked nothing alike.

Well, except for the tattoos. And the eyes, but Bullet's were far more purple than Riot's were, with just the thinnest line of red at the edges of his irises.

His hair was a pale blonde and probably chin length, but he wore it messily pushed back in a way that made him look like a rockstar, even though he was dressed like he'd just walked off a fashion shoot. His dark navy shirt had the sleeves rolled up to his elbows, showcasing detailed black ink all over his forearms, and he was wearing dark gray slacks and suspenders of all things.

He made the whole ensemble all seem so effortlessly cool, but he sort of looked like a model which helped—all angular features and lean muscles.

I'd intended to ask him if he was my soul bond, but there was no denying that fact once I'd laid eyes on him. My heartbeat had picked up, my mouth was dry, butterflies were aggressively attacking each other in my belly...It was a ghost of the reaction I'd had to Riot, but this wasn't actually real life.

Bullet's mouth, which seemed permanently curved into an amused smirk, twitched as he noted my thorough perusal of him and I glanced away, embarrassed that I'd been so blatantly checking him out.

I might not be able to remember this, but he would.

"Don't be shy, Grace. You can look at me all you like," he said confidently, reaching over to gently grip my chin with long, elegant fingers and guided my eyes back to his face. I sucked in a breath at the contact, surprised to see he looked just as affected by it as I was.

"Have I seen you before?" I asked, missing his touch instantly when his hand dropped away. I sort of wanted to snuggle him, but it seemed disloyal to Riot when he wasn't here.

"Oh yes," Bullet replied, still smiling though his eyes looked a little sad. "Almost every night of your life, actually."

"I'm sorry," I whispered, horrified at what that must feel like for him. I couldn't imagine how much it would hurt if Riot forgot me even once, let alone every night for years.

"Don't be," Bullet replied sharply before his mask of happiness slid back into place. "We've had thousands of first meetings, and I don't regret a single one of them."

"Don't you want me to remember you?" I asked, my throat thick with emotion.

"More than anything," he said simply. "It will happen. Sooner than you think."

I hesitated, wanting to tell him I wasn't sure I was ready for all that meant, but it kind of sounded like he already knew that.

"All powerful, remember?" Bullet teased, answering my unasked question as he tapped the side of his head, and I snorted before I could contain the unladylike sound. "Ask me anything," he commanded, sitting back with a smug grin.

"Okay then, all powerful one. I was thinking of visiting the library above the temple in Auburn before the memorial to find out more about the history of outreach trips and look for a loophole. Do you think that's a good idea?"

Bullet smiled brightly and I got the impression he was excited that I'd asked for his advice. What was I usually like in these dreams? Probably less relaxed, if I thought he was a complete stranger every time.

A stab of pain shot through my chest at the thought and I tried to imagine how I would feel in his shoes. It was an acute kind of agony to think of someone meaning so much to me, and me being nothing to them.

"You should go tomorrow," Bullet replied confidently. "You'll discover more questions than answers, but that's not a bad thing. You need to know the questions to ask to find the answers you need."

"You're very wise." I blinked at him, startled by the thoughtful words coming from such a seemingly playful, mischievous person.

"I make it my job to be wise when it comes to you, Amazing Grace." Bullet glanced at the walls as they seemed to ripple suddenly like waves. "It looks like our time is up," he sighed, shooting me an apologetic smile.

"What? Why?" I wasn't ready to go yet.

"Your alarm is going off, of course." He stood, grinning at me before sweeping into a dramatic bow. "It was a pleasure meeting you, my lady."

"Again," I supplied, my voice already sounding strange and distant. Bullet vanished from in front of me, his final two words bouncing around the room like a distant echo.

"Every time."

I woke up with wet cheeks and an ache in my chest, quickly silencing my alarm before it woke Riot. I desperately searched my mind, trying to force the details of the dream to appear, but as usual there was nothing but a *feeling* where I felt like the details should be. A sense of resolve, but a layer of sorrow as well.

Was it my sorrow or his?

I pushed the blankets back slowly, but Riot's arm snaked around my waist, tugging me backwards before I could sneak out of bed.

"Come back to bed," he mumbled into the pillow. "You're warm, and I want to make you come before you leave."

Sugar.

"That is a very hard offer to turn down," I squeaked, forcing down the guilt that came with the idea. I turned slightly to face him, running my hand through his messy hair and memorizing his features. I didn't want to leave any earlier than I had to and spend the day away from him again, but I couldn't help feeling like that sense of *resolve* I'd woken up with was related to my research plans for the day.

"Don't turn it down then," he yawned, cracking one eye open to look up at me. It seemed crazy to think of this muscle bound tattooed man as *cute*, but that was definitely how he looked first thing in the morning. Cute and cuddly and all mine.

"I'm going to the library," I said gently, lifting his arm up so I could wriggle away. "I have a *feeling* about it."

"Bullet's already cockblocking me and he's not even here," Riot muttered, and this time I couldn't help my giggle. "You sure about today, Gracie?" he asked, sitting up and leaning back against the pillows. I really should ask if he'd be comfortable sleeping without a shirt on, it seemed a crime to cover up that body.

"I can't not go," I said, crossing the room to my closet. My one black dress was already in a garment bag, ready to go for when I got ready at my parents' house, and I picked out a more casual, agathos-appropriate gray sweater and white skirt combination to wear to the library. "The whole community will turn out for the memorial, and it would raise a lot of questions if I wasn't there. Plus, the Elders might move the outreach thing forward if they think I'm not cooperating."

I paused with my hand on the coat hanger, tilting my head to the side. "Actually, my parents would probably try to have it moved up."

Riot made a disgruntled noise behind me, and I laid my garments over my forearm before moving around to his side of the bed to kiss his cheek. "I'll be back this afternoon. Early evening at the latest."

He grabbed my waist before I could pull away and I squealed as he tugged me onto the bed, capturing my mouth with his and giving me a *proper* kiss that had me incredibly conscious of my morning breath.

"Be careful, Gracie. Come back to me, okay?" he asked, pressing his forehead against mine, his concern brushing insistently at my skin.

"Always," I promised.

The temple in Auburn didn't look like a temple to outsiders. Specifically to humans. It was labelled as the town hall, and it was a three-storey red brick and white plaster behemoth that stood pride of place in central Auburn. A row of ionic columns along the front was the only external nod to the ancient rites that took place in the basement of the building. There were no humans that worked for the city of Auburn—it was and always had been an agathos settlement—but the altar was thoroughly hidden just in case, accessible only with agathos blood.

I visited this place constantly growing up. Aside from Chance, one of my fathers working here as a town planner, this was where the weekly classes took place for teen agathos every Saturday morning for three hours.

My boots echoed on the black and white tiled floor of the foyer, giving me flashbacks of the cramped first floor classroom on a hot Saturday morning, memorizing the tenets of our role for the Anesidora while staring longingly out the window where the younger kids were allowed to play on the grass.

There was no way I could get in undetected, but I had a vague enough excuse at the ready to cover myself. I was pretty sure that if I, renowned spinster, told anyone I was looking into the history of soul bonds, no one would push back. I'd most likely receive a pitying look and a healthy dose of awkward silence.

It wasn't a lie. I did plan to look at the history of soul bonds as well as seeing what I could find on outreach trips. Just because no agathos woman in *living memory* didn't have any agathos soul bonds surely didn't mean I was the first one *ever*.

I let myself through the oak double doors into the almost stiflingly dark small library that dominated half of the second floor. The walls, the shelves, the furniture and the floor were all the same glossy dark stained wood, and the entire space was illuminated by dim stained glass lamps that made the whole place feel both old and intimidating.

The librarian glanced at me over a pile of books on the counter, but didn't attempt any small talk, and I happily slipped past with a stiff smile, making my way towards the back of the room.

There were only a few agathos history books accessible to us, and they were kept in a private room that I absolutely despised going into. I wasn't claustrophobic generally, but it was a tiny windowless space dominated by a high table and stools in the center, and I always felt like I was in some kind of book prison when I had to go in there.

I paused outside the discreet entrance and quickly opened my pocketknife inside my purse, nicking the pad of my thumb on the blade and pinching until a small amount of blood welled. I swiped it over the piece of ancient marble embedded in the wall, then leaned against the heavy wooden door until it creaked open.

There wasn't exactly a huge range to choose from since the Elders were superstitious about how much of that should be written down— just one oak bookshelf at the back of the small room—so I grabbed a small selection and brought them back to the table to look through. I wasn't exactly sure what I was looking for, but I'd felt strongly that coming here was a good idea, so presumably I'd talked to Bullet about it in my sleep, which was a strange concept.

An hour later, I'd learned nothing I didn't already know. A woman had four soul bonds. The woman would feel drawn to them individually in Anesidora's own timing. If the draw to them stopped before all four were found, it was assumed that one of their intended bonds had died in childhood, and that had historically been a traumatic realization for the woman and there would always be a gap where that bond should have been.

Likewise, if one died after the bonds had come together, the pain of loss was said to be permanent. My heart hurt for Joy Lyon's bonded and what they were going through today.

There was nothing on the process of bonding, unsurprisingly, and just a brief mention that the cost of using Anesidora's gifts was shared among bonded.

There was very little in the texts about agathos men and their expectations and experiences, I noted with unease. There were far more male agathos than females, and the lack of attention they received in the texts was stark. It felt...intentional. Like they were expendable. Agathos women were created in Anesidora's image, at least that's what we were taught, and the men in the image of her lovers. The first she took was her public consort—Valor, in my mother's case—and the other three were her permanent lovers.

They were all gods. Did they care that Anesidora took all the spotlight? Perhaps not. My fathers had always seemed mostly content to orbit around my mother. Maybe that's the way it was meant to be.

Three of Anesidora's lovers were also her and her consort's children, but I tried not to reflect too hard on that. The gods' family tree was more bush-shaped, and I had to believe that gods didn't reproduce the same way mortals did for my own peace of mind.

There was a curious lack of information on outreach trips in any of the books. Nothing about where they went, or how the locations were chosen, or if the men ever came back.

A disturbing amount of *nothing*.

I was already determined not to go, but I couldn't help wondering what would happen if the Elders and my parents got their way. My parents' assurances that I'd get to travel and see the world—that an outreach trip was an *opportunity*—felt hollow. They couldn't lie, so they obviously believed what they'd told me, but I wasn't convinced that belief was built on solid evidence.

I stacked the books I'd been going through up on the table and massaged my temples. I'd hoped to find something that made me feel less like an aberration, but I wasn't entirely surprised that I hadn't. I doubted that someone—some*thing*—like me would even be written about.

I couldn't help but think that if another abomination like me had ever existed, the Elders would have done everything to cover her up. We were strictly forbidden from violence against each other or humans, *unless* it was in their best interests. It was a loophole I'd always found a little strange, but now I wondered if it was in place for people like me.

Maybe no other agathos in the history of our kind had been stupid or reckless enough to ask the dark goddess for help, and I truly was unique.

The regret still never came, though. I didn't regret Riot, whatever the consequences were. He was an endless calm in a sea of chaos, yet not emotionless the way so many agathos men were.

Riot didn't look at me and see all the things that I *wasn't*, because he was only interested in the things that I *was*.

The sudden creaking of the heavy door almost made me scream, and I clapped my hand over my mouth just in time to prevent a furious librarian from appearing. I spun in my stool to find Chance looking across the table at me with one eyebrow raised.

"You scared me," I breathed, dropping my hand to my chest to where my heart pounded rapidly against my ribs.

"Pay attention to your surroundings next time?" he suggested quietly, sounding like he was on the verge of laughing. It was rare I got to see any of my parents alone, and I'd forgotten how nice and calming Chance's presence was when it was just him.

"What are you doing here?" I asked as my heart rate settled.

"Well, I *do* work here," Chance replied, grinning. "Ever, the librarian, let me know you were here."

I didn't know Ever, but I supposed it wasn't too surprising he'd recognized me. Everyone around Auburn knew *of* me. It was why I'd left.

"I thought you'd have the day off because of the memorial," I said, leaning forward on my elbows to try to discreetly hide my reading material.

"I took a half day..." Chance's brow furrowed as he tilted his head to examine the spines of the books I had stacked up in front of me. It was incredibly frustrating the way agathos parents didn't believe in privacy. "Come on, let's get coffee. We have a little time before we need to go back to the house and get ready."

I couldn't think of a legitimate reason not to, so I nodded and hastily put the books away, holding them in front of my body to obscure the titles in the hopes Chance hadn't got a decent look at them. His appearance had taken me so off-guard, I'd momentarily forgotten that I was angry at all of my parents about the whole outreach thing.

I was marginally less mad at Chance than the others, but only marginally.

I followed him out of the library and through the lobby, smiling awkwardly at the few of his colleagues who were in today when he stopped to make small talk with them. Somehow, being here, I felt as small as I did when I used to visit him at work as a 10-year-old.

We settled in at a small agathos-owned cafe opposite the town hall and Chance ordered our drinks while I snagged the comfy white armchairs at the back, in front of an old fireplace that was always filled with oversized pine cones and votive candles in glass jars. We'd had a lot of coffee dates here when I was a kid and I'd always found it a strange place—all whitewashed wood and aqua colors with shells everywhere, even though the beach was miles away.

"So," Chance began, tugging up the legs of his slacks as he folded his lanky frame into the armchair opposite me. "How are you?"

Of all the questions he could have asked me, that one was actually difficult to answer honestly.

"Getting by," I settled on, shooting the server a grateful smile as he dropped off our drinks. He gave me a pitying look in return, which shouldn't have surprised me as much as it did.

I wondered if anyone had heard about the outreach trip already. Surely Verity Mae would have messaged me if word had spread?

Chance hummed quietly, taking a sip of his coffee. "We worry about you, you know. Always have, but more than usual these past six months. Milton isn't a nice place for a young lady, and you're there on your own."

"Is that why you all want to send me away? Was it the Elders' idea or did the suggestion come from Mother? Or Valor, perhaps?"

That was definitely *not* sweet, and if it had been any of my parents other than Chance here, I'd be in for a long and detailed lecture about all the ways I needed to work on my sweetness and contentment.

Since it was Chance, all I got was a disappointed look, which was a pretty effective chastisement coming from him. I wrapped my hands around my mug until the heat seeping into my fingers bordered on uncomfortable, and forced myself to swallow down the emotions I wasn't meant to be feeling.

"I understand that the announcement at dinner took you by surprise," Chance said patiently. "It took me by surprise too, when I found out. Your mother was not in favor of the idea at all, actually."

I cast him a disbelieving look and he chuckled. While my mother had concerns about me moving to Milton specifically, I had noticed her thinly veiled relief that I was leaving Auburn. My failure to launch was humiliating for her, and she'd always cared deeply about appearances.

"She has concerns you will fall prey to immoral vices being so far from home," Chance chuckled, like the idea was absurd.

Perhaps my mother knew me better than I thought.

"I live alone and unsupervised now," I pointed out. *And had definitely fallen prey to immoral vices.*

Chance gave me a confused look. "You wouldn't be alone on an outreach trip. You would be going with other singles. Men."

Was that what she was concerned about? Since I couldn't feel desire for anyone who wasn't my soul bond, I didn't really see what "immoral vices" Mother was stressed about, it's not like I'd ever expressed an interest in drugs and I only ever had a glass of wine socially. Not that it mattered, I wasn't going anyway.

"Do you want to tell me why you were looking at those books?" Chance asked gently. "Is this about the outreach trip?"

Unlike my other dads or my mother, Chance would let me get away with not answering. He'd definitely take any concerns back to the family though—he wouldn't be able to hide it from my mother even if he wanted to, that wasn't how soul bonds worked. Better to reassure him if I could.

"Not just about that. I was curious if there'd ever been a scenario like mine before." *Not a lie.* "I wanted to know if I was the only one."

Chance gave me a sorrowful look, shifting uncomfortably in his chair. "A year ago, we put that question to the Elders."

Of course you did. And yet, this was the first I was hearing of it.

Maybe the Elders had been the ones to propose I go into outreach, but I'm sure my parents' visit to them had planted the seeds of that idea.

That disagreeable, monstrous darkness that I wasn't meant to have rose up in me again, while I chanted '*be sweet*' silently on a loop, grinding my teeth.

"Did you consider mentioning that to me?" I managed to get out, not as softly as I'd intended to.

Chance scrutinized me carefully, like he was seeing something he hadn't noticed before, and I forced myself to breathe normally and relaxed my grip on my cup.

"It wasn't good news, sweet girl. We didn't want to upset you," Chance admitted apologetically. "There are other books at the temple, ones that are only available to the Elders and the Basilinna, that we were hoping to consult. To see if there had been a case like yours before."

I took a long sip of my coffee to delay answering. The more upset I got, the more I ached for Riot. He'd quickly become an anchor for me when my feelings got so big it felt like they'd sweep me away.

"I understand you have concerns, and this is a very big move for anyone," Chance said patiently. "But you could choose to look at it as an opportunity to travel the world, see places most agathos never get to see—"

"Perhaps I could look at it that way if it had been my choice to go," I interrupted. The words almost stuck in my throat, just *barely* scraping the barrel of truth. *Perhaps* and *could* were doing a lot of heavy lifting in that sentence.

"To be agathos is to relinquish choice," Chance replied sadly, startling me with his candor. It wasn't like Riot hadn't told me something very similar, but he was a daimon and programmed to think our way of doing things was wrong. Chance was born and raised in Auburn and worked in the belly of the beast. Mother probably fainted with joy when the call led her to him.

"You were the last soul bond that Mother found, right?" I asked casually, taking another sip of my coffee.

"I was," he said carefully, eyeing me like he wasn't sure where I was going with this. I wasn't really sure myself, but his comment had inspired a burning need to know if soul bonds were sunshine and rainbows all of the time.

If they were really the gift I'd always been led to believe it was.

"Did that ever bother you? Being last?"

Chance's eyebrows lifted in surprise, but he gave the question genuine thought.

This was why he was my favorite father.

"At the time? Not so much. I was 22, and felt like I'd been waiting forever," he replied with a wistful smile. "Of course, there is jealousy sometimes. Conflict, occasionally. Five individuals with their own wants and needs, it can be a lot to coordinate."

I'd always presumed Chance had given up the least—he was from Auburn, everyone moved to him when Mother had felt called here. I knew she'd struggled with his career, though. Many agathos used local government jobs as a springboard to move up, their sights set on Washington. Mother would have *loved* that, but Chance never seemed bothered by the idea.

"And Valor is your mother's consort, the public face of all of our unions. That is not a complaint, just a statement of fact," Chance continued.

I nodded silently, staring unseeing at the unlit candles in the fireplace. I wasn't even sure if I had a second soul bond, though it certainly *seemed* that way, but I definitely didn't like the consort idea. No matter what Riot had said about Bullet, I didn't think he'd like it either. Not when he'd talked so much about fairness.

"Are you looking for reasons not to want soul bonds?" Chance asked sympathetically.

"I already know you'll tell me they're a gift from Anesidora and you wouldn't give them up for anything," I replied wryly, struggling to keep the forbidden snark out of my voice.

"You're right, they are a gift," Chance said mildly. "But as you well know, for each gift, Anesidora requires a sacrifice. You can give good luck, but you receive bad luck in return. I can encourage self-restraint, but struggle with my own in return. We can take someone's pain, but then we suffer."

He gave me a pointed look and I wondered again if I was a bit slow for not realizing that sooner. Of course the gift of soul bonds came with strings attached. Nothing else was free, why would this be?

Not that anyone had ever thought to mention it before.

Chance's phone flashed on the small table between us, and we both looked down to see a message from Mother, reminding him to come home and get ready. I was sure if I checked my phone, I'd find the same one.

Perhaps with a little more...*encouragement.*

"We should get back," Chance sighed heavily. "Mercy will be glad to see you. She's been in a terrible mood all weekend."

"Because her emergence is coming up?" I asked, ignoring the burn as I quickly downed my coffee and stood. Whatever she discussed with me, it was unlike Mercy not to bottle up her unhappiness and put on a happy mask for my parents.

"Perhaps," Chance replied, sounding surprised. "I hadn't thought of that, but it is a stressful time. My guess was something at the community center didn't go well, but I'm sure she'll talk to you. See if you can find out what's on her mind."

GRACE

CHAPTER 16

I followed behind Chance in my own car for the short drive back to my parents' house, amazed at how unsettlingly foreign the streets of Auburn felt to me now. Until six months ago, this town was the only home I'd ever known, and yet I felt like I could be driving through any upper middle class suburb for all the connection I felt to the place.

Leon and Tobin were kicking a ball around with Creed in the front yard when I arrived. They spared me a wave before returning to their game, which stung a little, but I was used to it. The age gap between us—a strange one that had baffled the entire community and my parents when Mother had realized she was pregnant—was too big for us to have a regular sibling relationship.

But at least I'd had Mercy. She was more like a sibling to me than my little brothers were.

Everyone else seemed to be busy getting ready, so I made my way directly to her room—my old room—with my garment bag slung over my arm, makeup case in one hand and heels dangling from the other.

"Come in," Mercy called when I knocked on the door, and I slipped inside before Mother could dash out and accost me from the master bedroom across the hallway.

The room was still the same garish shade of lavender that Mother had painted it when I was young, with the same white wicker furniture she'd chosen, and the white quilt with ruffles around the edges she was so fond of. I'd found it monstrous when I was growing up, and I knew my cousin wasn't a fan either.

Mercy was sitting at the vanity with her back to me. Her naturally curly black hair had been twisted into the kind of prom-ready curls that Mother approved of, and was pulled back into an elegant updo. She paused with her eyeliner hovering in front of her face, giving me a weak smile when she saw me.

"No hug?" I teased, setting my things down.

"Of course you get a hug," she said, setting her makeup down, crossing the room and wrapping her arms around my waist.

"I missed you," I told her, giving her a quick squeeze before stepping back and fixing the sleeves of her high-necked black A-line dress I'd messed up. She didn't seem as bitter as she'd sounded on the phone yesterday, and I didn't want her to think there were lingering hard feelings because of that one conversation, but her mood wasn't quite as peppy as usual either.

Still, no need to make a big deal out of that. Despite what Mother thought, we were all entitled to have bad days.

"Come on, I'll do my makeup with you," I said, leading her back to the vanity and setting my own stuff up on the corner, bending over awkwardly to see my reflection. "How are you feeling today?"

I glanced at her carefully in the mirror, noticing a hint of sadness in her eyes that wasn't usually there, that she was valiantly trying to cover up.

I knew better than anyone what it was to cover up emotions.

"I found out this morning we have to go back to the community center," she replied, her voice a little too cheery to be natural. "We rushed yesterday to try to get it done, but it needs touch ups."

"It's the one just outside Milton, right?"

"Yep," Mercy practically squeaked. *Huh.* I struggled to think of what could possibly upset her or throw her off-balance about that. Maybe she didn't like spending time near Milton? She'd never visited me there, but neither had anyone else in my family except Chance, who'd helped me move in. I doubted Mercy would be allowed to visit my apartment even if she wanted to.

"Did anyone find a soul bond?" I asked, carefully applying concealer around my bruised eye. Those projects were mostly an excuse for mingling under the guise of charity. *Sugar, Mother was going to be furious if I couldn't make this eye look somewhat presentable in front of the whole community.*

"Find their soul bond?" Mercy replied with a borderline hysteric laugh before busying herself looking through her lipstick selection. "That would be something."

I frowned at her in the mirror, my concealer stick hovering near my face. She sort of had that look in her eye that I got when I was desperately wishing I could tell a lie, though I didn't think Mercy had that same darkness lurking in her that I did. There was probably an innocent explanation. Maybe she was jealous that someone else had met their soul bond, but didn't want to talk about it?

"If you ever want to talk about anything, I'm here. If you specifically *don't* want to talk about anything, I'm here for that too," I told her, giving her a smile in the mirror that I hoped was comforting. She didn't need me putting pressure on her to talk. I'm sure my mother was doing a fine job of that already.

"Can we not talk about it?" Mercy whispered, blinking back tears. "I think I did something bad and...I don't want to lose you."

I grabbed her hand and gave it a tight squeeze. "You never could, I promise. We don't have to talk about it now—you can tell me when you're ready—but please come to me if you need help, Mercy. I'm sure whatever you did, that it isn't as bad as you think, and you're never alone as long as I'm around. You don't have to go through this by yourself."

She squeezed my hand back before releasing it and returning to her makeup, and I forced myself to do the same, even as the unsettling realization that she didn't entirely believe me lingered at the back of my mind.

I fidgeted uncomfortably in the one black dress I owned, smoothing out the full skirt unnecessarily and tugging down the three-quarter length sleeves as we all waited in the foyer of the auditorium. Mother shot me a chastising glare, and I gripped my nude clutch tighter in both hands in front of me to stop myself from fussing, wishing I'd chosen more comfortable shoes than the nude pumps with the ankle straps that were currently murdering the balls of my feet.

I had taken extra care to look the part, twisting my hair back into a demure chignon that showcased the simple diamond studs my parents had gifted me for my 21st birthday, and applying my barely there makeup flawlessly, though my eye was still obviously swollen. Mercy and I looked like good little agathos robots, and I had a feeling we were both trying not to draw any attention to ourselves today.

Mother had given me a onceover and offered *zero* critiques, which was basically unheard of. Maybe she was feeling one percent guilty about the outreach trip. All of my parents had been unusually quiet with me except for Chance, and they hadn't even protested when I'd driven my own car here so I could leave straight after the service.

This auditorium in central Auburn, opposite the town hall, was the one used for all big agathos events north of New York. It was a starkly bright space, with white coffered ceilings, white carpet, white walls, even white pews. The only splashes of color were the gold chandeliers overhead, the black outfits of the guests and the pale gold curtains I could just glimpse in the main room through the double doors as we waited in the receiving line.

The mood at this memorial was even more somber than that of a regular funeral. Joy Lyon had died in a car accident aged 40, leaving behind her four bonded and three young children. Usually, after bonding, the women in our community were so well protected that this kind of thing didn't happen. Or it was never *just* the woman, at least. My mother had already made one comment about Joy's "independent spirit" that definitely hadn't been a compliment.

We approached the front of the line, me standing behind my parents with Mercy, Leon, and Tobin, since as a single woman I was counted as a child at these events. Us "kids" stood silently while my parents murmured their condolences to the four broken looking men in front of us.

One of them, probably Joy's consort, was taking the lead, stiffly thanking my parents for their words. He was dressed in a suit like the others, but his dark hair threaded with gray was messy like he'd been tugging at it, and the smudges under his eyes were almost purple. It had only been a week since she'd gone, and I wouldn't be surprised if he hadn't slept since, organizing the private funeral then today's public performance as well as looking after three grieving children.

My chest hurt, and I gave in to the urge to rub at my breastbone while my mother wasn't watching.

I felt sorrow for them, though I hadn't known Joy well and I didn't know her bonded at all really. They were 15 years older than me, and I'd just seen them around at events. I suspected the pain in my chest was more to do with missing my own soul bond. Comfort was a big part of what soul bonds provided, and it was difficult to be away from Riot at a time when I would have appreciated his emotional support.

266

The men's three preteen children were surrounded by a huddle of grandparents in the corner, and I was glad they hadn't been forced to stand with their dads to receive everyone like many agathos parents would have insisted on. At least one of them was sobbing loud enough for us to hear from where we stood, drawing disapproving looks from older members of the community who tended to frown upon excessive displays of any kind of emotion.

Their mom had *died* a week ago, it wasn't the time for observing social niceties. It was an effort not to openly glare at the judgmental spectators, but I was being on my absolute best behavior today. Just until I'd figured out a solution to this whole outreach issue.

We filed into the main room and my parents led us to seats in the center, stopping every few minutes to say hello to people. Tobin's small hand found mine, and I gave it a surprised squeeze, keeping him close. Us children were meant to walk a few steps behind our parents, so Tobin couldn't reach for Creed like he usually would. Even knowing I was probably Tobin's last choice for comfort, I decided to enjoy this moment of sibling bonding anyway.

Verity Mae sat across the aisle with her bonded, and she wagged her fingers at me while one hand rested on her impressively large bump. I returned the wave weakly as I took my seat, not feeling much in the mood for socializing.

In fact, I found it a little unsettling how chatty everyone was being. I'd been to memorials before—they were held for every member of the community who passed after a private funeral and rites had been conducted by the family—but they had all been for older people. Those memorials had adult children and less bonded standing to greet us, and while it was still sad, there was a sense of peace that their loved one had returned to Anesidora's embrace.

Today didn't feel like that for me, and there were others who looked more somber than usual as well, but there was also a lot of mindless chatter, like this was any other agathos excuse for an event.

Joy's four bonded made their way up the center aisle to the front row, and a few people craned their necks to see if they could spot the children in the foyer, waiting for them to make an appearance too. Apparently their fathers weren't going to force them on stage, and I was glad they had a little privacy in their grief.

Unsurprisingly, the Basilinna, Harmony Daubney took the stage first. Mercy had mentioned that Harmony was Joy's aunt, and as the highest ranking agathos in the Northeast outside of the Elders, it was expected that she would make the opening remarks.

The room grew completely silent under her surveying look. I was too far back to really make out her features, other than a black suit and dark hair, but she certainly had a surprising amount of *presence* about her.

She exhaled, briefly switching her attention to the four tense men in the front row, before returning it back to the expectant room.

"Today is a sad day," she began solemnly. "Today we must bid farewell to a beloved bonded, a mother, sister, daughter, granddaughter, niece, friend, and devoted member of our community, Joy Lyon."

I discreetly rubbed at the ache in my chest, wishing more than anything that Riot was here right now, and it was his hand I was holding instead of my thoroughly unnerved baby brother's.

"Joy was a bold soul, always willing to help almost anyone she came into contact with," Harmony continued. "She was a dedicated mother, although Anesidora only granted her three children."

That seemed unnecessary, I thought while everyone around me murmured sympathetically.

"Perhaps Anesidora always intended to call Joy home early. We must believe that she had a purpose, that she has a purpose for all of us—"

There was a scream of anguish from the foyer, and one of Joy's bonded stood instantly, rushing back down the aisle to tend to their child. My mother's lips pursed in disapproval, and the reality of how she and most other people in this room felt made nausea churn in my gut. I couldn't even focus on what the Basilinna was saying because of the sickly rage that was building inside me, my monster thoroughly in control.

The gossiping agathos would walk away from here whispering behind their hands about how Joy's children hadn't behaved, and how her bonded hadn't cracked down on them enough, how they hadn't put on a brave enough face, how the Basilinna would be disappointed at the display by her own family...

269

It all just felt so *wrong*. Like we were always focusing on the wrong things. Criticizing the wrong people, and celebrating the wrong achievements.

Why hadn't I ever noticed this before? I was frustrated with myself for not questioning things earlier. Before Riot.

The Basilinna finished her speech to delicate applause that felt entirely inappropriate for a memorial, and the stoic-looking man who'd been greeting everyone at the door took her place at the podium. Even from where I sat, I could see how stiff he was, and my heart went out to him for having to participate in this public display of mourning when he was so obviously uncomfortable with it.

"Uh, for everyone who doesn't know me, my name is Felix. I am—*was*—Joy's consort." He cleared his throat and took a deep, steadying breath before continuing. "I met Joy when we were 16. She followed the call right to my doorstep, and showed up with all her parents and siblings standing at her back." He huffed a quiet laugh at the memory and I rubbed my aching chest again. "It was the best and most terrifying day of my life, until the births of each of our children."

I discreetly pulled a tissue out of my clutch and dabbed under my eyes, wincing when I touched the injured one. I could feel Mother's stare on the side of my face, commanding me silently not to cry, but I refused to look at her. A small rebellion I would probably hear all about later.

"It seems ludicrous to stand up here and try to sum up Joy's life in just a few minutes. She glowed as bright as the sun when she was happy, and seemed to conjure thunder out of nowhere when she was mad. She was quick to anger, and slow to forgive. She loved *fiercely*. Joy was perfectly imperfect, and she was ours. And we thought we had forever, until we didn't."

The silence in the room was deafening. Every person in the room was listening with rapt attention to Felix's honest, heartfelt words, and I hoped that they were as moved by them as I was, because how could they *not* be?

"*Anesidora,*" he began, and I bowed my head in prayer along with everyone else. "I do not pretend I am worthy of understanding your plans, but I beg you to keep Joy safe in the afterlife. I pray that you will show us a way out of this grief. That you will guide our children on the difficult path they are walking. *Láthe biōsas.*"

"*Láthe biōsas,*" I murmured along with the rest of the room, tears streaming unchecked down my cheeks.

After Joy's parents spoke, everyone moved back into the foyer where hot drinks and plates of food brought in by members of the community had been set up on long banquet tables against the back wall.

For once, I was glad to be treated like a child at these events. It meant I was expected to follow my parents around like a silent shadow, and I didn't have to go make small talk with Verity Mae or Serenity, or any of the other people I'd once considered my peers.

My emotions were raw from the service, and I was worried that news had already spread about the Elders' plans for me. The last thing I wanted to talk about was the outreach trip.

Unfortunately, it didn't look like I was going to be so lucky on that front, as after only ten minutes milling about in the foyer—after Mother had sent me to the restroom to fix my smudged makeup—the Basilinna herself made a beeline for my family. Mercy and I discreetly exchanged nervous looks as the Basilinna struck up a conversation with my mother, and I absently ran my hand over Tobin's hair when he looked up at me with wide, wary eyes.

Even the five-year-old knew this was not a woman to be messed with.

"Ah, and this must be Grace." The Basilinna's attention turned to me, her face fixed in an unnervingly serene smile. I did not take it as a good sign that she already knew my name. The Basilinna for each region was chosen by the local Elders to manage the more logistical affairs of the agathos, as well as taking a leading role in administering rites during ceremonies.

She was responsible for the *entire northeast*. I should have been nothing to her.

"It is," Valor confirmed, giving me a warning look that clearly said *behave*.

"My name is Harmony," she said, extending her hand for me to shake. I tucked my clutch under my arm and took her hand with a nervous smile, sending a silent prayer to Anesidora that my palms weren't sweaty, before I pulled it back as quickly as I could without seeming rude.

There was something quite *unsettling* about the Basilinna's presence. It may have been as innocent as me not seeing her at these events usually, and definitely not expecting her to know my name, but it felt like more than that. Like my gut instinct was screaming *run* while I forced my feet to stay in place so I didn't further humiliate my family with my existence.

This was the first time I'd seen her close up, and she was a lot younger than I expected. Smaller, too. She had dark hair, agathos eyes, and faint lines around her forehead and mouth that made me think she frowned more than smiled. All the times I'd seen her—including this one— she was wearing a pencil skirt and matching blazer which always had shoulder pads. Maybe to make her look more intimidating? Her four soul bonds were fanned out behind her like bodyguards.

"I had a meeting with the Elders early this morning," Harmony said, turning to my parents to speak. "They are very excited about the possibilities for Grace in outreach. Eutychia will be a very valuable gift in...*remote* communities."

The disdain in her voice was impossible to miss and I clasped my hands in front of me, digging a thumbnail into my palm to keep myself from giving away my offense.

Eutychia was a useful gift anywhere. Who didn't need a little good luck from time to time?

"It is an incredible opportunity for Grace," Valor replied, speaking on behalf of the family. He inclined his head respectfully at the woman who was at least a foot and a half shorter than him. "We have prayed for many years for Anesidora to show us Grace's path, and we are grateful for the Elders' guidance on this issue."

Issue? There had never been a more accurate descriptor for how my parents saw me. I was an issue to be solved, preferably in a way that didn't further damage their reputations.

Chance grimaced at me like he knew exactly what I was thinking.

"As no female agathos has ever been on an outreach trip before, there will be additional things to sort out," Harmony said, all business. "Who she travels with, the lodging and so forth."

"Will she be expected to...*live* with *men*?" Mother asked, swallowing dramatically like the very idea made her ill.

If only you knew.

"Of course not," Harmony replied, reeling back as though she were scandalized. "We would never risk any agathos woman's reputation that way."

And just like that, any lingering concerns my mother might have had melted away into nothing. Her whole face softened as her posture relaxed, and all four of her bonded relaxed right along with her because her tension was their tension.

It had been a long shot to hope my family would come to my rescue, but it was abundantly clear now that they wouldn't. Not when they'd been personally assured by the Basilinna that my honor wasn't at stake.

Just my freedom.

I waited as I was expected to while my parents sucked up to the Basilinna—hands clasped in front of me, eyes cast down, *silent*. Mercy sidled closer, her arm brushing against mine in quiet support, and I appreciated her so much in that moment, knowing that she was going through a mysterious silent struggle of her own.

Harmony turned to leave, undoubtedly to do more hobnobbing at her niece's funeral, but she paused to give me one more assessing look, her mouth downturned.

"You are in a unique position, Grace. Your journey may end up in our history books someday. I do hope you've been praying for Anesidora's guidance."

I gave her a tight smile and bobbed my head in acknowledgment.

I'd certainly prayed to someone for guidance, and I'd got a far stronger response than Anesidora had ever given me. With unease, I realized I hadn't once prayed to Anesidora out loud since that night.

"You should leave," Mother clipped the moment Harmony was out of earshot. "Your eye looks terrible."

I wasn't about to look a gift horse in the mouth by arguing, so I tipped my head silently in acknowledgment, giving Mercy's arm a quick squeeze as I attempted to discreetly slip away.

"Oh, Grace?" Mother said quietly, wrapping her cold hand around my wrist to keep me in place as I passed and leaning in to speak directly into my ear. "Perhaps today's service will serve as a reminder to be grateful. I would rather you have no soul bonds than ones who speak of you the way Joy's bonded spoke of her."

Don't say anything. Nod. Stay silent. Walk away.

But the darkness in me twisted and hissed like enraged snakes, demanding I respond. That I protest, fight back, do *something*.

275

"You would be lucky to have your bonded speak of you with as much love as Joy's bonded spoke of her," I whispered, tugging my wrist out of her manacled grip. I doubted I would have been able to, had my words not taken her by surprise. Before she could respond, I slipped into the crowd, walking out of the building as fast as I could without drawing unwanted attention to myself.

Sugar, had I really said that?

I wasn't owed any bad luck, I had no excuses. I'd said that because I wanted to. Because the darkness in my mind had responded and I was sick of fighting it.

I'd said it because I couldn't tell a lie.

GRACE

CHAPTER 17

I drove back to Milton pushing the speed limit more than I ever had in my life, slightly terrified that if I looked in my rearview I would find my mother and one or all of my fathers on my tail with steam coming out of their noses.

I'd never talked back like that before.

Sure, I'd asked more questions than I should have, and I'd gently tested boundaries to see how firm they were. But I'd taken every insult Mother had thrown at me on the chin and never once objected, believing it wasn't my place. I was the child after all, she'd carried me in her body, given me life, put her own dreams aside to raise me. That's the message I'd always had drilled into my head.

I hadn't asked to be born, and I hadn't done anything to deserve the scorn she'd always shown me.

My hands shook and I clenched the steering wheel hard enough for my knuckles to turn white. I didn't regret talking back, but I was *terrified* of what would happen now. Possibly speaking up while the Basilinna was in town hadn't been the best idea. If anyone had the ability to move the outreach trip up, it was her.

Maybe I was codependent, or I was just being a big baby, but I wanted nothing more than to get back to Riot. To get back to that safe place where I felt like I could be myself without judgment.

The second I was within Milton's city limits, I exhaled a small sigh of relief. Not that the city itself would be a real barrier if Mother wanted to come find me, but she hated Milton so I always felt marginally safer from her wrath here.

A hitchhiker on the side of the road snagged my attention, their misery calling to me like a siren song. A voice in the back of my head told me to drive on, that I couldn't afford to be distracted, but I was pulling over before I'd even consciously decided to do so. No matter what I was going through, my agathos nature wouldn't let me ignore someone in need.

My heart sank when I realized I *knew* the hitchhiker—it was Rae. She looked worse than I'd ever seen her—gray and pallid, with dark shadows under her eyes, her usually bright hair matted and filthy.

"Grace?" she asked, peering in the passenger window as I lowered it. Her voice was scratchy and hoarse, and close up, I could see how bloodshot her eyes were.

"Hop in," I replied with a tight smile.

Rae stumbled against the car in her rush to get in, and practically collapsed in the front seat smelling of bourbon and a bunch of other unsavory things I tried desperately not to focus on.

"Man, it's been a crazy couple of days. I'm so glad to see you! Do you pick up hitchhikers often? It's dangerous, you know. You should be careful. Do you think there are any beds at the shelter tonight?" Rae asked hopefully, not stopping to take a breath. She was full of the optimism and sweetness that had drawn me to her in the first place, and I knew it was a place she went to in her head when things had been particularly bad.

"I have a feeling there'll be room for you," I murmured, moving the car forward so we were safely off the road and cutting the engine.

"Talk to me," I commanded softly, infusing my voice with Anesidora's magic as I held out my hand for Rae to take. With a slightly bemused smile, Rae rested her palm on mine, and I put my other hand over top, clasping hers gently as I let the magic of Eutychia flow through me.

I siphoned off some of Rae's emotional anguish while I held her there, piling it onto my own. Hopefully Riot was ready, because the moment I got home, I was going to wrap myself around him like a baby koala and never let go, and nothing about that idea scared me anymore.

Rae was talking about her weekend, and I forced myself to concentrate in spite of the uncomfortable clash of sensations that were ravaging my body.

"I know he's an asshole," Rae sighed, tipping her head against the headrest, oblivious to the energy passing between us.

"Your ex?" I murmured, trying not to wince at the stabbing pain in my head as I drew her agony in.

"Yeah," Rae laughed humorlessly. "Every time I go see him, it sets me back three steps. He just makes me feel seen, you know? Just for a little while, anyway."

It definitely wasn't the first time I'd given Rae luck, but it was the most I'd ever given her in one hit. Which seemed fitting, since this was the worst I'd ever seen her. Maybe this would lead to the life changing moment she needed. A chance at something *more*, something fulfilling.

Timing wise, it probably couldn't have been worse for me. There had to be balance. There was always a cost.

"You deserve someone who *always* sees you, Rae," I told her fiercely, my eyes watering with the effort of speaking, absorbing her pain, and transferring her luck. "Believe that you should always be someone's first choice."

She nodded silently and I patted her hand softly as the well of my magic emptied, pulling away and fastening my seatbelt.

Rae followed my movements before her gaze lifted to my face, her eyes wide. "I think you might be an angel," she said dazedly, probably a little high off all the good luck I'd given her.

"You give me far too much credit," I replied, my smile was more genuine this time even though my body was *wrecked*. I felt like I'd run a marathon while simultaneously being shoved through a meat grinder. It was...unpleasant.

"I'm going to drop you at the shelter then head straight home, I'm not feeling so flash," I told Rae apologetically, starting the car.

"Of course. I really appreciate it, Grace," Rae said, sounding genuine as she fastened her seatbelt. "I just...I feel like I get stuck, you know? And I want to do better and not make the exact same mistake fifteen times in a row, and then in the moment, I just...do. I just do the same stupid shit all over again."

The frustration in her voice was the most honest thing I'd ever heard from Rae. Usually, when she was sober and fresh off a bad decision, she was all sparkling optimism that *this time* was going to be different.

"You know there are programs at the shelter," I suggested lightly, keeping my eyes trained on the road. I probably shouldn't have even been driving feeling as terrible as I did. "I know it hasn't been something you've been interested in before—"

"I'm going to do it," Rae interrupted, sounding surprisingly determined. "I'm going to get my shit together, get a job, and meet someone amazing. Then I'm going to have a family one day and if I have a little girl, I'm going to call her Grace."

My mouth twitched as I tried to suppress a smile. "I know at least six other Graces, I don't know if I endorse that plan."

"Well, I do," Rae declared. "I'm going to call her Grace, and tell her she was named after the one person who never gave up on me."

I dropped Rae off and drove ten minutes or so back to my apartment in a daze, really hoping my bad luck wasn't going to be an accident.

The staircase seemed like it had tripled in length as I dragged my body up it. The key hole had somehow shrunk, and my keys weighed a ton. Everything felt *hard*.

The door opened suddenly, and I practically fell into Riot's chest with an *oof*, before closing my eyes and breathing him in.

"What did you do, Gracie?" Riot murmured, sounding a little exasperated. He scooped me into his arms bridal-style with my coat and heels still on, and carried me over to the couch.

"I'm too heavy!" I squeaked in surprise, making zero attempt to get out of his grip. Sugar, he felt so nice. So warm and strong and cozy.

Riot snorted like the very concept insulted him, sitting down with me on his lap like I weighed nothing. I could have objected more—it seemed like the polite thing to do—but I'd felt like a piece of my heart had been carved out of my chest all day being away from him, and I was only whole again now.

I rested my head on Riot's shoulder and exhaled the breath I felt like I'd been holding all day. His relief brushed softly against my skin, as warm as sunshine.

"What did you do?" Riot repeated, running his warm hand firmly down my stockinged leg to undo the ankle strap of my shoes and pull my heel off. An entirely inappropriate heat ran through me as he repeated the action on the other leg, considering how terrible I was feeling.

"I saw Rae on the way home and she was in terrible shape, so I gave her some luck," I rushed out, ripping off the bandaid. "A lot of luck. Like, all of it."

Riot huffed a silent laugh, his breath fanning over my hair. "Anything else?"

"I took a little of her pain, but that's all," I admitted, burying my face in his neck. On reflection, between my burst of courage with my mother and helping Rae, I had somehow managed to cause quite a bit of trouble for myself in one outing.

"Alright," he replied simply. "Any bad luck so far?"

"So far, so good."

His endlessly calm response was completely what I expected, I realized suddenly. Riot was a safe harbor for me to bring all of my emotions and baggage and bad choices without fear of judgment, never pushing me to slow down or speed up.

I hoped I could be that for him too. Or be *something* for him, at least.

At the same time, there was part of me that *wanted* to be pushed. It was the first time since I'd met Riot that I felt like someone was *missing*. More than one someone.

Maybe Bullet was that someone, the one who would push me.

"And how was the memorial?" Riot asked.

"Sad," I replied, closing my eyes and relaxing against him as both his arms wrapped securely around me. "Her four soul bonds and three young children were there. It was awful," I admitted. "They loved her so much and she's just...gone. Just like that."

I sat forward and Riot helped me out of my coat, lying it on the couch next to us before bundling me back up in his arms and rubbing soothing circles into the nape of my neck with his thumb. It was so good, I almost fell asleep, but we still had a lot to talk about, and I decided to start with the easy topics first.

"I pulled some history books this morning," I murmured drowsily. "To see if I could find information on outreach trips and how to get out of them."

"I'm guessing you didn't find anything," Riot replied, sounding amused.

"How did you know?"

"Call it a hunch, but it seems like the kind of information you'd lead with," he replied wryly.

"That's a valid point," I said, huffing a silent laugh. "Chance, one of my fathers was there. He told me that my parents had gone to the Elders about my...*situation*, a year ago."

Riot stiffened beneath me, and I cracked open one eye to peer up at him through my lashes. His mouth was set in a thin line, a muscle in his jaw ticking.

"That bothers you," I stated, forcing both eyes open as his anger scraped uncomfortably over my skin.

"I'm a daimon, I don't trust authority figures in general, especially not agathos ones. I don't like that your parents deliberately put you on the Elders' radar, and especially that they did it without your consent."

I chewed on my lower lip until Riot tugged it free, his thumb gently rubbing the spot I'd been gnawing. He hadn't said anything I hadn't thought of, but it stung more to hear it from someone else.

"Well, I'm definitely on their radar. The Basilinna was at the memorial—she's sort of the CEO of the agathos in the northeast—and she knew who I was. She was excited about what the Elders had planned for me."

"You probably *should* have led with that," Riot pointed out drily.

"I was enjoying not panicking about it for a moment," I sighed. "The more urgent threat is probably my mother. I may have said something a little *unkind* to her on my way out."

"Good," Riot muttered. "But between that, the outreach thing and the bad luck, I'm not feeling great about sticking around here, Grace. It feels like we're sitting ducks."

His arms were banded around my waist, but I could feel his hands twitching restlessly. I reached between us, sliding my hand into his front pocket—blushing profusely when I realized how close my hand was to *other* things based on Riot's sharp intake—until my fingers brushed against his lighter.

I pulled it out and held it up for Riot to take, and he rewarded me with one of those sultry little smiles that I felt *way* down low.

"Do I have a tell?" he asked, plucking the lighter from between my fingertips and immediately flicking it open.

"It's a pretty lighter," I remarked, inspecting the details up close for the first time. I hadn't noticed before that the deeply carved engraving was a dragon, its fierce face front and center, with a long body winding around the whole thing.

"It was my mom's," Riot said with a shrug. I paid close attention to his emotions, since he had barely mentioned his mom at all, but he didn't seem overly sad or angry. There was just a kind of resigned acceptance. "I was 17 when she died, so I had to move in with my dad. He didn't give me a whole lot of time to go through her things, but I swiped this on my way out the door."

"I'm sorry," I whispered.

"Don't be," Riot replied, his lip twitching slightly. "I never resented my abilities more than when I knew what would kill my mom, but I've come to terms with her death. I tried to prevent it, but I was a kid, and I had no idea what I was doing. I locked her in her room one weekend with food, water, and a bucket," he added with a grimace. "I guess I thought if I just cut her off, she'd kick the habit. Obviously, that was a terrible idea."

"You were a kid," I pointed out, snuggling in closer to him again. "No kid would know how to deal with that. They shouldn't have to."

Riot hummed absently as he idly toyed with a piece of hair he'd pulled free of my chignon.

"So, back to my get-the-fuck-out-of-Dodge idea..." he prompted, absently open and closing the lighter. "I know you're not sure about meeting Bullet just yet, but his place is always an option. Except..."

"Except what?" I asked, feeling a mixture of nerves and curiosity at the prospect of meeting what I was almost certain was another of my soul bonds.

"Shouldn't we wait until your bad luck has hit? We'd have to drive through a long stretch of agathos territory to get to Bullet's place. When does your luck usually run out?"

"Right," I sighed. That was a good point. "Within 24 hours, usually. I did give her a lot of luck though..."

I chanced a glance at Riot in time to see his grimace.

"I don't really want to just up and disappear anyway, I think that will cause more problems than it solves," I added decisively, feeling confident in that decision. "In the meantime, I thought maybe I could try praying to Anesidora again. I should have already, really. I just... haven't," I finished lamely. *Because I prayed to the Goddess of Night and I'm waiting for Anesidora to smite me.*

"Because she's been so forthcoming in the past?" Riot deadpanned, raising an eyebrow at me.

It was beyond inappropriate—blasphemous, even. I should have been scandalized. Maybe it was because I was drained, or because my emotions had been all over the place all day, but a laugh bubbled unexpectedly out of me, and I clapped both hands over my mouth to cover up my sacreligious response.

Both Riot's eyebrows were raised, his surprise mingling with something warm and fuzzy, wrapping around me like a familiar embrace.

"Do that again," he commanded roughly.

"Do what?" I asked breathily. Riot could switch from cool and unaffected to blisteringly intense in two seconds flat, and I didn't think I'd ever get used to the impact of all that intensity trained on me.

"Laugh. Laugh again."

"I don't...I can't just laugh on command," I replied lamely. "Say something funny."

"I'm not funny," Riot deadpanned. "I have no idea how I made it happen the first time, but you've never laughed like that before. *Properly* laughed. I'm not giving up until I hear it again. That was the prettiest sound I've ever heard."

"I don't know about laughing, but I think I'm going to swoon now," I whispered, heart flip-flopping wildly in my chest as the corners of Riot's lips turned up.

It should be illegal to be that handsome.

A knock on the door startled us both out of our weird, lusty reverie, and Riot tugged me closer to him as if it was instinct.

"Expecting someone?" Riot asked in a low voice, glaring at the door like there was an enemy army behind it.

"Definitely not," I whispered, shaking my head. Maybe it was a neighbor. Or someone selling something.

Or my luck had run out.

"Grace!"

Or my mother. My luck had *definitely* run out.

"Grace! Open this door, I have some things to say to you. It isn't good manners to leave your guests waiting in the cold," she groused. There was a low mumble of voices from the other side that told me at least one of my fathers was with her. Considering I was owed bad luck, I was guessing it was Valor.

"Sugar," I breathed. "I can't leave them out there, they'll have seen my car outside. I'll try to make them leave."

"Shit," Riot muttered, shoving one inked hand back into his messy hair as I extricated myself from his grip and padded quietly to the door. They wouldn't be able to see him from the doorway, but if they demanded to come in...

No, I wouldn't ask him to hide. I couldn't do it. It was one thing to keep this to ourselves until we understood it better, but even if I hadn't been programmed not to lie or cheat, I wouldn't disrespect Riot by treating him like a dirty little secret.

He was the first person to look at me like I mattered. Not as one small part of my community, or because I had abilities that were useful, or because I was a mutant puzzle that needed to be figured out. Riot just looked at me like I was Grace.

"Hello, Mother," I said, opening the door and positioning myself right in the entryway. "Valor," I added, while my heart worked triple time in my chest. Oh sugar, they looked so angry.

"Grace," he clipped, looking expectantly between me and the partially open door.

"Let us in," Mother demanded impatiently. "You need to practice your entertaining skills if you're leaving guests out on the doorstep. Though I'm sure your friends from home don't want to visit you here. Understandably," she added under her breath.

"It's almost dinnertime, why don't we go out? I know a great place near here—"

"Let us in, Grace," Valor snapped, eyes flaring angrily.

Why now? Only Chance had visited my apartment before and that was the day I moved in.

You know why, a resigned voice in the back of my mind supplied.

If Rae didn't use this opportunity wisely, I was never giving anyone luck again.

Be sweet, I half heartedly reminded myself.

No, don't be sweet. Be brave.

We had a good run. A whole week to ourselves. It had been nice while it lasted.

"Come in," I rasped, my throat suddenly dry as I stepped back from the door.

This was it. The bubble of peace we'd been luxuriating in was about to burst, but I was trusting that nothing worse than that would happen. I was trusting that my parents cared about their reputation enough not to do anything rash that might potentially put me or Riot in danger.

Well, me, at least. I wasn't convinced they'd be so compassionate about Riot. I'd just need to find a way to keep him safe.

Mother shrieked so loud, I was convinced one of my neighbors would call the police, jumping back dramatically into Valor's arms. Riot lounged on the couch like he didn't have a care in the world, ankle resting over his knee, arms spread along the back of the cushions. His only response to Mother's piercing greeting was a slight twitch of his eyebrow as he stared up at them, red and purple eyes on display.

He was the picture of bored arrogance, and his nonchalance settled some of the panic that was building in me, threatening to spiral out of control.

"*Grace*," Mother hissed. "There's a *daimon* in your apartment." She pointed a shaky finger at Riot like I couldn't see him. Valor quickly stepped in front of her like a shield, and I suppressed an inappropriate giggle.

"This is Riot. Riot, this is my mother, Faith, and one of my fathers, Valor."

Maybe if I stayed calm, everyone else would stay calm too?

"What is he doing here?" Valor growled. *Sugar*, if only Chance had been the one accompanying Mother today. He was far more reasonable.

"He's...well, I'm pretty sure he's my soul bond. One of my soul bonds," I corrected, tipping my chin up like I wasn't terrified of saying the words out loud. "He *is* my soul bond," I repeated with more conviction.

"That is *ludicrous*." Mother's voice was as angry as I'd ever heard it, even if it was barely above a whisper. "You cannot believe that."

"I cannot lie," I countered, defensiveness rushing to the fore. Not for me, but for *Riot*. Of the judgments she was making of him, written clearly all over her face.

"Daimons do not have soul bonds," Valor gritted out. He reached for me like he was about to pull me behind him too, but Riot was suddenly there, both arms banded around my waist, pulling me back against his chest.

"Don't touch her," Riot growled menacingly, his mouth just an inch away from my ear. A shiver ran down my spine that had nothing to do with fear.

His possessiveness was entirely daimonic, and I *adored* it.

"Grace," Mother warned, eyes flinty as she glared around Valor's back. "Come here."

"No," I replied, baffled that she would even suggest it. "Yes, Riot is a daimon and that is...unusual. He's still *mine* though. Our souls are intertwined. It's no different to—"

"Don't even finish that sentence," Mother warned. "It is nothing like a soul bond between agathos. We should have never let you move out here. Has this been going on the whole time? Is that why you moved here?"

"What? No, I only met him last week, after the baby shower. Maybe I wanted to live in Milton because I felt some kind of call, I don't know—"

"You did *not* feel the call, because he is *not* your soul bond," Mother snarled, and I recoiled against Riot at the venom in her tone.

"You will come back to Auburn with us," Valor demanded. "You will go straight to the temple for cleansing, then you will beg forgiveness from the Basilinna and the Elders and ask that they bring your outreach trip forward."

"No," I replied incredulously. "I'm not going to do that. I'm not going to do any of that. How could you think I would?"

Riot gave me an infinitesimal squeeze, and I felt his pride in me stroking gently at my skin.

"You have ruined yourself. Our life. Our reputation." Mother's words cut like knives, but they always did. The difference was, now I had someone standing at my back who would never let me suffer alone, and that made each blow easier to defend, each wound more painless to heal. "Think of your reputation, Grace!"

"I don't think it's my reputation you're worried about," I replied flatly. "I'm not sure it ever has been."

"If you don't come with us..." Mother began, indecision warring in her eyes for a moment before they hardened. "Then that's it."

"What's it?" I asked, leaning further back into Riot as his arms tightened around me.

"We can't let you in our home if you're knowingly continuing a relationship with a daimon," Valor said tightly. "This is a curse. You have displeased Anesidora. If you are not willing to repent and seek cleansing, we cannot help you. We cannot risk this *infection* spreading."

"Ah, there's that agathos compassion I've heard so much about," Riot muttered, his fury licking at my skin.

"He's not a curse. This isn't a curse," I said quietly, impressed at how steady my voice was when I felt like raging, the darkness in me rising in response to my anger. "But if you'd like me to stay away, I will respect your wishes. I would ask that you not say anything for now—"

Mother made a noise of a disagreement in the back of her throat, but I forged on.

"—as we are still seeking out the goddess' wisdom in this matter." It was the absolute barest minimum of truth I could scrape out.

My parents looked at me in silence for a long moment, probably reading each other's feelings the same way I was reading Riot's, except they were fully bonded and I imagined it would be more seamless.

"We will always do what is best for you, Grace," Valor said coldly, ushering my enraged mother out of the apartment without a second glance.

"That wasn't a yes," Riot murmured, his anger morphing into concern.

"No," I managed to get out around the lump in my throat. "It wasn't."

GRACE

CHAPTER 18

I looked around in confusion at the room I was in. I definitely hadn't been here before. It was a beautiful cabin—or was it a lodge?—somewhere surrounded by snow. All I could see out the window was miles of the stuff, blanketing the landscape.

It was warm inside though. A plaid wool blanket covered my legs, and I was curled up in front of a roaring fire.

I glanced down at my pewter gray zip up hoodie in surprise, peeking under the blankets to find matching sweatpants. Matching loungewear was not unusual for me, but this color was. Mother would have a fit.

Oh, this must be another of Bullet's dreams. Did I call him again, or had he set this up for me?

"I made you coffee, Gracie girl." I heard Riot's voice a second before a cup of coffee was set down beside me. Confused as to where he'd come from and how he'd so thoroughly snuck up on me, I squealed in surprise when he lifted me into the air, sitting back in the chair with me on his lap.

He shot me a smug smile before grabbing the coffee off the side table and handing it to me. I could smell my favorite hazelnut creamer in it, and I pecked him on the cheek gratefully for his thoughtfulness.

"I love you," Riot said easily, like he said it all the time, dropping a kiss on the tip of my nose. I was so shocked at the casual use of the L-word, I sat frozen in his lap, hands wrapped around my coffee cup, staring at him like I'd never seen him before.

Strangely, he didn't seem to notice my reaction. He was looking at the fire, humming something under his breath, fingers drumming absently on my thigh. Other voices filtered in too, from somewhere else in the house. There were at least two masculine voices I could make out—one teasing and playful, the other gruff and serious.

They felt comforting. I wanted to move closer to them, to hear what they were saying, but I was frozen in place on Riot's lap, my gaze somehow restricted to my immediate vicinity. Why couldn't I turn my head?

There was a musical sounding chuckle behind me, and I made a frustrated noise in the back of my throat as I tried to look for the source of it.

"Sorry, Grace. You can only see the parts of your future that I can see." Whoever was behind me tugged lightly on my hair. It was an affectionate gesture that felt incredibly familiar somehow.

"Bullet?" I asked the disembodied voice.

"The one and only," he replied smugly, sounding happy that I'd guessed.

"Why can't I see you?"

"This is a vision of your future, granted by La Nuit. Your future may not be my future," Bullet said sadly, standing so close I could hear his breathing, yet feeling a million miles away.

"No," I replied eventually. "I refuse to accept that."

"I know. You tell me that every time I show you one of these."

"The others that are here...are they my soul bonds?" I asked, feeling like I already knew the answer.

"Oh yes. I can only tell you that while you're asleep, since you'll forget. If you were awake, it might change your course. You're going to find us all soon, Grace. Sooner than you think."

"How sure are you about that?" I asked, giving up my fight to turn around and resting my head on Riot's shoulder. "My family knows now. They're going to try to separate us."

"They are," Bullet agreed. "You could go with them."

"I would never," I replied vehemently, annoyed he would even suggest it.

Bullet chuckled. "I didn't think you would, but the option is there. The path is open."

"I want to stay with Riot. I want to find you all. Tell me how to do that," I demanded, finding it surprisingly easy to be bossy in my dreams.

"I wish it was an easy journey for you," Bullet murmured, sounding surprisingly somber. "I wish I could see your path more clearly, but it isn't a smooth one."

"Tell me what to do," I pleaded, my voice barely above a whisper.

"Do what scares you. That's the answer to almost every question you have—how you'll find us, how it's possible for this future to come to pass, all of it. Do what scares you."

His voice was already fading, the dream around me starting to dissipate, breaking into smaller pieces that whirled around me and blended into the snow outside the window. I leaned harder into Riot, clutching the hot coffee in my hands, desperate to stay just a little longer. Bullet was sad, and he was mine. *He needed me here.*

"I want to stay with you," I insisted, my voice sounding tinny and thin.

"I know. I'll see you soon, Amazing Grace."

I woke up gasping for air, scrambling to hold on to the remnants of the dream that was already dissipating. I made a frustrated noise in the back of my throat, realizing that Riot wasn't even here when I cringed that I might have woken him up with my temper tantrum.

Where was he? I always woke up draped over him like a blanket.

"You're awake," Riot said, startling me as he walked through the door fully dressed, holding a cup of coffee. He set it down on the nightstand before climbing into bed behind me, pulling me back against his chest. I accepted the cup gratefully, sighing happily at the smell of my favorite hazelnut creamer before a tiny shudder ran through me.

"What is it?" Riot asked, moving my hair over one shoulder and dropping a kiss behind my ear.

"I don't know. Déjà vu, perhaps," I laughed lightly, trying to shake off the strange phenomenon. "Thank you for the coffee. Are you buttering me up?" I teased.

Riot hummed, still toying with my hair as I sipped my coffee.

"Don't go to work today," he said quietly. My throat tightened because it's not like I hadn't been expecting this. He'd let me deliberately avoid the conversation last night, but my alarm was going to go off any minute. My time for avoiding the subject was running out.

"Riot..."

"I wouldn't ask you if I wasn't worried, Grace," he said, guiding my chin to the side so he could see my face. "Your parents didn't make any guarantees when you asked for their silence."

"Believe me, I know," I muttered, looking down at the bedspread. "Can you trust that I know them better than you? Nothing matters more than reputation to my parents—Mother and Valor in particular. They won't drag me out of Hope House in front of all the agathos who work there, it would be mortifying for them."

I had to believe I could at least trust my parents that much. My entire life, I'd craved that feeling of absolute faith that my own family was in my corner, come what may, but I'd never found it. I could rely on Chance, possibly Creed, but Mother, Valor and Earnest always outnumbered them.

Besides, what was the worst that could happen, even if they did show up?

They couldn't break the connection between Riot and I no matter how they felt about it. Or could they? We hadn't consummated our relationship, which I was pretty sure was required to solidify the bond.

Maybe I should do that before work? How long could it possibly take?

I didn't think Riot would be on board with that plan though. He'd been very clear that whatever happened between us should be based on what we wanted to do, not what we were pressured into doing.

"Grace," Riot sighed, resting his forehead on my shoulder. "I know you've worked hard for the life you have, but you can't keep going on like nothing's changed."

I understood Riot's concern, but the idea of just walking away from the people at Hope House who needed me...what if someone needed luck and I wasn't there to give it to them? I only existed to ease their suffering, I couldn't not be there...

"Gracie," Riot breathed, running his nose along my shoulder and up my neck, a plea in his voice. "Fight your instincts. This is your life we are talking about."

I understood that, and yet...

And yet.

"Ask Bullet," I said hoarsely, closing my eyes against the lash of pain I felt from Riot.

With a disappointed exhale that I felt all the way in my bones, Riot shuffled behind me, grabbing his phone. I focused on drinking my coffee for the sake of having something to do, trying to ignore the tremble in my hands.

I had to go, I could feel it. Even if it was just to hand in my notice, because Riot was right. I couldn't keep pretending like nothing had changed. I had the feeling that Bullet was waiting for me, and getting some space from my family until I figured out how to move forward was probably a good idea, no matter how much my instincts raged at me to stay and be of service.

Riot's phone dinged and I stiffened against him, waiting to hear what he said.

"*Do what scares you*," Riot read, sounding unimpressed.

That strange déjà vu feeling washed over me again, making me shiver.

"Then I guess I'm going to work," I laughed weakly. "Unless he was talking to you?"

"Trust me, you going to work is definitely what scares me too," Riot muttered darkly. "Are you sure going to work scares you more than *not* going?"

"I'm going to resign," I sighed. "And that very much scares me."

I doubted Constance would even make me work my notice period. Aside from the fact that she'd probably be thrilled to be rid of me, she would be expecting me to quit for the outreach trip she'd endorsed me for anyway.

Riot made a pained noise before pulling something out of his pocket and sliding it onto my lap.

"A phone?" I asked, glancing at it in surprise. It was a basic-looking touch screen model, but it would be great to have a way to keep in touch with Riot during the day.

"Keep it on you at all times," Riot instructed. "Pick a skirt with pockets, strap it to your thigh, do whatever you have to do, okay? Fucking Bullet, what kind of advice is that?" he grumbled, shifting slightly behind me as he shoved his hand through his hair.

"Unpleasant but necessary advice, I think," I replied, downing the rest of my coffee and setting the cup aside so I could press a kiss against Riot's cheek, rough with days-old stubble. I tilted my head back to look at his face, finding his eyes already on me as they always seemed to be, filled with a mixture of awe, affection, and concern.

There was something very reverent about the way Riot looked at me. Like I could do no wrong. *No.* Like I could only do *right.* It was dangerous and a little addictive. He obviously didn't trust himself to make the right decisions, but I wasn't entirely confident I was equipped to either.

I'd stood up to Mother yesterday, though. *Twice.* I could do it again today, if she tried to talk to me at work. But I wouldn't be able to forgive myself if I just walked away from Hope House without a word. I wanted to check on Rae and properly tie up loose ends before I took a step into the unknown.

"We were never going to be able to stay in limbo forever," I told Riot softly. "Besides, even if my parents show up and try to convince me to leave again, you know I'll always come back to you."

Riot's lips twitched slightly, despite the concern I knew he was still feeling. "Oh yeah? Are you willing to make a deal with a daimon on that, Gracie?"

"I am," I replied confidently. "Are you?"

"It's not even a question in my mind, Gracie. I will always find a way back to you."

An hour later I climbed out of my car, smoothing down my pale blue knee-length dress with the peter pan collar that Mother had brought me for my 25th birthday.

It was hideous and I hated it, no matter how many times I'd tried to spin my negative thoughts into positive ones about the flattering way it skimmed my hips or how the color made my eyes look brighter. It made me feel like an oversized toddler, though it did have pockets, which was handy. The phone Riot had given me felt like a comforting weight against my leg.

I was wearing the dress in a flagrant grab for brownie points in case Mother turned up. I was determined to prove that I could still be a model agathos citizen, daimon soul bond aside. There was no need for her, or anyone else, to overreact and try to send me away.

One part of my brain argued that I didn't need her approval, I'd even told her as much yesterday. The other part of me, conditioned by a lifetime of being her daughter, still craved her acceptance. Her *love*, no matter how futile that was.

It was a cold morning, but I was so nervous that I carried my camel coat over my arm instead of wearing it, trying to mitigate the sweat situation. The *click click click* of my heeled ankle boots as I went up the stairs didn't give me that exciting, empowering feeling I usually got on my way to work. It made the ball of nausea and panic that had taken up residence in my stomach grow heavier with every echoing step.

Nothing is going to happen at work, I repeated silently. Constance had no time for any kind of personal problems here, and we couldn't talk openly about anything agathos-related with so many humans around anyway. Mother and one of my fathers might visit on my lunch break to reiterate the points she'd made last night and try to wear me down without Riot around, but I was ready for that.

Confrontation was not my forte, especially with my parents. Perhaps because I'd always felt like I was a burden enough as it was, and I didn't want to add to that.

Not today, though. I was completely prepared to stand alone and fight for my relationship with Riot, even if the idea made me want to pass out in a pool of my own vomit.

Credence was at the reception desk when I got inside, sparing me a quick wave while focused on a phone call. There was no Constance in sight, which was a good sign. If she was hanging around the entryway, it usually meant she wanted me to use my gift on someone.

My hands shook as I did my rounds, ticking things off my clipboard as I went. I smiled at everyone, changed sheets, straightened rooms and covered the front desk for a while so Credence could take a break. Rae was still sleeping, so I made a note to check in with her later before continuing my tasks. I did everything I was meant to in half the time with a brittle smile on my face, waiting for something to go wrong whilst hoping more than anything that nothing did.

Truthfully, I loved it here. Before Riot, before all of whatever this was, I'd felt lost at sea in almost every element of my life, except my job here at Hope House.

There had definitely been moments where I wanted to quit, especially when I'd seen people less qualified than me move up just because Constance didn't like me, but I'd stayed out of passion for the people here and sheer stubbornness, and knowing I was going to give it all up was gut-wrenching.

Even on my worst day, I couldn't help feeling like the people here needed me. Someone to counter the likes of Constance, who did her best to make sure only humans who fit her standards of "deserving" received the benefit of our gifts.

It would be hard to quit, and I might have to sell my apartment if I couldn't come up with another form of income soon, but getting some space from the agathos community was a smart idea. I *knew* Riot was right about that, even if it hurt my chest to admit it.

"Grace," Constance clipped from the doorway, scaring me half out of my skin. *Perhaps less internal pep talks, more focusing on my surroundings.* "Benedict can't make it today. I need you downstairs."

Ugh.

That wasn't a sweet thought, but I couldn't even come up with something to counter it. Downstairs meant laundry duty, which meant folding fitted sheets for at least two hours.

"Of course," I replied with what I hoped was a demure, compliant smile. I was planning to hand in my notice at the end of the day so I could rush off home and avoid the ensuing awkwardness, but I really didn't want to get on Constance's bad side in the meantime. She'd already proven once before that she'd call my parents to complain about me.

Constance narrowed her eyes at me as I slipped past her, like my graceful acceptance of orders couldn't be trusted, which was more than a little unfair. I'd always gracefully followed orders, even when I hated what was being ordered of me.

There was a cement staircase that led downstairs to the basement, accessible via a door behind the front desk. I had been down here a thousand times, but I almost jumped when the door clicked shut behind me, my hand resting over my pounding heart.

Get it together, Grace.

There were no boogeymen here waiting to jump out of the shadows and grab me. Constance, who was one of the most well-informed, well-connected agathos women in the Northeast, was treating me with her regular level of disdain and no more. The rest of the staff were acting like normal.

The only person acting strange was me.

I shook my head like I could physically clear the uneasy thoughts away before jogging down the stairs to the basement which at least had brighter lights and was a bit less...*ominous.*

It was also painted bright orange, which helped. The beige ceiling tiles were all a bit wonky, the paint on the walls was chipping, and the ancient stainless steel machines creaked and groaned like every cycle was going to be their last, but there was a comforting sort of normalcy about it.

There was a long table down the middle of the room with all the clean, unfolded linen, but I quickly switched over the wet stuff to the dryer first and emptied the rolling carts from under the chutes.

Efficient. I was going to be the Queen of Efficiency today. A totally respectable, hardworking member of the agathos community, who just *happened* to have a daimon soul bond. Take that, Mother.

Not a kind thought.

My heart ached fiercely as I settled into folding. I'd hoped it would get easier to spend the day away from Riot, but it never stopped feeling like I'd hacked off a limb when I left the house each morning. Would this feeling go away once we'd completed the bond? That seemed like a pretty good reason, honestly. That, and everything Riot and I had done together so far had far exceeded my expectations of intimacy.

Even though I'd accepted that Riot was my soul bond, the lingering guilt about saving myself and being *pure* was harder to get rid of. I desperately wanted to ask someone else if this was normal even with agathos soul bonds—how were you supposed to just switch off years of conditioning that all sexual touch was wrong?—but I had no one to ask.

I made a mental note to check in with Mercy after work and see if she was ready to talk about whatever it was that had been bothering her over the weekend. Maybe I didn't have anyone to talk to, but I could at least be that for somebody else.

Between my chaotic thoughts and the deafening sound of all the machines going, it took me a moment to realize the door had opened.

"Oh, hello," I said, spinning to face the two men who had just walked in, and pressing my back against the washing machine. "Can I help you? This area is for staff only."

Did they look sort of familiar? They were both in their late 40s or early 50s, wearing sharply tailored suits that looked completely out of place in Hope House.

"Grace Bellamy." The man who spoke had pale freckled skin and slicked back red hair. There was an almost apologetic note in his voice, and my eyes flicked to the sole doorway behind them.

"Will you come willingly?" the other one asked. He seemed older and more distinguished with his graying hair, and his tone wasn't quite as comforting.

"No," I replied. It didn't matter where they were planning on taking me, no one cornered someone in a closed room if they had un-nefarious plans.

"It will only make things worse if you fight," the older one continued. "You have nothing to fear. We only have your best interests at heart. We will take you to the temple. You will be grateful for it afterwards."

Sugar, that's where I knew them from. They were the Basilinna's bonded, the ones who'd been standing behind her like bodyguards at the memorial.

I shook my head silently, willing the tears that were already welling up not to fall. My parents really hadn't wasted any time.

Riot was going to be so mad. I should have listened to him.

With a labored sigh, like I was being immensely difficult, they both stepped forward as one and I stumbled sideways, moving around the long metal bench table in the middle. My chances of somehow getting past both of them to get out of here were...nil, basically. But I couldn't just let them take me.

307

"Don't do this," I pleaded as the redhead moved back to block the door and the older man moved around the table, basically herding me towards where the first guy was waiting. "I'm not a bad person. I use my gift. I help people. I've only ever missed one day of work..."

The redheaded guy was giving me a pitying look and I knew I was rambling, the tears I couldn't contain starting to spill over. I *was* a good person. Maybe not as good as I could have been. Maybe a little reckless sometimes. Maybe not as good of a daughter as I could have been.

But I didn't deserve this.

The older man restrained me with an infuriating level of ease, pinning both my arms behind my back, while I begged in broken whispers with tears streaming down my face as the redhead approached, eyes filled with sorrow as he pulled out a syringe.

"For your own good," he whispered as the man behind me found a vein and he handed over the syringe. "It's for your own good."

"Don't pretend that any of this is for my benefit," I managed to gasp out as the world started to spin. I stumbled between both of them, trying desperately to keep my eyes open, to force my muscles to function, but I couldn't fight the force of a sedative by sheer will, no matter how hard I struggled.

I'm so sorry, Riot. I'll find a way back to you.

CHAPTER 19

"You're off form today," Dare remarked, throwing a punch that I barely managed to block.

Probably because I'm waiting for my girlfriend's life to implode, feeling helpless to do anything about it.

I'd nagged Dare into spending the two hours he had off at Viper's shit hole of a gym because it was closer to Hope House, but it wasn't giving me as much reassurance as I'd hoped it would.

What was the distance limit on this emotion-feeling thing? I'd never felt Grace when we were apart before—usually all I felt was misery being away from her—but the proper exhausted achiness hadn't kicked in yet.

I didn't feel good though.

"Has your dad been giving you shit?" Dare asked, easily dodging my sloppy swing.

"What?" I asked, bouncing on my heels. "No, not at all. I dropped the stuff I took from him back at his place a couple of days ago, plus my key. Haven't heard from him since."

"*You gave it back?*" Dare asked, dropping his fists and staring at me. "What is this, *Invasion of the Body Snatchers?* Who even are you?"

Despite the foreboding that seemed to have crept up my spine and wound its way around my neck, I almost smiled.

"Didn't need it. And I don't want the drama with him," I replied with a shrug. Grace and I had enough drama in our lives with her family, I didn't need to bring any more to the table.

"I need to head back to the studio soon. Are we doing this or not?" Dare asked, moving his fists in front of his chin.

That foreboding feeling tightened like a noose around my neck. Maybe I was imagining things, but I couldn't help feeling like Grace needed me.

"I'm tapping out," I muttered, already unwrapping my hands. "Something doesn't feel right."

"What do you mean?" Dare asked, frowning as he followed over me to the benches and pulled off his own wrappings.

I glanced around the filthy daimon-owned gym. It was mostly empty during the day, but I still had to be careful of what I said.

The more I focused on it, the more *unsettled* I felt. No, it was worse than that. There was a sense of urgency that something was very *wrong*.

As soon as I got my hands free, I was ripping my phone out of my bag, hurriedly opening the friend tracking app.

"Fuck," I whispered, my hand tightening around the device, watching the little dot move across the screen. She'd never go willingly. There was no fucking way.

"What is it?" Dare asked, looking genuinely concerned.

"I need to get to Auburn. Like right fucking now."

"Auburn? You go to Auburn, you might not come back," Dare replied, looking at me like I'd lost my mind. "Seriously, Riot. Agathos' non-violence rules don't apply to us."

"I know, but they've got my girl, so not going is not an option."

Dare reeled back in surprise at that news, eyebrows disappearing under his hair that was sticking to his face after our workout. He didn't say anything though, and I appreciated our weird friendship more than ever at that moment.

"I'll come with—" he offered, but his phone rang suddenly, cutting off our conversation. "It's Bullet," he said, frowning down at the phone.

"You should take it," I advised. *Fucking Bullet.* Why had he told her to go to work?

"Hello?" Dare said warily into the phone, scanning my face like he could see inside my head if he tried hard enough. I leaned in close to listen, contemplating cursing Bullet out while I was at it.

"Find him a vehicle. One to get to Auburn, then a different one to leave in. Leave the second vehicle by the edge of the woods on Parkway," Bullet instructed. His voice was unsettlingly calm, but the constant shuffle of cards in the background gave him away. He was not relaxed.

"O-kay," Dare replied hesitantly, frowning to himself.

"You need to be gone before they arrive. You can't see her. Understand?"

311

"Why—"

"Trust the cards," Bullet clipped. *"Don't fuck with my future, Dare. Put Riot on the phone."*

"I'm going to fucking kill you," I snarled into the receiver.

"No, you're not. Trust me, this was the best option, but you know she's not safe from her people anymore, Riot. Fake identity, paper trail, eyes on her apartment, the works. You've got ten minutes to make that happen, then you need to be on the road. Auburn town hall, in the sub basement. Blood the stone to get through the door—not your blood. Got it?"

"What? No," I replied, trying to remember everything he'd just dumped on me while my panic threatened to wipe my mind blank.

You've got it," Bullet said decisively. *"You don't think you're the hero. You don't think you're capable. Do what scares you, Riot. Nine minutes."*

The call cut off and I shoved the phone at Dare's chest, swiping my bag and jogging across the converted warehouse to the metal staircase.

"I'll meet you outside in five," Dare called after me, and I was reassured to see he was moving with the same urgency I was. Why was Bullet so weird about Dare seeing Grace?

Could he be one of her soul bonds?

I shook off the thought, filing it away for when Grace was safe and I had time to analyze it, then jogged up the rickety stairs to where Viper's office was.

I fucking hated him, but he was a wheeler and dealer with connections everywhere, and I needed those connections right now, even though I'd probably have to sell my soul for the privilege.

I only had eight and a half minutes. He'd have to do.

312

"Come in," he called through the closed door before I knocked. He probably had cameras covering every inch of this place.

Viper looked up at me from behind his desk, smirking as he always did because he was a smug motherfucker sitting up here in the freezing cold office above his shitty decrepit gym-slash-pool-bar.

His chin-length brown hair was slicked back as usual, showing off the scars on his face he was so proud of. One cut from his inner eye down his entire cheek, the other was on his forehead, bisecting his eyebrow. Viper was the king of pissing people off, and his scars were proof of that.

"Riot, my man. What can I do for you?" he asked, leaning back in his chair and giving me an assessing look.

"I have a friend who needs to go into hiding. Keep an eye on her apartment, new identity, fake paper trail, the works."

"Riot, Riot, Riot," Viper said, shaking his head. "She's not going to come and ask me herself? You know what that means."

"I'll take the debt," I replied immediately, trying not to snarl at his arrogant expression. "All of it."

Viper's mouth lifted, eyes glinting. "Wonderful. Who's the girl? A daimon who messed with the wrong people, or have you found a human to occupy yourself with?"

Goddess, this guy was an asshole.

"Your silence is part of the deal," I warned him. "I need discretion."

"How intriguing," Viper chuckled, holding out his hand. "Fine, you have my word. New identity, fake paper trail leading her out of town, security at her apartment, and this stays between us in exchange for your *ongoing* service to me until the girl no longer needs hiding or for one year, whichever is longer."

Fucking asshole.

"Fine. Deal," I gritted out, clapping my hand into his and feeling the ripple of the goddess' magic pass between us as the deal was sealed. I ripped my hand back as soon as I could, already feeling the weight of what I'd just agreed to settling on me.

"She's an agathos."

Viper's brows shot up in surprise. In any other circumstance, I would have laughed at the uncharacteristic expression, since he usually vacillated between smug or smugger.

I rattled off her name and address, as I backed out of his office, not willing to waste any more time in getting to Grace. "Leave the paperwork with Dare."

"Try not to let them catch you, Riot," Viper called after me. "I'm not coming after you if the agathos lock you in their basement dungeon."

I flipped the bird over my shoulder as I jogged down the stairs, confident his cameras would pick up the gesture. I might be his servant for the foreseeable future, but I wasn't going to be cheery about it.

Bullet:

Three minutes.

Very fucking helpful, thanks.

314

I sprinted to the shitty bar in the corner and swiped a few supplies, shoving them in my bag while I sprinted towards the exit, hoping Dare had come through for me.

The nondescript metal door slammed shut behind me as I stepped out into the alleyway, the brightness outside almost offending my eyes.

The screech of brakes from one end of the alley drew my attention at the same moment shouts came from my other side.

"RIOT! What the fuck?!" my dad roared, taking me by surprise. I braced myself as he shoved me up against the wall, shoving him back as best I could.

Really could have used some of that Keres line of violent energy right about now. My dad was lost in the kind of rage most daimons suffered from—bloody, single minded and volatile. That I'd never experienced it was another reason why I was a bad, useless daimon.

"What is your problem, old man?" I grunted, shoving him back. My phone vibrated in my pocket and terror seized my lungs for a second. I did not have time for this shit.

"You working with fucking *Viper* now? That's why you bailed on me? You traitorous little snake. I'll fucking kill you!"

"What the fuck—no, I'm not—get off me," I grunted, shoving him back as he came for me again. Viper wasn't really direct competition to my dad, but he could get his hands on more *exclusive* products if people requested them, and my old man had always taken that as a personal insult.

Dare jumped out of the car and had one arm banded round Dad's neck, the other around his chest within seconds, dragging him off me.

"Keys are in the ignition. Go!"

The heavy metal door was already pushing open behind me, and I had no doubt Viper had cameras on the entrance and had been watching this interaction with his fingertips pressed together, Mr. Burns style, cackling gleefully to himself.

"I owe you," I yelled to Dare, already running to the driver's side of the black SUV, hoping Bullet's timer hadn't already run out.

I didn't look back as I drifted the car out of the alley, driving like a bat out of hell towards Auburn.

It was time to get my girl.

Our secret was out. Things couldn't go back to how they had been before, but once I knew Grace was safe, a part of me might be relieved about that.

Grace had been forcing herself to fit the agathos mold long before she'd met me—hiding every negative emotion she had, every questioning thought, every criticism of how the agathos did things, no matter how mild.

She'd followed the rules, and they'd led her to be the outcast of her community. She'd listened to her parents, and they'd betrayed her at the first opportunity.

No more.

Grace would never be allowed to shine among the agathos, but I'd build her a safe place where she could fucking *glow*.

As soon as I got her back.

GRACE

CHAPTER 20

I woke up in the dark. No, it wasn't completely dark.

Flames in wrought iron sconces flickered against the stone walls, but the ceiling I was staring up at was almost completely hidden in shadows.

I'd been at work. Those two men—the Basilinna's bonded—had taken me.

My parents had found out about Riot.

That's what it all boiled down to. My parents had found out about Riot, and they'd gone straight to the Basilinna.

Despite the fact that my wrists and ankles were bound and there was cold stone at my back, I felt remarkably calm. Maybe it was the effects of the drugs wearing off? I definitely felt weak and woozy, and my mouth was so dry it felt like I'd been chewing on chalk.

As the haziness cleared, I realized I was in the sub basement temple under the Auburn town hall, which was unsurprising.

Disappointing, but unsurprising.

I could have laughed at my own naivety. I'd been so adamant that *of course* no one would snatch me off the streets. I'd reassured Riot that wasn't the way they operated. I had been *convinced* of it. So infuriatingly, embarrassingly convinced that even if they didn't approve of my actions, they were still the good guys.

I'd let go of the idea that the daimons were the villains, but somehow hadn't accepted that the agathos weren't the heroes.

Not wanting to make it obvious that I was awake, I glanced down the line of my body to try to figure out if they'd really...

They had. They'd really laid me on the altar.

When the darkness inside me rose up, I didn't fight it. I didn't struggle and remind myself of all the ways I had to be good, to be positive, to be content. I just let it fill all the cracks inside me with a righteous, living *rage*.

Part of me was definitely scared, and another part of me wanted to *fight* them, to rage at them for thinking they had the right to snatch me away from my job, my life, and shove me into the box they'd designated for me.

Tears tracked silently down my cheeks at the rush of anger, and I resented myself for being a crier more than ever. I didn't want anyone to see these tears, to think they were for *them*. These tears were for me. For the stupid girl I'd been, thinking I could take on the agathos, my *family*, and win. For the girl who thought they'd just let me continue on with my life, even if they didn't wholly approve.

I thought I'd already said goodbye to my innocence when it came to the agathos, but I hadn't. Not really. Because the idea had terrified me too much to consider.

Do what scares you.

I had it wrong. I should have walked away. When Riot suggested we run, I should have jumped at the chance.

There was a low murmur of voices nearby that almost made me turn my head, but I forced myself to stay still. To not give them the satisfaction of any response from me. I'd spent my life performing for these people, and it had gotten me tied up on an altar in the basement.

The stone felt cold and unyielding beneath me. My legs dangled off the edge, the platform too short for me to properly lie on. I had only seen this place a handful of times in my life—it was used for rites a couple of times a year and we were only allowed to attend after we'd had our emergence.

Apparently, it was also used for whatever they planned on doing to me.

What were they planning on doing? What *could* they do? Could I fight it? I'd never heard of a bond being broken before, but Riot and I *weren't* bonded. The potential was there, but we hadn't sealed it, which I'd never regretted more.

My inner monster made it surprisingly easy to stay grounded, despite the uncertainty of my situation and the stupid tears tracking down my cheeks, and I wished I'd given it total control before instead of forcing myself into a box I'd never been meant to fit in. I *knew* that the people who'd brought me here were in the wrong. I'd been told my whole life that nothing was more sacred than a soul bond, and when I'd *finally* found one, they ripped me away from him like it was their right.

They were wrong, I reminded myself. I was going to prove that to them if it was the last thing I did. Maybe it would be.

"Ah, she's awake."

Harmony's businesslike tone made my skin crawl, but I clenched my jaw shut and stared blankly at the ceiling refusing to give anything away. These people didn't deserve any more effort at compliance from me.

"Would you prefer to check on her, Faith?" Harmony asked.

"May I?" my mother replied in a reverent tone, and I barely held in a disgusted scoff. She hadn't even waited *24 hours* to report me to the Basilinna. I sunk further into the darkness in my head and gave myself permission to hate the maternal concern she was pretending to show now.

"Grace," Mother clipped, peering over me. I stared blankly up at her, resenting how similar our features were. Thankfully the tears had stopped, but the evidence of them was definitely on my face and I couldn't wipe them away with my bound hands. "Are you well?"

Her eyes narrowed in warning, and in the very back of my mind, my snap reaction was to deflect. To smile and insist no one needed to worry about me, like I always had done. To *be sweet*, like I'd been trained to be.

"As well as can be expected after being sedated and kidnapped from my job," I replied flatly, getting a rush of savage glee from the way her eyes flared with outrage.

It didn't quite make up for 25 years of holding my tongue, but it was something.

"Save it," Mother hissed. "You had the choice to come of your own free will, you chose wrong."

"Seeing as I was knocked out and brought here anyway, it doesn't really seem like much of a choice, does it?" I deadpanned, channeling Riot's cool, unaffected tone. My stomach swooped nervously at being so blunt with her, but I ignored it.

Do what scares you.

"If I may," Harmony intervened, stepping up next to my mother and laying a hand on her arm. "This is a difficult situation, Faith, and you may be too close to it."

Mother stepped back with a stiff nod, and I fought not to respond to the glare she shot me, knowing my indifference would enrage her more than anything else.

"Grace," Harmony said gently. "We don't mean any harm. This is a difficult, unusual situation, I understand your concern." *She had no idea*, I thought bitterly, but she must have believed she did to be able to voice the thought out loud. "But this is for your own benefit. For the entire community's benefit. We have prayed to Anesidora for her guidance on this matter."

"And what did she say?"

"Excuse me?" Harmony said, looking startled.

"What did Anesidora say?" I repeated slowly. It was a genuine question. Anesidora never responded to my prayers, I wanted to know what she said when the prayers were *about* me. I doubted I was her favorite child—I was convinced I never had been—but especially since I'd prayed to the Goddess of Night. And hadn't prayed to Anesidora since.

"The signs were very clear that you were in need of our assistance," Harmony replied uncomfortably. "We thought outreach was the right path for you, but your parents told us you met the daimon last Sunday, we believe that is a clear sign from the goddess."

"A sign for *what*?" I asked, baffled. To move the outreach trip forward? The more she spoke, the more discomfited I became. I struggled discreetly against the rope, knowing there was no point.

"We believe Anesidora is sending a message by introducing you to the daimon the same day Joy died."

Joy? What did Joy have to do with any of this?

"The timing is too coincidental. This is Anesidora's blessing to you. To them."

"What blessing?" I sputtered. "Who is '*them*'? What are you talking about?"

"You are to take Joy's place among her bonded. She may be gone, but there is no reason for her soul bonds and children to suffer needlessly. Anesidora has given you all this gift."

I opened my mouth, but no words came out. How could they...no. Just...that wasn't how *anything* worked. Soul bonds weren't replaceable. They couldn't just *wish* me into Joy's old life. Even if it worked, which I was pretty sure it wouldn't, had anyone considered how that would make Joy's bonded feel? Her children? I'd seen their grief firsthand, heard her consort's misery when he spoke.

How could anyone think Anesidora would want this?

How could anyone support that kind of cruelty if she did?

"You are here for *katharmos*," Harmony continued, looking as though she was bracing herself before undertaking a particularly unpleasant task.

Of course. They thought I was tainted with miasma by associating with Riot. That I was polluted, and needed to be cleansed before repenting my sacrilegious behavior.

Fear temporarily stole the breath from my lungs, not because I was worried for my safety, but because I was worried their ritual would *work*. Not the part where they tried to force me into Joy's old life—even with the Basilinna herself doing the cleansing, that was absurd—but what if they could break *my* connection with Riot?

Riot had come into my life when I'd asked the Goddess of Night for her guidance. What if this ritual gave Anesidora the power to take him away?

We weren't even fully bonded yet. We should have bonded. *Why hadn't we bonded?!*

I attempted to gasp down a lungful of oxygen like I'd been held underwater at just the thought of losing him, and sucked down the scent of the pungent burning bay leaves instead.

"Stop this," I pleaded, my courage faltering as she approached the altar, hoping to see the smallest glint of mercy in her eyes and finding none. "I'm not hurting anyone. We're not hurting anyone. This plan—you must know it's insane. I can't take Joy's place."

"You are infected. You cannot understand Anesidora's plans with this infection upon you," Harmony replied softly, something akin to pity on her face. "You cannot receive her blessings in this state. You must be cleansed for your own good, for your family's, and for the community's, so your miasma does not spread. Once you are cleansed, we will pray for your new bonds to form."

Before I could respond, my mouth and nose was filled with salt water and I was choking and spluttering on the jug of ocean water she'd dumped over my face. I turned my head to the side, to cough up as much as I could while my lungs burned.

Harmony's bonded approached the altar with their own jugs, dumping more and more water over me, drenching my body in the cleansing liquid.

"*Apo pantos kakodaimones,*" Harmony began chanting, and the rest of the spectators joined in. *Away, every evil spirit.*

Every *daimon.*

I gritted my teeth against the strange fluttering in my chest. I would fight Anesidora myself to keep my connection with Riot. He was *mine.* She could visit the mortal realm and rip the bond out of my body if she wanted it back, and even then, I'd still choose him. Bond or no bond.

Riot and I gave each other a place to just *be*—no expectations, no masks, no judgment. I would never give him up.

Harmony assessed me with her head tilted to the side like she was expecting something to happen, and I stared right back, glaring with as much venom as I could considering I had water in my eyes. She sighed heavily, continuing to chant as she motioned for someone just out of my line of sight.

One of Harmony's bonded moved forward out of the shadows, carrying a ritual terracotta amphora with a grim depiction of an animal sacrifice painted on the outside in the traditional black-figure style, and handed it to an expectant Harmony. I knew without a doubt it contained some poor creature's blood, and my muscles tensed in anticipation of what they were going to do.

It was an aggravating feeling to be so *defenseless*. I was aggravated with *myself* that I'd never learned some kind of self defense, or anything that would help me in this situation. Why would I have, when I was supposed to find four men who adored me and would always be by my side? All those years spent learning the art of hosting dinner parties and how to sit like a lady as per my mother's instructions had resulted in zero practical skills when my life was on the line.

The unsettling chanting continued from every side as Harmony held the vase up to the ceiling in offering to the goddess, before tipping the blood over her hand and smearing it over my face, painting lines of it down my nose, over my forehead, down my cheeks.

It was colder than I expected, and I shuddered at the revolting sensation of it dripping down my already wet skin, pressing my lips tightly together to stop the blood from getting in my mouth.

The darkness, my monster, the thing that had been keeping me icy and detached from this situation was morphing, shifting into something fiery and furious. Something *reckless*.

325

I'd been reckless once before, and it had brought me Riot. Maybe I wasn't defenseless after all. Maybe I'd just been too *cautious*.

"Goddess of Night," I whispered, trying to open my mouth as little as possible while also struggling to speak from the salt water burn in my throat. *"I ask for your guidance—"*

"Stop it," Harmony hissed, glancing around her nervously.

"—I am proud to serve the light, but I care for Riot—"

"Stop it!" Footsteps drew closer to the altar, but I couldn't stop now. Not when a cool breeze blew through the closed room, drifting over my midsection as it seemed to wind through the space like a snake.

"—I believe that I can do both, that our lives don't have to exist in opposition to one another—"

With a satisfying *whoosh*, the flaming torches in the sconces went out, like an invisible force was traveling around the room, extinguishing them all one-by-one.

My lips curved into a tight-lipped smile that was probably a little feral. I was beginning to think the Goddess of Night liked me.

"Light the candles!" Harmony ordered as bodies scrambled around in the dark. "Keep chanting!"

"Apo pantos kakodaimones," echoed, my mother's distinct voice the first to speak.

I was shivering so hard in my drenched dress that I could feel rope burns developing on my wrists and ankles despite my best attempts to hold still, but no one seemed particularly bothered about me possibly freezing to death while they fumbled around in the dark basement to relight the candles. I could hear amphora vases knocking together, and men hissing instructions at each other in the darkness as they struggled to find matches, but I wasn't about to make this easy for them.

"—*You have shown me that the agathos are wrong about the daimons, but maybe they're not so wrong about us. Maybe we're wrong about ourselves—*"

"SHUT UP!" Harmony screeched, her hands landing on my forehead in the dark, scrambling around until she pressed both hands over my mouth. I fought to turn my head to the side, but one of her hands moved to my hair, holding me in place.

I hadn't even known what I was saying, what exactly I was asking for, but I'd planned to keep talking. To make it clear exactly how I felt about the people who had trapped me in this room. To maybe gain an ally in a shadowy goddess I'd been raised to fear.

The sole door that led to the altar room opened with a *bang* that echoed against the stone, letting light into the pitch black space and startling the Basilinna who was looming over me. She snatched her hands back like she'd been burned, whirling away from me to face the entryway. I couldn't see past her, but I didn't need to.

The achy hollowness inside me eased. The thread that always felt like it was stretched too thin whenever I was at work slackened. Rage didn't so much brush at my skin as curl around it like a welcome second defense, a shield against the world.

Riot was here, and he was *furious*.

BULLET

CHAPTER 21

Glowing hands emerged from the blood red river, grasping at the white dress that trailed through the water, but The Devil wouldn't let him take her. His face was no longer hidden in shadows like it had been in this dream before. It was Riot, with his dark hair and stormy expression. Black leathery bat wings stretched wide behind him and curled goat horns emerged from his head, at odds with his messy black hair.

In his arms was my pretty little Fool. Our pretty little Fool.

Unlike The Devil, her features were clear. Smooth brown skin, long black hair that curled at the ends, opal-colored eyes filled with uncertainty, framed by long thick lashes.

A white rose dangled from her fingers, and a golden crown sat on her head—a distorted, sloping thing, shaped like a jester's hat.

I watched them cross, struggling through the river filled with snatching hands ready to rip her away, my feet frozen in place on the riverbank. There was no skin on my face. My body was hidden by thick black armor, but I could feel the smooth skeletal bones of my skull.

A skeleton alone on the banks of the river, I waited.

If I looked over my shoulder and skyward, I could make out two more figures on the looming cliff behind me. One standing in a chariot on an unreachable ledge, dressed as a warrior in armor decorated with crescent moons. His face was also hidden in shadows, his posture tall and proud.

The journey to him would be difficult. No one could be carried up that cliff face. She would have to climb alongside us.

There was an easy path from The Chariot to the final figure at the top of the cliff, standing on the divide of the known and unknown. The World. His body, wrapped in a purple toga, faced the unknown, but his shadowy face looked down over the river below, watching The Devil's struggle to safely guide The Fool through treacherous waters.

"It is time," the Goddess whispered.

And then I woke up, slumped over the table, surrounded by the cards I'd been reading right before I'd passed out, smiling from ear to ear.

Amazing Grace.

The love of my life, the person I knew better than anyone, who I'd visited every night without fail. The woman who owned my soul for however many days I had left on this earth.

The woman who didn't know me at all.

It didn't matter. It was time. She was coming.

THANK YOU

Don't be mad, it's just a little cliffhanger! A teensy one. A baby cliffhanger, at most. And book two is not far away, I promise. I've had too much fun with these characters to stay away for long, and I can't wait to spend more time in Bullet's head. Prepare yourself for more *Hamilton* jokes, definitely a few *Les Miserables* references, and I'd be remiss not to include some *Phantom of the Opera* shout outs.

Thank you as always to Lucy, who never complains when I bombard her with ideas and chapters right from when I first came up with the idea all the way through the editing process. I couldn't ask for a more supportive and amazing friend.

A special thank you to my lovely friend Kari, for beta reading and hyping me up whenever my confidence flagged. I also have to thank TS for never letting me get too far into my own head, and being such an incredibly supportive friend and sprint buddy!

Thank you also to Julia for being the best PA I could ever ask for, and to Red Line Editing for reining in my wild comma usage. And of course, I have to thank my husband and amazing kiddo for barely complaining when I holed up in my writing cave to get words on the page, and listening patiently when I whined my way through the editing process. And finally, thank you, reader! Thank you for taking a chance on a new series, I hope you enjoyed it.

That's all from me! The State of Grace series will have five books in total—you can preorder book two via Amazon if you like.

Colette x

ALSO BY COLETTE RHODES

STATE OF GRACE:
Run Riot
Silver Bullet
Wild Game
Dare Not
Saving Grace

SHADES OF SIN:
(MF monster romance)
Luxuria
Superbia

THREE BEARS DUET:
Gilded Mess
Golden Chaos

LITTLE RED DUET:
Scarlet Disaster
Seeing Red

KNOTTY BY NATURE:
(RH omegaverse with T.S. Snow)
Allure Part 1
Allure Part 2

EMPATH FOUND:

The Terrible Gift

The Unwanted Challenge

The Reluctant Keeper

DEADLY DRAGONS:

The (Not) Cursed Dragon

The (Not) Satisfied Dragon

STANDALONE:

Dead of Spring (MF - Hades & Persephone retelling)

Blood Nor Money (RH - vampires)

Fire & Gasoline (MF - wolf shifter fated mates)

ROMANCE AUTHOR

Made in the USA
Middletown, DE
25 February 2024

50337849R00190